TEMPTATION

Vegas Edge 1

ROSEMARY WILLHIDE

LUMINOSITY
PUBLISHING

LUMINOSITY PUBLISHING LLP

TEMPTATION
Vegas Edge 1
Copyright © March 2017 Rosemary Willhide
PAPERBACK ISBN: 978-0-9956898-6-2

Cover Art by Poppy Designs

DEDICATION

TEMPTATION is dedicated to my publisher, editor, amazing cover artist and friend, Kate Miles, from Luminosity Publishing. Without her, this dream wouldn't have come to fruition. I still remember the day after countless rejections Kate was the "Yes" I'd been waiting for, and the perfect patient and kind person to work with. Not only did she guide my first series and polish it up, she gave me the time I needed to write TEMPTATION. Every book I write is better when she adds her own special Kate magic to the mix. I'd be lost without you. Thank you. This one's for you, KJ.

PROLOGUE

ADAM

I spanked a girl, and I liked it.

It was love at first *smack* when my bare hand made contact with a willing submissive's round cheek on my inaugural evening at The Purple Peacock, a secret BDSM club.

I took to the lifestyle like a bee to sweet honey. In fact, I was so enthralled I became a silent partner in the club. The Purple Peacock gave my fellow kinksters and I a place to explore our fetishes and write our own rules. Safe, sane, consensual, and private was our motto.

The private part was my idea. It was an addition I demanded, and my partners Sebastian Harris and Eli Reece agreed. As a prominent casino mogul on the Las Vegas Strip, I had to be careful.

By day, I was, Adam Maxwell, the elusive, take no prisoners, ball busting executive and CEO of Maxwell Industries. By night, I was a Dom who couldn't resist a curvy brunette that had never been spanked. It was my kryptonite.

Being in control in the boardroom and the bedroom was a rush, a drug I could never get enough of. I excelled in both realms, and did not mix business with pleasure.

Each submissive was carefully vetted by Sebastian. They knew the deal, my deal. I would be their first taste of the lifestyle, no strings attached, no grand expectations, no muddied liaisons.

My life was streamlined. I worked hard, and played even harder. And right now, my cock was bone-hard as my hand readied to spank, Kristi, the dark-haired beauty draped across my lap.

I circled my palm over the curve of her cheeks, while she squirmed in anticipation. My other hand dipped between her thighs. *Fuck!* Just as I suspected, she was drenched.

"Good girl, princess," I whispered. "You're so wet for me. Are you sure this is what you want?"

Her words came out in breathy pants. "Yes. I mean, yes, Sir."

I teased her swollen clit. "I'm going to spank you eight times, and you're going to count. If you're good, I'll allow you to come while I fuck you. And make no mistake, you will be face down, ass in the air, and used for my pleasure. I'm going to fucking own your pussy tonight. It's mine. Are we clear?"

"Oh, God," she cried, with her pussy gushing all over my hand.

"I'll take that as a yes. Welcome to the lifestyle, princess. Enjoy the ride."

Smack!

CHAPTER ONE
JESSICA

"Jess, I'm living for you in this dress," touted my bestie, Tilly Treviño. "Seriously, your tits are giving me life!"

"Easy, lady. My eyes are up here," I joked and adjusted the "girls" in my plunging, burgundy dress.

Tilly laughed. "Yeah, I guess we don't want to give anyone the wrong idea. Especially here."

"I know, right. Thanks for doing all the legwork and finding out about this place."

"No need to thank me, *mija*. If your plan works out, it'll help both of us. Now stop fidgeting, and let's make our way to the bar. I need a drink."

"Me too. I'm more nervous than I thought I'd be. A Red Bull and vodka would help."

"Don't be nervous. You look amazing. You can do this. Just don't ask too many questions, and blow your cover. You don't want to sound like a reporter. Come on."

Tilly and I pressed through the crowd at The Purple Peacock, an exclusive Las Vegas BDSM club, on the down low. You had to know someone just to get an invite to today's munch. *A munch?* It sounded like a blowjob, pussy eating orgy. In reality, it was an afternoon gathering of people in the BDSM lifestyle, or they were like me, curious. I fantasized what it would be like to be one of the women in the kinky novels I read when I couldn't sleep. A date with a Dom, a submissive, and Boomer, my vibrator, worked better than a sleeping pill. When I confessed to Tilly that I named my vibrator, Boomer, she asked if it was Australian. Maybe it was. Or maybe I masturbated to thoughts of Chris Hemsworth tying me up and flogging me. That always brought the big *boom*. At any rate, I was curious. I was curious and sick of writing my entertainment column "Sin City Nights" at the *Las Vegas Times*.

I wanted to be a real reporter and sink my teeth into something gritty, like secret worlds of decadence. Going undercover as a submissive in the BDSM lifestyle would be killing two birds with one stone. I'd fulfill my fantasy and jumpstart my career. Plus, Tilly could take over my column. She was right. It would work out for both of us if I didn't blow it.

I whispered to Tilly, "Is this a bar or a bed?"

"It's a bar that's on point." She patted the dark, purple leather loveseat made for two. "Let's sit, and get you a drink. I can tell how nervous you are. Your chest is turning all red and splotchy."

"Shit. I hate that." I rested my forearms on the marble bar and exhaled.

The bartender approached. "Welcome to The Purple Peacock, what can I get for you ladies?"

"I'll have a vodka and Red Bull. Tilly, what do you want?"

The bartender crossed his arms. "Sorry. There's no alcohol served at the munch. And the private rooms are closed too."

Tilly used all of her Latin charm. "So, when you say alcohol you don't mean, Tequila, do you? Where I come from, *mi amor*, it's a food group."

The bartender didn't flinch. "Miss, it means all alcohol. We have very strict rules. Now, I'll ask again. What can I get for you?"

Wow! Denied! I'd never seen my beautiful bestie not get her way with a man. She was everything I wanted to be, outgoing, confident, curvy, and sexy as hell. I was an awkward, blonde bean poll with tits. I thought I looked like a human PEZ dispenser. You could dress me up and put the "girls" on display, but I was more comfortable in running shorts and a tank top.

Tilly didn't let this bartender get the best of her. She motioned for him to come close. "What's your name?"

He locked eyes with her. "Patrick. What's yours?"

"I'm Tilly, and this is my friend, Jess."

"Tilly, that's a ... beautiful ... name."

Oh, he was toast!

"Thank you. Now, I'd love a margarita, but I don't want to break the rules, so what if you make me a virgin, and then buy me a drink if I come back sometime in the evening?"

Patrick's face flushed. "A virgin? Well, I suppose that could be arranged just for you."

"And I'll have..."

I was too late. Patrick was off making Tilly a virgin. Good luck, buddy!

I plopped my bag on the bar. "That was a close one, *mi amor*, but look at him. He doesn't even notice the other guests. Including me."

"Sorry. I guess I don't know my own strength." She gestured to a man with a crew cut wearing all black. "I'm wondering if that's the guy you should ask about getting some one-on-one time with a Dom. He's been working the room all afternoon."

"Maybe." For the first time, I took a long, sweeping look around The Purple Peacock. "I'm not sure this is what I was really expecting. Were you? I mean, sure, the bar looks like a four-poster bed with those big, brass poles, and it's a little night clubby, but it's also kind of elegant.

"You're right." Tilly pointed to a painting on the wall. "And check out the peacock. That's like, legit art if you ask me."

A stunning portrait of a purple peacock had me in awe. It was surprisingly mesmerizing. I couldn't take my eyes off it.

"It's a real beaut, eh?" The man with the crew cut startled me. "Sorry, Miss. Didn't mean to spook you. I'm Sebastian Harris, one of the owners."

I touched my fingertips to my blotchy, warm chest. His Australian accent threw me for a bigger loop than the peacock. "Oh, hi. I'm Jessica Blake and—"

Tilly interrupted, "And you're Australian! I love your accent, Sebastian. Do you know what a boomer is? Is it battery operated?"

Desperate for her to shut it, I kicked her. "Pay no attention to my friend, Tilly. She's just a big fan of ... booming ... Aussie ... things."

Sebastian folded his arms with a quizzical expression. "No problem, Miss Blake. What brings you to our munch? Have you been in the lifestyle long?"

Shit! I forgot my prepared speech about my interest in BDSM and why I wanted to be submissive, or a sub as they called it. My hand flew back to my chest, and it was on fire. This wasn't how it was supposed to go down. I'm a reporter. I ask the questions.

I stammered and licked my lips. "Well, I'm not exactly ... you know ... in..."

Tilly intervened, "What Jess is trying to say is, she isn't in the lifestyle, but—"

"I'm curious." I steadied myself and looked Sebastian in the eye. "I guess you could say I'm ... sub-curious."

He nodded with a slight grin. "Well, aren't you a slick one. A little cheeky, but slick. So, tell me Cheeky Miss Blake, would you and your lovely friend like an invite to the club in the evening? Would that sub-due your curiosity?"

"Oh, I see what you did there. Nice one, Mr. Harris," I retorted. "By the way, my friends call me, Jess."

"So, we're friends now?" he teased. "Shame. I didn't get the bloody memo, mate."

Sebastian bore no resemblance to Chris Hemsworth, but he was kind of sexy in his own way. His confidence, charm, and that freaking accent ticked all the right boxes. Plus, I needed him. He was my gateway "boomer" to some time with a Dom.

"I'll have my people send your people the bloody memo, mate."

"Well, in that case, Jess, what night would you and Tilly like to come?"

"Uh, I don't know." I looked to Tilly for help. A night at the club wasn't the only thing I was hoping for. How could I get what I wanted without blowing my cover?

"Is there some sort of a newbie night?" Tilly asked. "In case we have questions. I mean, what exactly happens in the evening? Is it like, wham, bam, spank you, ma'am?"

"Ladies, I assure you, everyone that walks through our door is properly vetted. Our motto here is safe, sane, consensual, and private."

"That's good to hear," I interjected. "I was so curious, I was tempted to go online to look for a Dom."

Sebastian bristled. "I strongly advise against that. Inexperienced, potential subs searching for a Dom online are an easy target for a fake. Trust me. I know. If you're really that interested in learning about the lifestyle, I could set you up with someone."

"You'd really do that?"

He cocked his head. "What are mates for, Jess?"

"Thank you so much." I reached for my bag, to give him my card. *What an idiot!* My card said, "Jessica Blake – *Las Vegas Times*."

Luckily, Sebastian beat me to the punch. "Here's my card. Email me if you're serious about this." His tone turned stern. "I have a Dom who is particularly fond of first-time subs. But don't waste his time. You'll have to go through a proper screening and fill out copious amounts of paperwork. If everything checks out, I'll arrange a meeting, and he will take it from there. Just a meeting. Nothing else."

My stomach fluttered, in a booming—Chris Hemsworth, flog me—sort of way. "Thanks." I was one step closer to making my fantasy come true.

"My pleasure. I'll be off." He offered his hand to Tilly. "Good to meet you. Hope to see you here again, in the evening."

She smiled. "I hope so too."

He placed his hand on my shoulder. "I'll be in touch, mate. Take care."

While he took his leave, he tossed one last comment over his shoulder. "By the way, nice dress. You look lovely in red."

"It's burgundy, actually." I exhaled in victory and grabbed Tilly's hand. "Thank you. Thank you so much for helping me."

"You didn't need me. But, I'm happy to help."

With a smirk, Patrick set down Tilly's drink. "Here you go, virgin."

She took a sip. "Not bad. If I didn't know better, I'd say this isn't a virgin at all."

"I'll never tell," Patrick quipped and sauntered to the other side of the bar.

"Is there really tequila in there?" I asked.

"Maybe. Whatever it is, it's delicious. Grab one of those plastic cups. I'll share."

When I reached for it, my elbow knocked my bag off the bar. Almost everything inside spilled on the floor. "Shit." I hopped off the loveseat to gather my things, especially my business cards.

"Do you need help?"

"No. I'm good." I snatched up the last card, stood, and froze when I spotted him across the room. The casino king of Las Vegas was at The Purple Peacock. He was here, in the flesh. I'd never seen him in person before. How could I? He was so reclusive, and gorgeous, and ... oh ... God... *Well done!* It really was Adam Maxwell. His piercing blue eyes, jet-black, perfect hair, and gladiator muscled frame left me dumbstruck. Not to mention his razor-sharp jawline that could slice you in two, just by looking at it. *Wow!* I couldn't stop staring. His magnetic presence captured me and wouldn't let me go.

Tilly tapped my arm. "Jess, what is it?"

"It's ... Adam Maxwell." I heaved.

"You're lying. Where?"

I whispered. "Over there in the corner, on that round bed."

"Oh, *mierda!*"

"My thoughts exactly." Tilly taught me all the dirty words in Spanish. I was fluent in filthy "fuck me" phrases.

"Look at him," Tilly said. "He's so hot. It's insane. I love a guy with an ass chin."

"A what?"

"You know, he has a sexy cleft thing."

"Why do you call it an ass chin?"

"Because my ass should sit on his face, and experience it first-hand."

"Down girl. Besides, it looks like he's taken."

A tall, thin woman with a mane of long, stick straight, dark hair flopped down on his lap.

Tilly shook her head. "That's no girlfriend. That's just a *punta* with a thirsty ass."

"How can you tell?"

She picked up her margarita. "Watch."

Within seconds, Adam shrugged her off, got up and checked his phone.

"Told you." Tilly offered me her drink. "Here."

"Thanks. I need cooling off." I brought the margarita to my lips. For a moment, I swore Adam looked in our direction. That was all it took to turn me into a thirsty ass. I downed Tilly's drink until reality socked me between the eyes. "Oh, my, God. We've got to go."

"What are you talking about?"

"Aren't you forgetting something? Adam Maxwell just isn't the youngest casino mogul in Vegas. He's also the *Las Vegas Times*' number one advertiser. He's basically our boss. Without him, our little paper wouldn't exist." I set the glass back on the bar. "We need to get out of here."

"He has no idea who we are. We're fine."

"Didn't you hear what Sebastian said? The Purple Peacock's motto is safe, sane, consensual, and private. They aren't going to grant me time with a Dom if they find out I'm connected to the media. Hell, they'd probably throw us out right now if they found out we worked for the paper. It's too risky."

"Is it? Because he's headed this way."

Shit! I made the mistake of looking and nearly turned to stone. Somehow, I summoned enough fortitude and strength to bolt for the door without glancing back for one last glimpse of Adam Maxwell's radiating, red-blooded, powerful form.

What was he doing at The Purple Peacock? Was Adam Maxwell a Dom? I had so many questions.

* * * *

"What've you got for me, Blake? Anything?" My boss, Hal Cook, leaned against the doorway of my dingy little office, with an expression of impatience and irritation. I'd seen this look many times over the six years I worked at the paper.

Deep down Hal was a pussycat. He gave me the entertainment column fresh out of college when I was twenty-two and eager to do anything, even the fluffy "Sin City Nights." Sure, he grumbled and fussed from time to time, but it was for my own good. It made me a better writer, with a hunger for something more.

"I'm still working on it. But, I promise, I'm close."

He took out his handkerchief and dabbed his sweaty bald head. "You've been saying that for months. Damn it, it's hot in here. Is the AC not working again?"

"It's working, but it's August in the desert."

"Listen, kid." He shut the door and pulled up a chair close to my desk. "I really need you to follow through on this big story you've got cooking. I don't have to tell you that subscriptions are down, and if weren't for Adam Maxwell's advertising budget, we'd all be out of a job. Newspapers like ours are dying on the vine. So, you've got to deliver for me. I don't know how much longer I can pay you and Tilly to write the same column."

"But I'm still writing the column, and I have all my contacts from the clubs back when I used to go out. Tilly's like my assistant. She helps out everyone."

"She used to be part-time. Now, she's full-time because she's the one out in the field."

"Oh? I didn't realize."

"You've got two choices. Either bring me something big, and I can justify making you a feature reporter, or... Well, I can only pay one person to write, 'Sin City Nights.'"

I slumped back in my chair. Hal's words were like taking a punch to the gut. "Message received. It should be Tilly's. She works really hard."

"Well, she's ambitious. Just like you used to be. What happened to the spunky twenty-two-year-old with all the questions?"

"She's still here. I'm just burned-out on reporting celebrity dirt. I want more." *So much more.*

"I've got faith in you, but time is running out."

"I hear you. I won't let you down."

Tilly rapped on the door and sprung into the room. "Everyone decent in here?"

Her charms were not lost on Hal. He chuckled, and they exchanged a quick greeting before he left. She perched herself on the edge of my desk. "Did you hear from Sebastian?" she asked with excitement in her voice.

"Not yet. I was just about to check my email when Hal came in. The wait is killing me. I wonder how long it's going to take to process all my paperwork. I filled out less forms when I bought my townhouse."

"It's good they're so careful. That means you'll be safe too."

"Safe, sane, consensual, private, plus proof of birth control and blood test required. I did everything he told me to do, with the exception of where I really work. Tell Tony at the Palms I owe him, big time."

"What's a little favor for a friend? He didn't think twice about verifying your employment at the Ghostbar. A few years ago, you were like an employee. You were always there. You're the one that broke the story about the contestant on that reality show dealing drugs. The place has been packed ever since."

"It was the only time I felt like a real reporter. After that, I just lost interest in who was seen with who, and what they were wearing."

"Well, I love it. Every night is different. Different celebrities, different clubs, and the men!" Her dark eyes sparkled. "Real men. Not men from the pages of a book. When was the last time you got laid? And not by Boomer."

Oh, this again! "Boomer never lets me down. Especially since I buy my batteries in bulk. But the men in the clubs ... I don't even remember their names. They were bangs with no boom."

"A bang with no boom is better than nothing."

I scrunched up my face. "Is it? I'm pretty sure I'm dead inside."

"Then, let me bring you back to life. There's a red-carpet premiere tonight for a new club at the Paris. What more could you want? Come with me."

"I can't tonight."

"Come on, Jess. You don't go out anymore."

"I don't have to. My little birds tell me everything I need to know."

"Oh, I see, so I'm a little bird now? Shall I chirp for you?"

"Could you?" I laughed.

Tilly broke out into her best bird/JLo impression. She cracked herself up. "I can see the headline now, 'Las Vegas Entertainment Reporter Flaps and Dances Her Way onto the Vegas Stage.'"

"They'll call it, 'Tilly's Got Talent.'"

"Whatever it takes to get my *mija* out of the house for some fun."

"Okay. You have my word. As soon as I get my story and become a feature reporter, we'll go out and toast to both of us. 'Sin City Nights' will be yours. You'll have your own byline if you want it."

"No way. I'm going to keep it amorous, like you."

"You mean, anonymous?"

"Yes. That's what I meant. Anonymous. I'll get more dirt that way."

"Smart *chica*."

"I learned from the best." She moseyed to my side of the desk and tapped on my laptop. "Check your email. I'm dying to see if you heard from Sebastian."

I flipped it open. "I'm kind of dying here too." I scrolled through, and my stomach fluttered the same way it did at The Purple Peacock. An email from Sebastian came in ten minutes ago. In the subject, he wrote "A Dom for my mate." I gasped. "It's here." I clicked on it and read it to Tilly. "Jess, please respond to this email immediately upon receiving. You are to meet your Dom for an interview only, promptly at noon tomorrow. Do not be late. Dominick Cane will be waiting for you at The Palisades Resort and Casino in the penthouse of the Luxury Tower. You'll have to show ID to security to get on the proper elevator. If I don't hear from you before eight p.m. this evening, your meeting is canceled. Good luck. I hope you find what you're searching for. If I can be of any further assistance, please let me know. All the best, Sebastian Harris."

I sat motionless and quiet, with my eyes transfixed on the email.

Tilly broke the silence. "Well, this is it. Email him back."

"Oh, yeah ... right. This was what I was waiting for. Except ... I have so many questions."

"Ah, Jess! You're killing me. You just need to go for it. Look at you. Your chest is turning red. You'll have to wear a turtleneck to the interview."

I glanced down at my red spotted chest, and for a moment, panic sat in, until I re-read Sebastian's email and it sunk in. Everything was coming together. My intense temptation overtook my nerves, and the heat from my chest traveled south between my legs. I was going to meet "my Dom" tomorrow—just like the women in the books I devoured. I pressed my knees together and hit reply on my email to Sebastian. I typed:

"Dear Mr. Harris,
Please tell Dominick Cane, I will see him
tomorrow at noon.
Thank you, Jessica Blake –
a.k.a. Sub-Curious."

Send!

CHAPTER TWO
JESSICA

Right before I rang the bell at Dominick Cane's penthouse, I took one last glimpse of my chest. *Whew!* No blotches. I could do this. After all, my outfit received the Tilly seal of "on fleek" approval. She said my black pencil skirt and fitted white top were a classic look that would knock his belt off. She meant socks, but somehow belt suited the occasion better.

It was noon on the dot. I pressed the bell and waited—and waited some more. Finally, the door flew open. "Miss Blake. I'm Dominick Cane. Please, come in."

Jesus—Christ—Superstar! What the hell was going on? It was Adam Maxwell and all of his hellfire hotness. *Shit!* My legs felt like two cinder blocks sinking into the floor. I couldn't move or speak.

"Miss Blake, are you going to come in or would you like to conduct our meeting out here in the hallway?" He smirked. "You seem rather attached to that particular spot on the carpet."

God Almighty, his voice. It was so low and velvety. If only I could re-discover the use of my own. "Uh."

He took two calculated steps toward me. "I'm a busy man, Miss Blake. You're free to leave if you like, but if you're staying..." He motioned inside the penthouse, and then our eyes locked on one another. "Have we met before?"

His gaze dug into me, causing me to quake in my heels. "Um ... no. I–I ... no, Mr. Cane."

"Strange. You look very familiar. And a little unsure of what you've gotten yourself into. It happens. Maybe it would be best if you did go."

Interesting. While I was worried about blowing my cover, he appeared concerned about his own. Both of us were bluffing. "I'd really like to stay. I was just a little nervous." I marched inside. "I'm fine now."

I wasn't fine. I was sweating bullets. My palms were so slippery I nearly dropped my bag, with my mini recorder taping every word.

He motioned toward the plush, grey sofa. "Please have a seat. Can I get you anything?"

My mouth was dryer than Vegas in a drought. "Some water would be great."

"Absolutely."

He headed to the right, toward the panoramic window with the view of the strip and ducked around the corner. My eyes were glued to his rounded, perfect butt in his navy trousers. Adam Maxwell was a walking Adonis. Who was he trying to fool with his phony name? Dominick Cane, my ass! Oh, now I got it. Dom—Cane, like a Dom with a cane. He had some sort of BDSM alias. *Smart.* Better to meet first before revealing the most sought-after bachelor in town was a kinkster.

I sat down in the middle of the sofa and took a quick peek around the sleek penthouse. Its clean lines and modern décor were fit for a king. The thirty-five-year-old king of Vegas. After all, The Palisades was one of his casinos. He tore down the old Copacabana and revitalized this part of the strip years ago. I covered the grand opening and waited all night for a chance to interview him. He never showed. Adam Maxwell was notorious for eluding the public eye while toying with the press and gaining more publicity than anyone in Vegas. He was as mysterious and private as a superhero. Perhaps now I knew why.

I settled into the sofa, slipped my hand into my bag, checked the tape recorder, and secured my bag next to my hip. It was so snug against me it was practically in my lap. The butterflies in my stomach morphed into bats. Thank God I didn't have anything besides Red Bull and Tic Tacs this morning. Maybe I had too much Red Bull. My heart rate sped up when I heard Adam's footsteps approaching.

I turned my head in his direction, and our eyes met again. A trace of a smile played on his lips, and it sent a sizzling flare bubbling up inside me. *Sweet baby Jesus!* My body never experienced such a pure chemical reaction to a man before. His presence was so overwhelming, my head dizzied.

He placed two large crystal tumblers on the glass coffee table and reclined into the leather chair next to the sofa. "Are you sure you're all right, Miss Blake. You look a little pale."

"Oh, yeah, totally." *Lies, lies, lies!* "I'm ... good."

His grin widened. "Well, I do like a good girl."

And, now I'm wet! I wriggled in my seat and stared at the sexy cleft in his chin. *Don't call him ass chin! Don't call him ass chin!* I blew out a ragged breath. "Thank you for the water."

"My pleasure. It's important to stay hydrated in this weather." He gestured to the glass. "Please."

"Yes, Mr. Cane." I scooted forward in my seat, grabbed the glass, and chugged the water like it was beer, and I was at a kegger. Not exactly ladylike. "I guess I was a little ... thirstier than I thought."

Amusement danced in his eyes while I wiped away tiny droplets of water from my mouth. *Did he find me funny? Or was he imagining me naked?* Either way, it didn't do a thing to decrease the wetness between my thighs. The struggle was real!

Without taking his eyes off me, his well-manicured rugged hands wrapped around his tumbler of water. He swirled it, saying, "Would you like some more water, Miss Blake? Or shall we discuss your interest in my lifestyle? Sebastian mentioned you seemed rather curious. Did you have any questions for me?"

"Questions!" I proclaimed a little too loudly. "I mean, sure, I might have a few things I wanted to ask you."

I put the glass on the table, shifted back into the sofa, and accidentally sat on my bag. I reached to pull it free from underneath me, and *click* ... the recorder turned off. *Shit!*

"What was that?" Adam inquired in a harsh tone.

"My phone." I swallowed hard and calmed myself. "I forgot to turn it off."

He furrowed his brow and placed his water on the table. "Never heard a phone make a clicking noise before. I'd appreciate you turning it off. I don't have a lot of time."

"Yes. Of course. Sorry about that." I was steady as stone on the outside, but was truthfully so thrown, I bobbled my bag in my trembling hands, and it tumbled to the floor. The recorder was ejected and landed next to Adam's expensive, freshly shined, black shoes.

It all happened so fast. I lunged for it, but Adam snatched it up and stood. I found myself on my knees before him.

"What the fuck is this?" Adam seethed.

"It's nothing," I answered, maintaining my cool.

"You're fucking recording me, and I want to know why."

I retrieved the rest of my stuff, shoving it back in my bag. "I wasn't. I forgot I had it with me." I hoped I sounded more confident than I felt.

"My number one rule is, never lie to your Dom. Now gather your things and get out."

I was shaking, but rose with my poker face intact. "Okay. I'll go."

He handed me the recorder. At the same moment, we both spotted one more thing on the floor and made a play for it. Adam beat me to it. *Oh no!* It was my business card. How could I be so stupid?

His eyes narrowed as he read it aloud, with an intense, quiet anger. "Jessica Blake – *Las Vegas Times*. What the fuck is going on? Are you a goddamn reporter?"

"Um... I–I ... look, I can explain."

He closed the gap between us, and his hulking frame loomed over me. "Start explaining," he spat out, "and don't lie to me again."

My head spun, and my mouth failed me in the most epic way possible. "I won't, Mr. Maxwell. I swear."

"What did you call me?" His eyes burned with fury. "What kind of game are you playing, sweetheart? My number two rule, do not play games with your Dom."

I backed away. "I–I'm not ... playing a game, I–I..."

He cocked his head. "I've seen you before, haven't I?"

"No. I don't know what you're talking about?"

His jaw clenched, and he shook his head. "Stop lying. I remember now. You were at the last munch at The Purple Peacock. I saw you there. Red dress."

"It was ... burgundy," I mumbled.

He threw his hands up in frustration. "Jesus! Unbelievable. You're here to do some kind of undercover piece about the club, aren't you?" His anger grew with each word. "You want to expose us to the masses? Not a fucking chance! I'll let you in on a little secret, Miss Blake, without me, the *Las Vegas Times* wouldn't exist. I could call your boss and have your skinny ass fired right now..."

As he raged on, his words sounded garbled and muddy to me. I clasped my head in my hands.

"Miss Blake? Jessica? Are you okay?"

"Yeah." I tried to focus, and there were three blurry Adams waving in front me. "I'm ... okay... I–I ... just need to..." I took one step, and my legs gave way.

Adam caught me before I hit the floor. "Oh, great," he uttered sarcastically.

His grip on me was a little too tight, and I squirmed. "You can let go now. I was just a little dizzy. I'm fine."

"Easy, sweetheart. You're not fine." He plopped me back on the couch, and his face softened somewhat. "Fuck. What am I going to do with you?"

"You don't need to do anything." I glanced down and quickly covered my splotchy chest with both hands. I was so embarrassed. It looked like a Jackson Pollock painting.

He sat on the coffee table and sighed. We were quiet for a moment, and then Adam reached over and removed my hands, holding them in his. A minute ago, he was yelling at me, and now his touch was soothing and gentle. Our gaze met, and the anger in his eyes dissipated. "My number three rule. Never hide who you are and your flaws from your Dom. Are we clear?"

"Yes," I whispered.

The pads of his thumbs brushed against my palms, causing little flickers of heat firing through me. I pulled my hands away and resisted the urge to conceal my chest, placing them on my lap instead.

Adam took note. "Good girl."

Those two simple words relaxed me, and I regained my composure. "I guess I have some explaining to do." I shrugged. "Unless you want to call my boss and have me fired."

"Make no mistake, Miss Blake. That option is still on the table. I'm afraid you've landed in a world of trouble. Consider this a negotiation to save your job."

"A negotiation?"

"Yes. You have found yourself at my mercy." He crossed his arms relishing his position of power.

"Or are you at mine?"

"You think so? Care to enlighten me?"

"Well, I can't imagine you would want the world to know you're a Dom. Why else would you use an alias when arranging a meeting? Freedom of the press, Mr. Maxwell."

A smug look crossed his face. "Impressive, but not a wise move. You signed a non-disclosure agreement. Break it, and I'll see to it you lose your job, and I'll sue you. I'd win too—I always win."

Shit. He was right. "Oh. I forgot about the non-disclosure."

"How about we start over again, with the truth? Why are you really here?"

"Well, the truth is, I write the 'Sin City Nights' column at the paper."

"*Hmm.* I know it well. You're a good writer."

"Thank you. But, I want to be a serious journalist. My boss said if I could come up with something different, something no one else was writing about, he could bump me up to a feature spot. But, it had to be salacious and sinful, like Vegas. I started reading a lot of fiction about Doms and subs, and I thought I could go undercover as a submissive, find out what it's really like, and do a story about how it compares to the best-selling books women are reading."

He rolled his eyes. "Don't tell me. You're one of those."

I scrunched up my face. "One what?"

Adam stood. "One of those women who read BDSM books which fill their heads full of unrealistic expectations."

"I don't have any unrealistic expectations. In most of the books I read, somehow the woman gets the man to change. I think that's why they call it fiction."

Even if he tried not to show it, he appeared somewhat charmed by me. "What were you expecting? You'd waltz in here, and I'd be so taken with you, I'd ask you to be my submissive? You're not even my type."

Annoyed, I snapped, "Dude, I'm a blonde with big tits. I'm everybody's type."

Adam stifled a chuckle. "Did you just call me, dude?"

"Sorry. Sir ... D u d e."

He leaned in close enough for me to feel his breath against my cheek. "You're clever. I'll give you that, but don't push it. I still haven't decided if I'm going to have you fired." He backed off and studied me. "Most of my subs have been brunettes, with more meat on their bones. You're a little too thin for my tastes."

His comment cut deep. I'd been teased my whole life for being too skinny. Thoughts of junior high taunts echoed in my head. Adam Maxwell hit a nerve. "Fine by me, because, you're a little too much of a jerk for mine."

I jolted out of my seat, and he caught me by the arm. "We're not done here yet. You can't walk away in the middle of a negotiation."

"Watch me." I shrugged him off, grabbed my bag, and fled to the door.

"I wouldn't do that if I were you. Just one call to the *Las Vegas Times* and you'll be unemployed."

Fuming, I turned and stared him dead in the eyes. "Go ahead. Call them. If this story's a bust, I'm going to lose my job anyway."

"Miss Blake. Don't leave like this. I thought we were sparring with one another. But, I seemed to have upset you somehow?"

"It doesn't matter. I don't need you. I can find another Dom online."

"I'm afraid I can't let you do that."

"You can't let me? Who do you think you are?" Now I was in a rage. "I know I came in here under a false pretense, but I'm curious about being a submissive. I really wanted to learn about your lifestyle. And just so you know, I was never going to mention The Purple Peacock or your name in my story. But you... You're such an ass!"

"Watch your language, young lady."

"My language? Do you actually hear the words coming out of your mouth? Or are you used to spewing so much bullshit it doesn't register? You said not to hide my flaws. Well, dude, this is me and my skinny, flawed ass leaving." I bolted to the door, twisted the knob and gave him one last parting shot. "And for the record, I don't think you're a very good Dom, Mr. Cane."

* * * *

I raced home in my silver Nissan with adrenaline zipping through me. I couldn't bear to go back to work. Did I really call Adam Maxwell an ass? My boss, Hal would kill me if he knew. I'm so screwed. What was I going to do?

As I pulled into my townhouse's cul-de-sac, I managed a smile when I saw my neighbors, Stacy and Roger washing their motorcycles. They were the closest thing I had to any kind of family besides Tilly. Actually, they were better than family. They looked out for me, and never pried into my personal business. I didn't nose into theirs either. I wasn't even sure if they were in a serious relationship, or just best friends that lived next door to each other and enjoyed the same interests, like motorcycles, cooking, and animals. There was only one major difference. Stacy was a cat person. She lived with five rescues, and always had room for more. Roger was a dog lover. His adopted pooch, Harley, was his little buddy. They were inseparable from the minute Roger brought him home from the Humane Society three years ago.

Our townhomes formed a horseshoe in what used to be one of the nicest neighborhoods in town on the edge of Summerlin. Over the past couple of years, it became more transient. The place next to mine was still vacant after Mrs. Goldman passed away last fall.

Roger waved me over, so I walked across the cul-de-sac to see what was up. "Hi, guys. Aren't you dying in this heat?"

Stacy aimed her hose at Roger. "I'm fine, but Roger needs cooling off."

She squirted him, and he retaliated. They carried on like a couple of teenagers, even though they were both well over forty.

I laughed. "If I wasn't in my work clothes, I'd join you."

Roger hollered, "Truce. I'm calling a truce. Hoses down."

"You first. Drop your weapon," Stacy stated like the police officer she was.

He threw down the hose and held his hands up. "I surrender, Officer Sibley."

She sprayed him one more time. "And, now we're done."

"Who am I to argue with the law?" Roger joked.

"Good man. I'll run in and get some towels. Don't forget to tell Jess about her visitor," Stacy said while heading toward her townhouse.

"I had a visitor? Who?" I asked.

"Yeah. It was some lady," Roger answered. "She was knocking on your door when we came out to wash the Harleys. I'd never seen her before. She said she was looking for you. I hope you don't mind, I asked her what she wanted. You can never be too careful."

"No. I don't mind. I'm glad you did. What did she say?"

"She acted all high and mighty and said I should mind my own business. I told her I could give you a message and the lady said, 'Just tell her Lauren was here.'"

"Lauren?" My stomach sank. As if this day couldn't get any worse. "Roger, that was no lady. That was my mother."

"Your mother? I thought you didn't have any family."

"I don't. Not really. It's a long story."

"You don't need to explain anything to me."

"No. I do. You and Stacy should know, in case she comes back."

Stacy rejoined us, tossing Roger a towel, and handing me a bottle of water. "Should know what?"

"Thanks." I screwed open the water and took a swig. "Roger told me about the woman that was here. She's my mother."

"Your mother?" Stacy exclaimed.

"Look, I know you must feel like I lied to you, and I'm sorry. My mother and I haven't spoken since my dad passed away ten years ago. Actually, to be more specific we haven't spoken since my dad's estate was settled and I was awarded all the money. I don't know why she thought she was entitled to anything. They'd been divorced since I was six. She remarried, several times, but was in between husbands when he died. She pissed me off, acting like the grieving widow until she found out he didn't leave her anything. Since I just turned eighteen and was no longer a minor, there wasn't any way for her to have access to my inheritance." I drank another sip of water and sighed. "The entire time she acted like an actual mother I knew I was being played. I felt it in my gut. The day we left the lawyer's office she came clean. She said she was broke and needed half the money to start over."

"What did you say?" Stacy asked.

"I held my ground. I said, no."

"Good for you, Jess," Roger replied.

"Thanks. I felt good about it until..." I stared at the ground, still in disbelief. "Until she said, 'You're going to regret being so selfish when you hear the truth that I've kept hidden all these years for your benefit.'"

Roger placed his hand on my shoulder. "Hey, you don't need to tell us anything else. We get the picture. If she comes back, I'll tell her to fuck off."

"And I'll write her a ticket for trespassing," Stacy added. "You don't need this kind of crap."

"Thank you. You know, if I were a hugger, I'd give you both one right now."

Stacy smiled. "And I wasn't soaking wet, I'd let you." She squeezed Roger's bicep. "I'm headed to work. The cats have been fed."

"Okay. Stay safe."

"I will. Jess, Roger is working a double shift tonight too. Be sure to lock your doors."

I saluted her. "Yes, ma'am."

Stacy hurried into her house, while Roger gathered up their motorcycle washing supplies.

"So, if you're working a double, does this mean I get to have a slumber party with Harley?"

"I hate to impose, but if—"

I interrupted in glee, "You're not imposing. I'd love to. Where is he?"

"Harley! He was laying on the tile after lunch. Some tough life. Let me get him." Roger hustled to his townhouse and opened the door. Harley bounded toward me, all fifty pounds of him. He was Border Collie mix with a double dose of personality. How could anyone have dumped this sweet boy in a shelter?

"Hey, mister. Is someone spending the night with me?"

Harley wiggled his little nubby tail and pranced around me doing a four-legged happy dance. His shiny black coat gleamed in the sunshine. He was too cute for words. I loved the freckled markings on his mask and chest. But the speckled spots on his paws were my favorite. I called them his leg-warmers.

I bent down to pet him. "Who's a good boy?" He gave me a smooch. "Harley is."

"I don't know who spoils him more. Me or you?" Roger said.

"I think it's a tie. Is it all right if I take him with me on a run tonight? I'll wait until the sun goes down, so it isn't so hot."

"Sure. He'd love that."

"Good. After the day I had, I could use a jogging buddy to help me kick my stress to the curb."

"You mean your mother? Or is it something else?"

"Oh, trust me. You don't want to know. Just ... work stuff."

"I hear you. I'm looking for another job myself. These double shifts at The Golden Nugget are killing me. I keep applying at one of Adam Maxwell's casinos. Everyone says he treats his employees the best."

"Don't believe everything you hear," I mumbled.

"Anyway, I better hit the shower before work." He knelt down. "Okay, Harley. Be a good boy for Jess. And I'll see you in the morning, buddy."

There was something so special about their bond. The way big, burly motorcycle riding, Roger turned to mush around Harley always touched me. Maybe I wasn't totally dead inside.

He kissed Harley's head and stood. "Thanks again, Jess."

"Of course. I'm happy to have him."

"I'll touch base with you in the morning."

"Sounds good. And if I'm ever not home and you need to drop him off, you have a key. Just let him inside and leave me a note. It's no problem."

He handed me Harley's leash. "Oh, that's right. The keychain has a red ribbon on it."

"It's not red, it's burgundy." Were all men so unobservant?

"Do you have enough food for him?"

"Yup. I still have half a bag. But, I have to go to the store later. Maybe I'll pick him up some chicken, and a new toy."

"Oh boy. Harley's going to start liking you better than me."

"Trust me. That will never happen. You're his person."

A huge smile split his face. "Very true. From the second I saw this little guy at the shelter." He reached down and patted Harley's head. "Okay. I'll see you later. Bye, Harley. Thanks, Jess."

"You're welcome. Come on, buddy." Harley hesitated for a second and then followed me to my door. I looked back, and Roger was still there. He waved one last time.

With all the shit I'd been through today, it was comforting to know Roger and Stacy had my back. They were good people. Some of the best I'd ever met.

* * * *

After a trip to the store, and a five-mile run I was in desperate need of a shower. I peeked into my office, and Harley was sacked out with his new toy—a baby blue shark. He was so tired he didn't attempt to destroy it when I gave it to him after dinner. He carried it upstairs, hunkered down on the cool tile, and fell asleep.

I stripped down, cranked up the hot water in my shower, and scrubbed myself nearly raw. As if it could erase Adam Maxwell and the visit from my mother out of my mind. It didn't.

While I was toweling off, I wiped the steam off the mirror. The words, "Dude, I'm a blonde with big tits. I'm everyone's type," swirled in my head. How could I have said that? I was no one's type. I peered into the mirror. Adam Maxwell was right. I was too skinny. They called me, "B.W.B.," in junior high, and into high school. It stood for "Boney with Boobs." The ones that didn't pick on me for my body called me owl or Ferbie. My blue eyes were too big for my face. When I wore my glasses, kids hooted at me.

A few years ago, I got laser eye surgery and thought I was growing into my looks, filling out more. But I guess what my mother, Lauren said was true. I was an Ugly Duckling. No wonder staying home with a good book was more appealing to me. It was just too "peopley" out there. The world could be a cruel place.

I checked my phone and had a text from Tilly. I left her a message earlier saying my meeting with "Dominick Cane" was a bust, and not to worry about me. Looks like she was using her charm to lure me to a new club. Not a chance, *chica*. It was only nine-thirty, but I was in for the night.

I also had a voice mail from my boss, Hal. "Hey, Blake. Hal, here. I was looking for you today. Tilly said you were working on something big. So, uh, did you come up with anything? You've got a week. I'm sorry to give you a deadline, kid, but I can't wait any longer. I'll be in Arizona for a family reunion until Wednesday. I'll see you when I get back. Hopefully, you'll have something for me. Talk to you later. Bye."

Well, no time like the present to go looking for a Dom. I settled into my bed, fired up my laptop, and typed BDSM, Dominants in Las Vegas, into the search. Christ almighty! There were thousands of pages. I clicked on a website called, "Fetish Confidential." It looked nice. It was well designed, very informative, and no typos. The grammar snob in me appreciated that. I made a profile and called myself, Sub-Curious28. It wasn't long before I received chat requests.

Shit. I had fifty requests in five minutes. This was too much. I closed the computer down. I could sift through potential Doms tomorrow when I wasn't so exhausted. Besides, my Kindle was waiting. Last night in my book, *The Apprehensive Submissive*, Alice was about to go the dungeon of pleasure and pain. Her Dom, Lucas, said, "Enough was enough. He was going to own all of her holes tonight." Nobody ever owned any of my holes. They barely rented.

I grabbed my Kindle and picked up where I left off. Oh, yeah, this was good shit. As I read, I imagined I was Alice, kneeling before Lucas and his "steely sword of man meat." He owned her mouth like a "random glory hole." God, it had been so long since I sucked a cock. I slid my hand over my breast, down my stomach, and checked to see how wet I was. Oh, so wet. Lucas did the same to Alice. "Good girl, kitten. You love having your face fucked like a nasty little whore. My whore." I fucked myself right along with Lucas's pace. We were nearing the edge until Lucas grunted and released Alice's mouth. "Turned around, ass in the air. It's time to own your slutty snatch."

Not able to resist temptation, I whipped open my nightstand, picked up Boomer, and put my ass in the air. I placed the Kindle on the bed, turning pages with one hand and turned on Boomer with the other. As I read about "Lucas's triumphant ownership of Alice's hot pocket," my go-to image of Lucas morphed from Chris Hemsworth to... *No!* Adam. It was Adam taking me to "heaven's gate, by fucking me with his stony slab of sausage."

Filthy visions of Adam spanking my ass filled my mind, while Boomer ramped me up to the point of no return. When Lucas gave it to Alice like "a pig banging her beaver blanket" I cried out, "Fuck me, Adam. I want you." And I came. I came twice. *What the hell?* That never happened before. Damn you, Adam Maxwell. Get out of my head!

CHAPTER THREE

ADAM

"Then, she called me an ass!" I scoffed. "This was the worst potential sub you have ever sent me, Sebastian."

I was at The Purple Peacock with my associates, Sebastian Harris and Eli Reece. Recanting my tale of Jessica Blake and her smart mouth.

"Sorry mate," Sebastian said, without an ounce of remorse. "She seemed lovely to me. A bit of a corker."

"I love a feisty sub," Eli added. "I thought you did too. I'm sure your meeting wasn't completely tits-up."

I exhaled in frustration. "I'm going to start needing a translator when I talk to you two. Tits-up? Is that a British thing?"

"Yes. It means it wasn't, uh, you know, total rubbish." Eli explained.

I slammed back the rest of my Jack Daniel's. "Totally rubbish from beginning to end. Did you not hear me say she was a reporter and didn't work at the Palms? What's up with that, Sebastian? What happened with the background check?"

Sebastian bristled. "She was properly vetted. I always do my job. I called The Ghostbar at the Palms myself. Can I help it if she has a mate that lied for her? Maybe you're angry at the wrong person. It wouldn't be the first time."

"What's that supposed to mean?"

Eli and Sebastian exchanged a look and then stared into their drinks with shit-eating grins on their faces.

"What the fuck? Do you think this is funny? Some impertinent reporter lies her way into my penthouse and calls me an ass? You find this amusing?"

Eli covered his mouth to conceal his laughter. "It's quite comical, really. Think about it. When it comes to women, you're an awful arse."

Sebastian chuckled too. "It's true, mate. The real question is what did you do to make her pissed with you?"

I shook my head in disbelief. "Fuck both of you. I didn't do anything. She's the problem. All I said was she was a little too thin for my tastes, and she got all offended."

"You're a bloody idiot," Eli said.

"What the fuck are you talking about?" I sneered.

Eli took a swig of his lager. "You can't and shouldn't criticize a woman for her looks. I have a female cousin back in the UK. She eats loads of food and is thin as a post. Her sisters teased her without mercy. To this day, it affects her."

"Eli's right," Sebastian concurred. "Even if she wasn't going to be your sub, she should be built up and respected. We don't want her flying off on her own, trying to find a Dom online. It's too dangerous."

"Well, fuck me. I am an ass," I admitted.

Sebastian raised his Chivas Regal Scotch. "Cheers to that."

"And you're a dick," I replied half-joking. "Just do me a favor. No more blondes."

Sebastian sipped his drink. "As you wish. But, if I'm being honest, I think Jessica Blake has gotten under your skin."

"Not possible." I craned my neck to check out my options for the night. "In fact, I'm trying to decide where I should bury my cock for the evening. I haven't given Jessica a second thought. So what if she called me an ass, a jerk, and ... dude." I smiled when I thought of the way she said "Sir Dude." Her giant blue eyes grew twice their size. She knew she was being a smart-ass. "Anyway, like I said, not interested."

"What about Lisa?" Eli suggested. "You have a fetish for first-timers. She's been cocktailing here for a while and never had an experience with a Dom. She's very eager."

"I don't think so. Don't get me wrong. She's a sweet girl, and brunette, which I like." I looked in her direction, across the room. She was taking a drink order. "But, Lisa will need more. I sense she's the type to fall hard and fast. So, her first Dom needs to be committed to her, or she'll get hurt. And, since it's been pointed out, I'm an ass. I'm not the Dom for her."

Sebastian gestured to the door. "There's Brandy, our new hostess. She was all over you at the last munch."

"As much as I'd love to get my hands on her, I'm not going there. I haven't told you this, but Brandy has become invaluable to me at Maxwell Industries, and she's not really a submissive."

"She isn't?" Sebastian asked. "Then why is she here?"

"Brandy looks good at the door," I answered. "She's the first thing our invited guests see when they walk in. She's charming, but won't put up with any crap. I trust her completely."

Eli stood and threw back his last bit of lager. "I'll leave the matchmaking of your cock to you two. I have an early morning."

"Eli, are you feeling all right?" I inquired. "You never let work get the in your way of your cock before?"

"What can I say? You can't be a commercial real estate tycoon on no sleep." He tossed some cash on the table. "Plus, as you know, Gracie is tops with me. At the moment, she's the only female in my life."

"That Golden Retriever has mellowed the Master of the cane," Sebastian quipped. "I'd never thought I'd see the day."

"Yeah, me neither. The self-proclaimed Master of the cane and pussy whisperer," I added. "Man, this is a tragedy."

"It's puppy love, actually. I've gone soft." Eli grabbed his crotch. "Except where it counts." He headed out. "Enjoy the burying of your cocks, mates."

"What's with him?" I asked.

"You got me. When we first got to the States, he'd crack a fat for every woman he'd see."

"Crack a fat? Seriously, I'm going to need a new dictionary."

"You know, an erection. He's the horniest fucker I ever met."

"Could be the long hours. He's trying to build and run his business all by himself. I sent a couple of assistants to help out, but he's such a fucking control freak he sent them right back."

Helen, our friend and employee, picked up our empty glasses and put them on her tray. "I went to Eli's office too. But, we didn't get any work done." She grinned. "My ass was black and blue. Best work day ever."

It was good to see Helen smile again after her breakup. "You're looking well, my friend." I offered her the chair between Sebastian and me. "Please, sit. Lisa can look after your tables."

"Thank you." She put down her tray and sat with the most exquisite posture. Her palms laid flat against her thighs, just like Jessica's this afternoon. *Christ*. Why did she pop into my head?

Sebastian's arm fell around the back of the chair. "I'm very proud of you, Helen."

"For what?" She asked in a breathy voice.

"For how strong you've become since the breakup. You've blossomed."

Helen beamed. "I couldn't have gotten through it without all of you. I was such a mess. When Dylan left so suddenly ... I ... missed the lifestyle, and was so desperate for discipline ... I..." She stopped herself and drew her shoulders back. "Anyway, that's the past. And now, I've moved on. I've started painting again."

"That's wonderful." I lightly stroked her chestnut locks. "Are you going to paint us another purple peacock?"

"It's a surprise," she answered with excitement.

Sebastian patted her hand. "That pleases me, my pet."

Jesus! Could he be any more in love with her? Sebastian was such a stubborn son of a bitch. He wouldn't admit it. He claimed they were only BDSM friends with benefits. I suppose on occasion we were too. But, I didn't insist she move in with me after her breakup. Helen was always game for a little playtime in one of our private rooms. I'd never met a more natural submissive in all my years in the lifestyle. She was also a bit of a pain slut. Which was Sebastian's number one fetish.

Helen's eyes darted back and forth between us. "Um, with permission. I would like to please both of you tonight."

My cock stiffened in response. "You have my permission. I would love to share you if that's okay with Sebastian. Maybe he wants you all to himself."

"Fuck off, Maxwell," Sebastian growled. "You heard our friend. She asked to please both of us. She's been such a good girl. So, she has my permission too." He spread her legs, slid his hand between her thighs, and Helen gasped. "Good. You're already wet. Just remember, tonight, this is mine." He shot me a sideways glance. "Adam, you can fuck her ass."

Helen writhed in the chair, with nipples protruding in her purple tank top. "Yes ... oh ... yes, Sir."

Sebastian continued playing with her pussy. "I want you to go to the private room with your favorite king-size four poster bed, get naked for us and wait in your pose by the door." He removed his hand, and it glistened with her juices. "Don't touch yourself, or you won't be allowed to come." He helped peel her out of the seat. "Now go."

Helen couldn't scurry off fast enough.

Sebastian didn't take his eyes off her as she hurried in the direction of the private room.

"Are you sure you want to share her?" I asked.

"What?" He turned his attention back to me. "Why wouldn't I?"

"Because... Are you really going to make me say it?"

"Say what? Come on don't be a wanker. Out with it. My balls are turning blue."

"I'm talking about Helen. She's yours."

"Fuck you." He shoved out of his seat. "I'm beginning to think Jessica Blake is right. You are an ass."

I rose and threw some cash on the table. "Enjoy, Helen."

"You're not joining us?"

"No." I always liked sharing a willing submissive, even if the couple is fully committed to one another, but this was different. "I have an early morning too."

"Suit yourself, mate. But Helen and I are just friends."

I fibbed in agreement, "Absolutely."

As I headed to the door with half a hard-on, Brandy stopped me. "Adam, where are you going?"

"Home. It's been a long day."

"Do you need anything before you go, Sir?"

Brandy was about as subtle as a neon sign.

"No. Thank you. Good night."

* * * *

When I arrived at the penthouse, the lights of the Vegas Strip streamed through the window. I flopped down on the sofa and spotted Jessica Blake's water glass still sitting on the coffee table.

I snatched it up, holding it to the light, and saw the faintest bit of her lipstick. Jessica's lips were full and heart-shaped. *Hmm...* I'd never noticed the shape of a woman's lips before. I could just picture her on her knees with that smart mouth wrapped around my cock.

My dick swelled. The hard-on I had earlier was back with a vengeance. I put the glass back on the table, undid my pants, and my erection sprung free. I gripped my cock. I was in need of serious relief. After a few pumps, drips of pre-cum oozed. My head fell back as I imagined fucking Jessica's face. Her huge blue eyes bulging in wonder as I plunged deep into her throat. Would she be able to take it all?

The pressure built while I jacked myself with both hands vigorously. I envisioned Jessica bouncing on my cock with her big, creamy tits jiggling in my face. *Fuck!* The things I wanted to do with those. She may have called me an ass today, but her nipples poked right through her tight, white shirt, like two round pebbles, that needed to be bitten—hard.

My balls tightened, and I groaned as I shot an enormous load. *Ah, Christ!* My cum jutted forth like it was being fired out of a cannon, one thick ribbon after the next. I squeezed my cock and shafted myself until the last wave spilled out.

I looked down at the incredible amount of jizz all over my Armani shirt. What the hell? I never came that hard when I'd whacked off before. Damn you, Jessica Blake. Get out of my head!

CHAPTER FOUR

JESSICA

"*Dios mio*, Jess," Tilly cried out. "How did this happen?"

"Is it really that noticeable?" My hand flew to the fresh bruise on my cheek. "Can you help me cover it up?"

"I can try."

"Thanks." I shut my office door and sat on the edge of my desk. It was Wednesday, my deadline, and my undercover submissive story hit another bump.

Tilly pulled her makeup bag out of her purse. "Lucky for you, I wear more makeup than a drag queen. What did you do, run into a building?"

"No. The back of hand ran into me?"

"Someone hit you? Who do I need to kill?"

"No one. I can't say."

She slammed her makeup bag on the desk. "What do you mean you can't say? I don't like this one bit." Tilly stared at my left cheek. "I need you to tell me what happened or I swear to God, I'll hug you and start crying."

"Don't do that. I'll tell you. But you can't say anything to anyone."

"Never. You talk. I'll conceal."

"Okay. Deal. You know the meeting I had with Dominick Cane?"

"Yes. You said it was a bus."

"Actually, I said bust. Like I got busted and blew my cover."

"Right. A bus. Go on."

"Anyway, Dominick Cane wasn't his real name. My meeting was with Adam Maxwell."

"What? Adam Maxwell is a Dom? You met him?" she squealed.

"Yes. And you can't tell anyone that either. He was so pissed. He still might call Hal and have me fired. I tried to forget about it, but... God, he's such an ass."

"Adam he's ... not the one who...?"

"No. It wasn't him."

"Good." Tilly continued her makeup magic. "It would be a shame to punch such a pretty face."

For a second, I thought about his perfect, gorgeous ... face... *Shit!* "Anyhow, I signed up on this fetish website. I spent most of Sunday in a chat room, talking to a Dom from Vegas. He seemed nice. He wasn't pushy or aggressive. The other guys I got chat requests from, sent me dick pics before saying hello. So, Dom Aiden seemed like a saint by comparison. I told him I was new to the lifestyle, and he answered all of my questions. So, I agreed to meet him."

"Alone?"

I blew out a shaky breath. "Yes. And, before you lecture me. I get it now. It was stupid."

My hands trembled, and Tilly grasped them in hers. "Jess, what did he do to you?"

"Nothing sexual. God, I've been trying to erase it from my mind. I'm usually pretty quick to move on, but I realize what kind of danger I put myself in. I should've at least called you and said where I was going. I'm an idiot."

"Don't say that, *mija*. You're the smartest woman I know."

"I don't feel smart. But, it was easy to be lulled into a false sense of security."

Tilly resumed her makeup skills on my bruise. "Take a breath and tell me."

"Okay." I exhaled. "At first it was going great. I mean, I made it pretty clear I wasn't necessarily interested in being his submissive, but learning about the lifestyle. And he looked a little smarmy, but was friendly enough. Then my tape recorder, it started to rewind, and he heard it. He ripped my bag out of my hands, fished out the recorder, and ... it was scary. He emptied the contents of my purse on the floor, and demanded to know why I was recording him. When I came clean and told him who I worked for, he became completely unhinged like he had no control over himself. I mean, Adam was angry when he discovered I was a reporter too, but I didn't feel threatened."

"What happened?"

"I scrambled to grab my stuff and get out. When I made a run for the door, he yanked me by the arm and backhanded me across the face. He said, 'If you tell anyone about this, you'll get worse.'"

"Oh, Jess. I'm so sorry." She wrapped her arms around me.

"What are you doing?" My body went rigid.

"I'm hugging you. And you're going to like it." She squeezed me tight. "It's okay to cry if you need to."

I broke our embrace. "I don't need to cry. I need to figure out what I'm going to do. Today's my deadline with Hal. I've got nothing."

"Your deadline? That's what you're worried about? What about the creep who hit you?"

"What about him? There's no point in dwelling on it."

There was a quick rap on the door. Skip, the fair-haired feature reporter poked his head into the room. "Hey, I just heard something. Do you have a second?"

"Sure. What's going on? Is Hal back?" I asked.

"He texted me and said he's on the way," Skip answered and took off his glasses. His normal upbeat demeanor was tempered as he approached my desk. "Jess, there was a murder in your neck of woods this afternoon."

"Oh, my God. Are you sure?"

"You live in The Willows right off of Lake Mead, right?"

"Yeah."

Skip sighed. "This was the next development over, in the Arbors. I don't know much, but right now, it looks like it was random, and they don't have any suspects. So, please be careful."

"I will. You know, my neighbor Stacy is a cop. She told me a couple of weeks ago people were being held up a gunpoint outside the grocery store close to the Willows. Maybe there's a connection. I could help you if you need a backup."

"No. I've got it. You focus on that secret story Hal keeps talking about. He told me to tell you he'll want to know something today when he gets in. Must be big. I couldn't get him to spill any details."

"Oh, it's big," Tilly exclaimed. "It will blow your brain."

"She means mind," I interjected.

"Mind. Brain. What's the difference? Jess is going to blow something."

"You can say that again," I muttered.

Tilly and I laughed, but as usual, jokes went over Skip's cerebral, sweet head. "So, anyway, I'm going to get to work. Be careful."

"Thanks. I will."

He headed out and left my door open.

"Do you want to stay with me for a while?" Tilly asked while finishing up concealing my bruise.

"No. I'll be fine. I have Stacy and Roger."

"Okay. But if you change your mind, you can always crash with me." She held up a little mirror so I could see her work. "What do you think?"

"Much better than when I tried to do it. I knew I could count on you." I swept some of my hair to the left. "If I could just cover it a bit more. I don't want Hal to ask any questions."

"Here. Let me help you. I'll turn you into a blonde Jessica Rabbit."

"I wish. Adam Maxwell said I was too thin for his tastes. What an ass!"

"That's Sir Ass, to you."

Our heads snapped to the door. *Shit*! It was Adam Maxwell, casually dressed in snug jeans and a T-shirt that matched his ocean blue eyes. He had never turned up at our tiny paper before. Was he really going to have me fired?

I hopped off the desk. "If you're looking for Hal, Mr. Maxwell, you're out of luck. He won't be in today."

"Yes, he will," Tilly piped in. "Skip said he was on his way."

I elbowed her, hoping she would share in my blatant lie. "No. He won't. Don't you remember?"

"Yes. That's right. Silly me." She gathered up her things and gave my hair one last tweak. "So, I'm going to go, and let you talk to Mr. Maxwell." She fumbled her way to the door. "I'll just close this. I wouldn't want you to be disturbed by anyone."

"Nice to meet you." Adam smiled. "Whoever you are."

She looked like she was about to say something, but giggled instead, and shut the door.

I glanced at the ground, covering my cheek with my hand. "That's my friend Tilly. She works here too. She's taking over my column."

"And what will you be doing?"

I shrugged. "It looks like I'll be out of a job."

He closed the gap between us. "That's what I came to talk to you about. I have a proposition for you. I'd like to make you an offer."

"No thank you, Mr. Maxwell. I don't like the way you negotiate."

"I think you'll want to hear what I have to say."

I lifted my eyes to meet his, and my heart accelerated. "What are you doing here? Are you trying to get back at me or something?"

"No. It's nothing like that ... I..."

"Look, I apologize for not being upfront with you. Is that what you wanted? Are we good now, because I have work to do."

"Miss Blake, I assure you, that's not why ... I..."

"Then why? Why are you here?" My voice grew louder. "To insult me some more?"

"If you would just let me finish a sentence, I think you'll..."

"I'll what? Think you're not an ass?" My words flew out in rapid succession. "I highly doubt there is anything you could say that would change my mind. Of all the people I've ever met you are the most..."

"Stop." He grabbed my wrists and peered deep into my eyes. For a moment, I thought he was going to kiss me, but he released me and brushed the hair off my face. His brow furrowed when he looked at my cheek. "What's this?" The pad of his thumb wiped away the makeup.

I trembled under his touch. "It's nothing. I'm clumsy."

"Sweetheart." He grasped my shoulders gently and spoke in a soft voice. "Please don't lie to me."

I swallowed and pressed my lips together. "I ... found a Dom online. I met him in person and..."

"Did he do this to you? Did he hit you?"

My eyes fell to the ground. "Yes," I whispered.

Adam slammed his fist into my desk and paced. "Damn it. Who is he? I want his name."

"I'm not telling you that. I can't tell anyone."

"I told you it wasn't safe to go looking for a Dom online," he scolded.

"Well, it would've been if I hadn't blown my cover, again."

"There's no excuse for putting your hands on a woman like that. None."

The online Dom's face flashed through my head. My stomach churned, and heat prickled across my skin. "It's not that big of a deal." I glanced at my blotchy red chest, hid it with my hands, and leaned against my desk.

Adam came to me with an expression of genuine compassion. "It is a big deal." His eyes locked on mine as he drew near and lightly touched the bruise on my cheek. "Does it still hurt?"

Tiny flickers filled my belly. "No ... it's ... okay." Why was he being so caring and charming? *Stop messing with my head, you gorgeous bastard!*

"Good." He cupped my chin, and with a slight smile, advanced even closer.

In a confused panic, I skirted back on the desk. "You're not going to hug me, are you?"

He placed his hands on the outside of my thighs. "You're a real piece of work, Miss Blake." He brought his lips to my ear. "I wouldn't dream of hugging you. I'm an ass, remember?"

Adam's faint scent of sandalwood mixed with warm laundry wafted over me. *Shit! That's nice.* In one long breath, I blurted, "You left out jerk."

He laughed low in his throat. "I suppose I did." He pulled up a chair and propped his feet up on my desk. "So, shall we begin?"

"Begin what?"

"Our negotiation. The way I see it, you need a Dom for your salacious story to save your job, and I've decided to help you."

"But, then it won't be an undercover piece."

"Exactly. That's one of my lines in the sand. You can't go undercover again."

"Why not?"

He shot me a killer grin. "Because, you're really, really bad at it. You're, just the worst."

"I kind of am." I chuckled.

"Now we're getting somewhere. Also, you can ask me anything you like about the lifestyle."

"Anything? But why? Why would you help me after I deceived you? You said it yourself. I'm not your type."

He folded his arms, which made his massive biceps balloon even more. "That's true. You definitely aren't."

"No biggie. You're not my type either."

He smirked. "Sweetheart, I'm tall, dark, and handsome. I'm everyone's type."

"Well, you're clever. I'll give you that," I retorted.

"The truth is, helping you is good business. After I thought about it, a story like yours could create a stir. The better the *Las Vegas Times* does, the more people see my hard-earned advertising dollars at work."

"So, I'll get to be a real reporter?"

"That's right. You'll get your story. And, I'll get you, to do with as I please, for as long as I like."

My breath caught in my throat, and I stuttered, "But ... I–I might be a terrible submissive."

He nodded, delighting in our negotiation. "It is quite possible you don't possess a single submissive bone in your body. I will thoroughly enjoy finding out. So, do we have a deal?"

His piercing sapphire eyes blazed with such fire, they could have burned my clothes right off. I was standing on the precipice of everything I wanted. The temptation within threatened to override any leftover shreds of sense. Was I about to make a deal with the devil? A sexy wicked devil.

I released a ragged breath. "Can I ... can I think about it?"

Hal burst through the door. "Hey, Blake, I'm back, and I hate to do this to you but... Mr. Maxwell?"

Adam rose from the chair and shook his hand. "Mr. Cook. It's so nice to finally meet you in person."

Hal's normal bluster was reduced to dull sputter. "Please, c–call me ... Hal."

Adam released him from his firm grip. "Thank you, Hal. I'm engaged in a rough negotiation with Miss Blake. I understand she wants to be a feature reporter, and I've offered some assistance. But, I can't quite seal the deal."

Hal nearly blew a gasket. "Jess, whatever Mr. Maxwell wants, give it to him."

"I like the way Hal thinks." Adam offered his hand to mine. "Do we have a deal, Miss Blake?"

I hopped off the desk with grand confidence, even though I was quaking on the inside from head to toe. "We have a deal, Adam."

Amusement flashed in his eyes when I called him Adam for the first time. "Very nice, Jessica." Both of his hands embraced mine as he drew me close. "I'm pleased."

Hal blurted out, "This is great. Good work, Jess. I can't remember the last time I was so curious about what one of my reporters were working on. I have so many questions."

I gazed into Adam's eyes and whispered, "So do I."

CHAPTER FIVE

JESSICA

"Do you mind if I tape our interview?" I asked. Fidgeting with my mini recorder.

Adam swiped it from me. "Hasn't this thing gotten you into enough trouble?"

It was two days later, and I was back at Adam's fancy pants penthouse, overlooking the Strip. The view from his cherry wood dining room table was magnificent, even to a jaded local like me.

He studied my recorder a bit closer. "Isn't this a little antiquated? Do they even make cassette tapes anymore?"

I retrieved it from him. "It was my dad's. So, yes, it's old school, but I like it. And you can still buy cassettes, on eBay."

"Good to know." He took a seat next to me, at the head of his table. "You're welcome to tape anything I have to say that is on the record. As long as we're clear, my name or The Purple Peacock will not be mentioned or remotely hinted at in any way."

I nodded in agreement. "Yes, Sir."

A slight smile touched his lips. "Good girl. Let's begin, Miss Blake."

I pressed record. "Oh, you can call me Jess if you like. My friends call me, Jess."

"Well, we'll see. This is just a business deal after all. Isn't it?"

"Totally. It's just business." His reminder of our deal wasn't going to sway me from asking the tough, hard-hitting questions. "So, Mr. Maxwell, are you a sadist?"

"You're cutting to the chase, aren't you, Miss Blake? No foreplay, just right into the rough stuff." He unbuttoned his cuffs and rolled up the sleeves on his pricey, designer shirt. "I don't think everyone can be pigeonholed into a specific label. It's too black and white. It's my opinion most people have an inner streak that leans toward sadism or masochism, maybe some have a little of each. It depends if it's ever tapped into and recognized. For example, people who pay good money to be tortured in an exercise class. They're being pushed past their limits and get off on the adrenaline rush. I would say they have a masochistic side, even if they don't realize it. Does that make sense?"

"Actually, it does. I ran track in junior high. My coach pushed me way beyond my limits. I broke a couple of records. It was exhilarating. Does that make my old coach a sadist?"

"Coaches, fitness instructors, dentists, all sadist." He chuckled. "I'm partially kidding to make a point. When it comes to BDSM, don't get too hung up on labels. Everyone is as different and unique as anyone in the vanilla world. There's no one kind of cookie cutter Dom or sub. They explore and discover a dynamic that works for them. Next question."

I looked down at my extensive list of questions on my notepad and stopped myself. "Wait. You didn't answer the question. Would you consider yourself a sadist?"

He cocked his head. "You're not going to let me get away with anything, are you?"

"No, Sir Dude. I'm not," I quipped.

He rubbed his hand over his chin. "I would say I have sadistic tendencies in the bedroom and in the boardroom. A little pain always makes the interaction more satisfying. Being in control and getting what I want gives me that adrenaline rush. There's nothing like it." His eyes raked over me. "Your chest is getting red."

"Shit. I hate that."

Before I covered it with my hands Adam, reprimanded, "Don't. Remember my rules. This will never work if you can't trust me enough to be vulnerable with me. Flaws and all." He took my hand in his, and his touch made me tingle in all the right places. "And on the record, I don't see it as a flaw." He raised an eyebrow. "It's kind of, endearing."

"Mr. Maxwell, did you just give me a compliment?" I asked in a breathy voice.

"I suppose, I did."

"You're still holding my hand." He let go, and I instantly missed the close contact, but I soldiered on maintaining composure. "This will never work if I can't trust you to keep it strictly business."

"Touché, Miss Blake. What's your next question?"

"You mentioned rules. Do you have a lot of them? Are there more as you get deeper into the relationship?"

"Relationship?" His expression turned serious. "Define what you mean by relationship."

"A relationship. You know. It starts out as casual and evolves into something more over time. Did I say something wrong? You're looking at me like I've sprouted an extra tit in the middle of my head."

"Jessica..." He paused, choosing his words carefully. "My arrangements with my submissives don't evolve into something more. They end. This isn't one of your books. I'm sorry if I gave you the wrong impression."

A brief pang of something I couldn't identify pinged me in my gut. But, I quickly recovered. "Well, be still my cold, dead heart. You're such a romantic." I laughed nervously. "You didn't give me the wrong impression. I was just curious about your past arrangements."

"That's a relief. I wouldn't want you to think this could lead to anything beyond our deal. I don't like to engage in things I don't excel at. And I don't excel at romantic entanglements. I've been told I'm an awful boyfriend, so I don't bother."

"I get that. I suck at relationships too." Truer words were never spoken!

He appeared relieved. "Then you understand where I'm coming from. You're a good writer, so you write. I'm good at, this," He gestured to the Strip. "So, I continue to roll the dice, and build my empire one casino at a time."

"Do you think you're a good Dom?"

"Contrary to what you said the other day, yes. I do think I'm a good Dom, but a better teacher."

"What do you mean?"

He leaned forward with a wicked look in his eyes. "I love the art of play. I can find out more about a woman in one hour of playtime than most husbands know about their wives. Like the way her body responds the first time she's spanked tells me so much."

Lord, have mercy on my kinky soul! I pressed my knees together. "What ... um ... what does it tell you?"

The corners of his mouth upturned into a panty-drenching grin. "It usually tells me she wants more, much more. I can teach her how pain brings pleasure, and how surrendering control makes a woman feel free ... and wet..."

He rose out of his seat and turned off the recorder. "You're wet, aren't you?"

My words escaped in a hushed tone. "What makes you say that?"

Adam moved behind my chair, and his scent invaded my senses. "It's written all over your body. Your breathing, your flushed cheeks. The way you're squirming slightly in your seat." He swept my hair to one side and trailed his fingertip along the back of my neck. "You need to come."

Every cell in my body vibrated with electricity. He was right. I needed to come.

Both of his hands clasped my shoulders. "How long has it been since a man made you come?"

"Uh ... so long," I murmured.

"Sit on the edge of the table and face the Strip. I feel like playing."

Without hesitating or thinking, I perched myself on the end of the table, overlooking Las Vegas Boulevard. Doing what he asked brought an even greater ache between my legs.

"Good girl," he said with a low rasp to his voice. Adam positioned himself in front of me, with a focused intensity in his eyes. "Now, I'm going to ask you again. Are you wet?"

"Yes, Sir," I whispered.

"It would please me to make you come. Is that what you want?"

I closed my eyes and exhaled. "Yes..."

"Open your eyes and look at me. We aren't fucking, and we aren't getting naked. This is just about what you need right now. Spread your legs."

I hiked up my periwinkle summer dress, and opened up to him, delirious with arousal.

Adam slid my thong to the side. "Your panties are soaked." He dipped a finger inside, making me gasp. "Jesus, you're ready to explode. If you think my hand feels good, wait until I'm deep inside you, fucking you hard with my cock. I'm going to make your pussy weep until you can't take anymore."

I careened backward, bracing myself with my palms, and thrusting my pelvis with his rhythm. He was so right. I was ready to explode. Adam dove another digit inside me, and his fingers fucked me more expertly than any dick in recent memory.

I bit my lip to keep from screaming, but it was no use. The moans coming out of me grew louder with each plunge toward climax.

My head relaxed back as he held me on the threshold of orgasm. If only he would rub my...

"I can feel it, sweetheart. You're about to burst. Consider this your first lesson from me." Adam grunted and slowed down his strokes.

My head snapped upright in response. "Oh, please."

"Please, what?"

"Please, Sir."

"Tell me what you want. Say it, Jessica."

"I want to come." I gasped. "I need to. Please."

His finger thrusts amped back up. "That's a good girl. I'm almost ready to let you."

"Almost?" I panted.

He grabbed my throat. "Doms love control and orgasms. Being my sub means submitting all your pleasure to me. At this moment, your pussy is mine."

The pad of his thumb brushed over my sensitive clit, and I winced. It would have been so easy to let go and come, but I held back. Pain and pleasure mixed together in this burgeoning implosion between my legs.

Finally, working my hooded flesh, he gave me just the right amount of friction. Every muscle in my body tensed. He squeezed my throat and violently fucked my pussy with his hand.

"Now, Jessica," he growled. "Come. You can come now."

I shrieked as I toppled over the edge. My arms gave way, and I collapsed on the table. Adam released my throat, pressing his palm flat against my chest, securing me in place while my orgasm pulverized me in sharp waves of ecstasy.

When I stopped flailing like a mad woman, and my eyes focused, Adam was smiling down at me. He reached under my dress and peeled off my wet thong. "I'm going to keep this. You'll get it back when you least expect it." He looked at it dangling from his finger. "Blue. It matches your dress. Very nice."

"Periwinkle." I heaved and hauled myself up. "They're both periwinkle."

"Periwinkle it is." He tossed my thong, and it landed on the limb of an indoor plant, hanging like a Christmas ornament. He nodded. "I might redecorate in here."

"What are you going to call it? Thong chic?"

"Something like that."

"I guess, I should go now?" I hopped off the table and lost my balance.

Adam captured me by my midsection. "Easy." He held me against his steely frame. "Did I say I wanted you to leave?"

"Um ... I just assumed." His erection dug into my stomach and robbed me of my breath. *Shit.* He was huge. "What ... what would you like me to do?"

"Not what you think, sweetheart. Not yet, anyway."

Being this close to him stirred everything in me. Even after that monstrous climax, I wanted more. I wanted him inside me. I wanted to feel that huge cock fuck me senseless. I peeked up at him with parted lips, begging him to kiss me.

He grazed his index finger along my jawline. "On second thought, I think it would be best if you went home."

I lowered my head in defeat. "Yeah. You're probably right."

"Jessica." His deep voice resonated in my belly. "I want you to go directly home, draw yourself a bath, and relax. Think about the way you came, how you fell apart all over my hand. Imagine every single moment my fingers slid inside you." He took a deliberate step away from me and continued, "And, don't even think about touching yourself. If you do, I'll know. Any questions?"

"Just one. Can I take a shower instead?"

He slight grin touched his lips. "Fine. A shower instead. But everything else applies. Think about everything that happened this afternoon, but no masturbating. Are we clear?"

My pussy was already throbbing in need, but I gritted my teeth and obeyed. "Yes, Sir."

Besides, he would never know...

* * * *

I dashed home, bobbing and weaving through the Friday afternoon Vegas traffic. Driving without panties was one more thing I found exhilarating about today. So far, being a submissive trumped breaking records in the hundred-meter dash. What else would I discover about myself while I was working on my story?

My cul-de-sac was quiet when I parked my car in the driveway. Roger and Stacy were probably at work. I kept meaning to touch base with Stacy about the murder at the Arbors, but the past couple of days, we hadn't run into each other.

I hopped out of the car, anxious to follow Adam's instructions. When I hurried inside, I got a furry surprise.

"Harley! Hello, mister."

He did a quick sit. Then excitement took over as he twirled around me. What a greeting. Too bad humans couldn't greet one another with more butt wiggling enthusiasm.

There was a note laying on the end table in my small TV room:

Hey, Jess. I got called in last minute for an extra shift. I hope you don't mind looking after Harley. He had a long walk this morning, and I fed him right before I left. Don't let him tell you differently. LOL! Thank you so much. I'll be over in the morning to pick him up. I'll text you to make sure you're awake. Take care,

*Roger. PS Stacy wanted me to remind you to
keep your doors locked. She's working late.*

"Well, Harley, looks like it's just you and me tonight.
You want some chicken?" His ears perked up like two
antennas. "Okay, come on. It's practically the only thing
I have to eat in this place. Don't tell Roger. He said he
fed you already."

Harley trotted along like he understood every word
I said. I gave him a little morsel of chicken, and we
padded up the stairs. He made a beeline for the tile in
the den, and I made one for the shower. After all, I had
to follow orders.

Minutes later, the scalding water pelted my pale
skin. I slathered my passion fruit body wash all over me,
leaned against the wall, and did as Adam asked. I
thought about everything, but took a mental inventory
of specific things that caught me off guard, things I
didn't know would turn me on, like having my throat
grabbed. I placed my hand around my throat reveling, in
the memory of his expertise. My fingertips found their
way to my nipples, and I teased myself, which I wasn't
supposed to do.

Being disobedient fueled a growing need in my
pussy. *Shit.* Adam said not to. Then I closed my eyes,
remembering how wet he made me by simply saying the
word, spank. A spanking. Maybe I would get a spanking
for not obeying. My hands floated over my stomach and
rested just above my mound. Should I? My horny
rationale was that this particular masturbating session
was purely work related. I had to finger myself, to get to
the spanking, to help my piece for the paper.

A girl's got to do what a girl's got to do. I helped
myself to a piece of me. I spread my lips with one hand,
and my fingers rubbed my clit with vigor. The initial
delight I took in having a go at my lady boner suddenly
faded. I stopped and was overcome with an odd feeling

deep inside that I didn't understand. Adam ... Sir... He would be disappointed.

I shut off the shower, plucked up my towel, and dried off. While throwing on my old black jogging shorts and tank top, it dawned on me. What the hell am I going to do with my Friday night? I couldn't dare read the rest of *The Apprehensive Submissive*. I'd never make it to the end without... My doorbell rang.

"Harley!"

He scampered down the hall as if he said, "Hey, Jess, there's someone at the door."

"Yes. I know. You have to come with me, buddy. You're my protector. Come on. Run with me."

We flew down the stairs, and I peered out the peephole. What the hell? It was Adam.

I cracked opened the door a little. "Uh ... hi."

He shoved his hands in his shorts and raised an eyebrow. "Hi. You don't look happy to see me."

Harley was going nuts trying to get to Adam, but not barking.

"I'm just surprised. How do you know where I live?"

"Your address was on your paperwork you filled out for Sebastian. Have I interrupted something? I'll go if you like. You seem a little busy?"

"No. It's fine. I just wasn't expecting you, and my place is a mess. Plus, I have company."

"Company?" For the first time, Adam looked a little unsure of himself. "Male company?"

"Yes," I teased. "And I'm in love with him. Adam, meet Harley."

I threw open the door, and Harley bounced out to the porch to say hi. His exuberance didn't faze Adam one bit.

"Hey, Harley." He calmed him down. "Good boy. I didn't know you had a dog."

"I don't. He belongs to my neighbor across the cul-de-sac. He's a dealer at the Golden Nugget. He's been working a lot of doubles, so Harley stays with me."

"So, your neighbor works for the competition?"

"Actually, he'd like to work for you. He said the other day he's been trying to get a job at one of your casinos."

"What's his name?"

"Roger Walker. He's a great guy."

"Consider it done."

"Well, in that case, won't you come in, Mr. Maxwell?"

The three of us stepped into my townhouse. Harley spun in circles, barked once, and tore down the hall to my kitchen.

"He wants out. Harley has a ficus tree he likes to nap under, you know, after he waters it." I motioned left to my TV room. "You can take a load off in there if you like."

"Thank you. But, I'm fine right here. I probably won't stay long."

As I hurried to the kitchen, I thought to myself, *Whatever, Sir Dude.* I let Harley out and took my sweet time sauntering back down the short hallway. I caught him scrutinizing me, like I was a riddle he couldn't solve.

"So, Mr. Maxwell, what can I do for you?"

He folded his arms across his chest. "Well, when you left the penthouse, I gave you strict instructions. I'm here to see if you obeyed."

"Oh." I exhaled with nervous knots tightening in my stomach. "I drove right home and got in the shower."

He stalked around me like an animal in heat, brushed his fingertips over my collarbones and sniffed my neck. "You do smell fresh from the shower. Good girl." He brought my hand to his lips. "What about..." He shoved his free hand in my shorts. "What about this?" He fondled my pussy. "Did you touch yourself?"

I nearly evaporated under his touch. "I–I couldn't help myself. I'm sorry."

Releasing my hand, he pressed two fingers inside me. "Where's your bedroom?"

"Ah… It's—up—stairs."

Adam whipped his hands out of my shorts. "You're going to be punished. Get your ass upstairs."

"Yes, Sir."

He took a step back and let me lead the way to my bedroom. My heart thudded so loud I felt it in my ears. Exactly what kind of punishment was awaiting me? "Sir, in my defense…"

"Sweetheart, there's no defense. It was a simple request, and you were a disobedient submissive. I need to teach you a lesson."

My bedroom looked like thieves had ransacked the place. I'd made a giant mess getting ready for our "interview" today. I couldn't decide what to wear, so clothes and shoes were strewn everywhere.

"Wow! Were you robbed?" Adam joked.

I gathered up everything on my bed and tossed it on the chair close by. "I told you the place was a mess." I kicked some strappy sandals under the bed and turned to face Adam and my punishment.

"Are you always this untidy?" he asked in a low tone, fully back in Dom mode.

"Sometimes."

"Are you always so disobedient?"

"I'll try to do better, Sir."

"Good. Now, turn around."

I did what he asked, and he yanked down my shorts, leaving my butt completely bare. He placed the palm of his hand against my ass cheek, and every nerve ending in my body came to attention. His arm coiled around my waist with his massive hard-on, burrowing into my back. "Lay on the bed, face up. I want to see if you taste as good as you feel."

I angled my face to his. "Really? You're not going to punish me?"

With flaring nostrils, he whispered, "Just do what I say, sweetheart."

My pussy pulsed in anticipation as I stepped out of my shorts and reclined on the bed, just like he said.

A wicked smiled crept across his face as he opened up my legs. "I need you tell me when you're about to come. Are we clear?"

"Yes, Sir," I gasped.

"Now, spread yourself a little wider for me. Let me see."

I arched my back, granting him more access.

"Good girl." He knelt on the bed, peering down at me with carnal longing in his eyes. His index finger swiped along my slit. He growled in appreciation. "So wet."

He grabbed my hips, and his mouth came down on my pussy. First, his tongue slithered gently over my clit. Then he ate me like a famished wild man.

If this was a punishment, then color me disobedient for life! I was already nearing the point where my greedy gratification took over. My heels dug into the bed, and I pressed myself into his lips that suctioned around my clit. One hand released my hips, so his thrusting fingers could find their way inside my wanting hole. My pussy flooded with juices as my internal muscles clenched around his probing digits.

The craving to climax all over his tongue had me convulsing in pleasure. "Oh, God. I'm close ... I'm about to..."

He stopped! *No!* My head snapped up, and Adam wiped his mouth with the back of his hand. "And that, sweetheart, is your punishment. Have a nice night." He sauntered toward the door.

"Wait!" I jostled to my knees, still quivering from the inside out. "You can't leave me like this."

"I can and I will."

"Can't we negotiate?" I asked in desperation.

He shook his head. "I don't negotiate when it comes to punishments."

"But, you didn't hear me out, when I said I couldn't help myself."

"I think you're grasping at straws, Miss Blake. But, go ahead."

Relieved, I collected myself, ready to litigate my case, even though I was a plaintiff with no pants. "The truth is I did exactly what you said, I thought about the way you, made me come, and at first I was so turned-on, I touched myself. But, then I felt ... bad, I guess, because, I knew you would be disappointed in me. So, I stopped."

His expression was hard to read, but the hunger in his eyes, gave me hope. Adam took one precise step toward the bed. "That actually tells me a lot."

"Am I forgiven?"

"Absolutely," he said with a slight smile. "But your punishment still stands."

And yet a tremendous erection created a pop tent in his shorts, like a get out of orgasm jail, free card. "Are you sure there isn't anything I can, do?" I summoned all my inner sexy, which wasn't much, and crawled across the bed. *Oh yeah!* This was working like a charm until I tripped myself up, and face-planted with a splat. *Why does God hate me?*

An audible gasp and chuckle escaped from Adam. "Uh, are you all right?"

"Yes," I said with my face still plastered on my comforter. "I came in a little too hot."

He hoisted me up by my armpits and brushed the hair from my face. "Yes. You did. That was an interesting tactic, Miss Blake. Just what were you hoping to accomplish?"

My breath hitched, staring into his cobalt, brilliant eyes. "I thought I could take care of you the way you took care of me at the penthouse."

I slid a tentative hand over his crotch, and he snatched up my wrist. "Do you know how tempted I am to fuck the shit out of you right now?" He pushed his hardness into my stomach. "Feel what you do to me. I've thought of nothing but fucking you since the day you and your smart mouth left the penthouse. But, you need discipline. Get on your knees."

I flew to the floor and kept my head down.

His shorts hit the honey beige carpet, and he stepped out of them. "Jessica, look at me."

"Yes, Sir." My eyes slowly skated up his sculpted, strong legs, and found their way to his— "Oh..." My mouth fell open at the sight of his handsome, lengthy girth of cock.

"You're going to suck me dry, sweetheart. And I don't plan on being gentle. Does your smart mouth have any questions?"

"No, Sir." I gulped.

"You'll need a safe word."

I peeked up at him. "How can I say it with my mouth full?"

"Such a smart-ass." He palmed the back of my head. "If you're almost to the point that you can't take anymore, hit the floor with your hand, and I'll make sure you can say your safe word if you need it. You can choose anything you like."

My eyes met with his third one. "Blow-pop."

A hint of a grin spread across his face. "Fine. Blow-pop. Now, open up for me like a good girl."

I licked my lips and took his tip into my mouth. Almost immediately drops of his pre-cum awakened my taste buds. He hissed and pushed more velvety inches inside. Once he settled into firm, even strokes, his hands gathered up my hair. He twisted it and wrapped it around his wrist, creating an anchor to control the fucking of my face. His tip shoved deep into the back of my throat, and I gagged.

He quickly came out of my mouth. "Take in a big breath. I'm going to fuck your throat."

I inhaled, and my throat expanded. His cock plunged back inside while he held my head still, grunting with each forceful thrust. Salvia was dripping down my chin, with my cheeks bulging, and eyes watering. Then, my pussy flushed in desire. I wanted this. I wanted his cum.

He pulled out of me and growled. "Good girl. Now use your hands. Jack that cock."

I gripped his dick and stroked him with both hands. We both moaned while I watched his veins pulsate. *Shit!* This was one glorious cock. And I was the one bringing it pleasure. I brought one hand to his balls and squeezed them gently. Then I glided my index finger over his smooth perineum. It made him crazy.

Adam groaned. "Get your mouth on me, now."

I took in a breath, and his hands gripped my head. He slammed me to his base and shafted my face in fast, furious strokes. I held onto his muscled thighs, and accepted every brutal thrust he gave me.

"That's it. Fuck. Take my cum, take it all."

He blew his load, and I swallowed down every drop of his tasty cream. A proud, euphoric feeling swept through my core and settled in my pussy. I was still desperate to come.

Adam extracted himself from my mouth. "Nicely done, Jessica." His hand caressed my cheek. "I'm pleased."

I wiped my mouth off on my tank top and heaved. "Are you pleased enough to, um?"

"Still negotiating?"

"You can't blame a girl for trying."

"Did it turn you on, surrendering your mouth for my pleasure?"

"Yes. More than I thought it would."

"Sit on the bed," he ordered with a look of indecision.

I hopped up on the bed, pressing my legs together. I was so wet with arousal, and the throbbing in my pussy was excruciating.

"I do admire your determination," Adam said in a matter-of-fact tone. "Spread yourself. I want to see how you enjoyed getting your face fucked."

I stretched myself wide for him, and his hand surveyed my wetness. The corners of his mouth upturned in a devilish grin. "You're drenched. It would be so easy to send you over the edge." One finger dove inside. "You have such a tight little pussy. I'm going to love making you scream when I fuck you."

I wilted back on the bed. "I want to scream for you... Please... Please make me scream."

He removed his hand. "Not yet. But I am willing to negotiate."

I popped back up. "Okay. Anything."

"Anything? Be careful, Miss Blake, you're showing me all your cards."

"That's because my Queen of Diamonds is desperate!" I blurted.

"Relax. I'm feeling generous. I'm going to give you a choice. You can either not come and accept your original punishment, or you don't stop coming until I say so."

"That's a serious choice? Of course, I want the second thing you said."

He leaned down, brushing his lips across my cheek. "Very well. Lay back, sweetheart. You're under my control now."

I slid back on the bed and reclined. Why did he appear so cocky about my choice? Who wouldn't pick it? That look of intensity gripped his face as he peered down at me. Excitement mixed with curious trepidation coursed through my lower abdomen. What had I done?

My heart rate spiked when Adam's voracious mouth landed on my clit. He sucked my pink erection until I cried out in sweet anguish. His tongue's swift strokes over my slit brought my first orgasm forward in no time.

My heavenly climax gave me the relief I had craved since the shower. All the pressure finally released and left my pussy flesh sensitive to Adam's touch. I squirmed and nudged his head away.

"Oh, I don't think so." Adam pushed himself off the bed and rifled through the pile of clothes on the chair. "Remember, you chose this. We're not stopping until I say you've had enough."

He found the belt on my bathrobe and tied my wrists over my head. "Where's your vibrator?"

"What? I don't..." I couldn't lie, especially now. "It's in my nightstand."

He retrieved it and fired it up. "Now, you're going to keep still for me and take this like a good girl. I promise I won't push you too far, but you're going to be forced to orgasm."

My body calmed and came off its high from the first release. Oddly enough, being tied up at his mercy made me feel brave. "Push me. I want you to."

Over the next hour, Adam took me on a ride of sweet torture, where adrenaline charged pleasures and agony mingled together, casting me into a crazy, yet blissful void. Time and space disappeared, and my mind honed in on his soft, rich voice, guiding me through each peak and valley. My body was fried, wrung out, covered in sweat, and tingled with a satisfied peace. If sore was the next sexy, then, I was one sexy beast.

How did he know how to do this to me? We barely knew each other. And yet...

While he put his shorts back on, he kept his eyes on me, looking at me with admiration. "You did very well, sweetheart. I'm impressed."

"I'm spent. That was ... you're really ... ugh. Not even my mouth can move. You must be relieved."

He let out a small laugh. "Well, it has been rather busy. Along with the rest of you." He headed to the door. "Close your eyes for a little while. I'm going to your kitchen and see what I can find. I'm starving. You must be too."

"I am, but you won't find much in my kitchen, besides take-out menus."

"I'll figure it out. Just rest."

"Can you let Harley in?"

"Sure. I'll take care of it," he said in a low voice, and left.

* * * *

When my eyelids flipped open, it was dark in my bedroom. I hurried to the bathroom, freshened up, and threw on a clean pair of shorts and a tank. I padded downstairs not sure what time it was. Where was Harley? Was Adam still here?

The light from the TV room led my way in the darkness, and I smelled something delicious.

"Hey. You're still here?" I asked.

"Absolutely." Adam was chilling out on my sofa checking his phone, with Harley by his side. "It would be irresponsible to leave you after our session. I take my role as your Dom seriously, even if it is just a business arrangement. I wanted to make sure you're okay, see if you had any questions for me."

"I always have questions." I shrugged. "Like what smells so good?"

"I ordered Thai food. It's in the kitchen. Are you hungry?" He started to get up.

"Yeah. Stay put I'll get it."

A few minutes later we dined picnic style on a feast of orange chicken, pad Thai, and potstickers. Adam also had them deliver a nice bottle of Shiraz. Harley tried to join in, but as usual, gave up and flopped down in the hallway.

"This is so good," I said between bites. "Thank you. I didn't realize how hungry I was."

"You do have quite an appetite," Adam observed. "That pleases me."

"Are you surprised? I hope you didn't think I was one of those girls that starves herself."

"I did wonder. Especially when I saw the contents of your pantry. There's nothing in there but an assortment of chips."

"I like chips. I'm a connoisseur. There's kettle cooked, blue corn, chips cooked in avocado oil. Oh, and don't forget the ones made from sweet potatoes. That's like eating salad."

"I'll remember that." He sipped his wine. "So, how are you feeling?"

"Sore, but okay. No complaints."

"I'm sorry, I'm not always an overly affectionate Dom. I probably should have stayed in your room and held you for a while."

"Held me? Dude, trust me, we're good. I don't need all that lovey-dovey shit."

"Then, I think we understand each other. Do you have any more questions?"

"Only a million. Can I get my recorder?"

"I'd rather you get a deck of cards if you have one?"

"I think so. Why?"

He placed our empty plates and containers on the coffee table. "Because I have a few questions for you too. How about we make it interesting. High card gets to ask a question."

I hopped up from the floor. "Okay." After rifling through the drawer on the end table, I grabbed an old deck of cards in a black velvet box. "As long I can ask some extra nosey questions. I have those too—here." I handed them to Adam.

He opened them. "These are, as you would say, old school, like your tape recorder. Were they your Dad's too?"

I parked myself back on the floor. "That sounds like a question. I don't believe we've decided who's asking the first one."

"Fair enough, Miss Blake."

"I'm just kidding. I don't mind talking about my dad. He was amazing. That's us in the picture on the wall. He taught me how to play softball that summer."

"Look at those blonde pigtails. So, you were quite the tomboy, softball and track?"

"I guess so. I think I still am in a lot of ways."

"Are you close?"

I lifted my wine to my lips, debating how much I should divulge. "Well, he passed away when I was eighteen. A brain aneurysm."

"I'm so sorry, Jessica. I had no idea."

"Don't be sorry. You didn't know. It was ten years ago. I'm a big girl. I can handle talking about him without falling apart. I just focus on what a great dad he was, you know, the good things. Which doesn't mean I don't miss him. I do. I miss him every day. He was my person."

"Your person?"

"Yeah. Your person. You know, the person who is always there for you, who loves you unconditionally. The one you can count on. Like Harley and Roger, my neighbor. Roger is Harley's person." Harley heard his name, trotted over, and plopped down between us. "Does someone want attention?" He rolled on his side, for a belly rub.

Adam petted his stomach. "Harley, you're being a bit submissive."

"He's a lover, not a fighter."

"When he spends the night, does he sleep with you?"

"Sometimes." I scratched him behind the ears. "He's either all in or all out."

"What do you mean?"

"If he sleeps in my bed, he's right up against me, and if he's not in the bed, he's down the hall in my den. So, he's all or nothing."

Harley had his fill, got up, shook and went back to the hallway.

"See, that's so him," I exclaimed. "He got what he wanted and left. Typical male."

"Is that what you really think?" Adam asked with a puzzled expression.

"That, Mr. Maxwell, will cost you. If you get the high card, I'll answer that question."

He shuffled the deck, made two piles, and we drew a card. "A Jack, Miss Blake. Beat that."

I flipped over my card. "A lousy three. You win."

"What I'd really like to know is why you said you suck at relationships. What do you mean by that?"

"That's a loaded question. How much time do you have?"

"Until this bottle of wine is empty."

I chugged my last swallow. "Deal. Hit me again. I'll have it gone in no time."

He poured me half a glass. "Wine this good is meant to be sipped, slowly. Now, there's a question on the table."

I lifted my pinky in jest and slurped the tiniest drop. "But, of course, Mr. Maxwell. So, are you ready for this? I was engaged."

"Really? What happened?"

"Well, for starters, I should have never said yes to his proposal. We were only twenty-one. But when my dad died suddenly, Danny's family asked me to move in with them. And since my mom's life was and still is a total shit show, I did. The truth is, I was more in love with his family than him. Growing up it was just me and my dad, which was great, but Danny had a big family, and they were close, like a living Norman Rockwell painting."

"Did you break it off?"

"Eventually. Danny's mom wanted to plan the wedding, and every time she talked about wedding dresses and centerpieces, my chest turned red. At first, I thought it was because I'm not that girly. I could give a rip about flowers and all that crap. Then, I realized, Danny and I just didn't fit together. Something was off. I just couldn't put my finger on it. So, I broke up with him. And for the longest time, I felt like the biggest jerk. His family wanted nothing to do with me. I think that's what hurt more than ending it with him. Meanwhile, I did him a huge favor."

"How so?"

"Danny's gay. He came out of the closet four years ago. We're good now. He lives in California, but if I ran into him, it's like totally cool."

"Was he your only serious relationship?"

"Well, that's another question. But, I'll give you this one for free. The answer is yes. After I got the column at the *Las Vegas Times*, I went a little nuts. I partied way too much. Maybe it was a way to numb the loss of my dad and Danny. I don't know, but I was out almost every single night. There were plenty of men, but it's kind of hard to form anything beyond a hook-up at a nightclub. Plus, I obviously can't pick the right ones."

"Interesting. Shall we draw to see who gets the next question?"

"Sure. I hope it's me. I got the ding-dong daddy-o of questions."

Adam flipped over his card. "Hmm ... a six."

I turned over mine. "Ha! A nine! Oh, a six and a nine, sixty-nine." I laughed. "That's an awesome number. I think I might be getting a little tipsy."

He topped off my glass. "I like tipsy Jessica Blake. You seem so relaxed."

"Thanks. I think. What was I earlier?"

"You were lovely. I just meant, sometimes you strike me as being a bit on edge, or guarded, and definitely driven. Which aren't bad things."

"What can I say, Sir Dude, you might be growing on me. I mean, good food and sex, and if I'm not mistaken, I don't have to worry about you staying the night and taking up all the room in my bed."

"You aren't mistaken. I do have to go soon. You better ask your question."

"Okay. It's something I've been curious about for a while. It's about your ex, Monica Preston."

"Monica? We ended our engagement six years ago. That's hardly a secret. Unfortunately, our breakup was tabloid fodder for even national publications." He downed the rest of his wine. "Why would you ask me about that?"

"Hey, I'm not trying to piss you off. I've just always wondered if I was right about something I put in my column. Your broken engagement was one of my first stories."

He sighed. "Right about what?"

"Everyone else reported the breakup was mutual. But I had a hunch and did some digging. I found a friend of Monica's that said she broke up with you. I confirmed with some of my sources at the clubs. Was I right?"

He rested his back against the couch. "That was you? I remember that. It's one of the reasons I started buying advertising with the *Las Vegas Times*. I was intrigued. I remember thinking, who is this nosey reporter that wouldn't publish our statement and leave it at that. You were right. She ended it with me."

"I knew it." I moved to my knees. "So, here's the part that never made sense to me. If she ended it with you, why did you stick by her side when her dad was on trial for fraud? Gosh, I tried so hard to talk Hal into letting me cover that story. But, I had just started working for the paper. Skip got it. And between us, he sure did take it easy on Blair Preston."

"Wow. You ask insightful questions, Miss Blake. I wouldn't want to get on your bad side."

"Will you answer them?" I asked pleading.

"I think I did earlier. She broke up with me because I'm a horrible boyfriend. And she was right. I stood by her side during the trial because I thought it was the right thing to do. Plus, her father, Blair, tried to claim he was mentally unfit to stand trial, and was evaluated by a psychiatrist. The psychiatrist, Olivia, is an old friend of mine. She deemed him mentally stable. He was furious and thought I should have helped him, so I ended up paying for his legal team. He already resented my success. I didn't feel I had much choice. Obviously, that was a complete waste of money. His Ponzi scheme landed him in federal prison for the rest of his life. Monica was left penniless, and I helped her start over again. She owns a boutique in one of my casinos."

"But, did you do all that because you wanted to win her back?"

He paused and gazed into my eyes. "I should go."

"Go? Are you kidding? We just got to the best part!"

He rose from the floor, placed his wine glass on the coffee table, and offered me his hand. "I think that's enough questions for one night. I want you to get a good night's sleep, and rest tomorrow. I need you ready for Sunday."

I clamored to my feet and slugged back my wine. "Sunday? What's happening Sunday?"

He took my glass from me and set it down. "Easy." He cupped my chin with his hands. "You'll find out when you get to my penthouse. Seven-thirty. And don't be late."

"Or, I'll be spanked? I was kind of hoping for that today."

"I normally don't like to think of spankings as punishments. I prefer the term, fun-ishments."

"Okay, now you're just making crap up."

He laughed more heartily than I had ever heard him before. "You'll just have to wait and see, Miss Blake." He glided to the door. "Sunday morning I'll send you an email. It contains a list of things I'd like to slowly introduce into our playtime. Look it over and let me know if you have any objections."

I followed behind. "What kind of things?"

He turned to me with a cocky expression. "Again. You'll have to wait. I'm not answering any more questions tonight." He opened the door. "Be sure to lock up. This neighborhood is—"

"Is perfectly fine, Mr. Moneybags."

Adam stood on the porch with a smirk and moonlight gleaming down his sexy ass chin. "Such a smart mouth. Good night, Jessica." He strutted to his car, like a baller.

"Good night, Sir." I almost hated to see him leave. "Oh, just one more thing."

He opened the door to his black Mercedes. "What's that?"

"Are you ever going to kiss me?"

"Not until you're mine, sweetheart. Not until you are all mine."

He slipped into his car and sped away, disappearing into the night.

Was I going to be his? What does that even mean to a man like Adam "no entanglements" Maxwell? Now I had even more questions. My temptation to find out the answers would have to wait. Sunday couldn't get here fast enough.

CHAPTER SIX
JESSICA

At ten a.m. on Sunday morning, I was in bed waiting for Adam's email to arrive. I couldn't remember the last time I woke up this excited. I kept refreshing my laptop and procured all my favorite things, Red Bull, kettle cooked chips, and Harley. Poor Roger worked another double, so Harley spent the night with me again. He cuddled close, and his expressive brown eyes followed my hand each time it dove into the chip bag.

Of course, I shared a few nibbles. "Don't tell Roger. He'll think I'm spoiling you."

Harley sighed, and I tapped the refresh button again. *Bingo!* It was here:

"Good morning, Jessica, I hope you are well-rested and ready for this evening. I've attached a list of items that I enjoy using in a scene. (Some refer to Dom/sub playtime as a scene or a session – good information for your article.) Please put a Y by the ones you'd be willing to try, an X next to the ones that are a hard no, and a question mark next to the ones you are unsure of. I know how you love your questions. You'll find I'm not into anything too extreme. That's why I'm a good fit and teacher for new subs. Think of me as a starter Dom.

As my submissive, my expectations are that you will be respectful and honest with me, communicate openly, and obey me. You already know, you will be punished if you don't. Normally, my punishments include being sent to the corner, orgasm denial, or both. All Doms have different forms of punishment, some do spank their subs in the heat of the moment, but I don't. I want you to enjoy your "fun-ishments" like spanking, flogging, etc. I never have spanked any of my subs in anger, and I never will. So, don't manipulate the situation to earn a spanking. I do not play games. If I feel you are not respecting my rules, you will be dismissed, even if your article isn't finished. I've been somewhat easy on you because of our business arrangement. If you choose to come to my penthouse tonight, you will be treated the same way I've treated all of my other subs. No negotiating. Once your article is complete, our Dom/sub relationship will be over, and we will both move on. I do hope to open you up fully and give you the proper training to serve your next Dom well if you decide to remain in the lifestyle. I see potential in you, Miss Blake, as a successful journalist and submissive. There's a powerful fearlessness in you if you choose to own it and make it yours.

Please get the attachment back to me before two this afternoon. I want to give you time to think about each item, but I also want to plan our scene according to what you're comfortable with. If you send the attachment back, I will expect you at the penthouse at seven-thirty sharp wearing a little black dress, heels, and nothing else. I also expect you to spend the night. Please eat a light meal ahead of time. I will not be wining and dining you. (Friday was a rare exception.) This is not a date. This is training.

Remember our motto at The Purple Peacock, safe, sane, consensual, and private. If you've changed your mind, that's okay. This is for you to decide. The choice is yours.

Adam."

"Well, don't sugarcoat it, Sir Dude. Tell me what you really think," I muttered to myself.

He was direct and somehow aroused me and pissed me off at the same time. *Ugh! You make me crazy, Mr. Maxwell.*

I clicked on the attachment, and to my surprise, there wasn't anything on the list that made me recoil. No fisting, clit clamps, or ball gags. He appeared to be a pretty basic bondage, blindfold, crop, and butt plug kind of guy. The dungeon in *The Apprehensive Submissive* had some serious shit, like electric probes, cages, and full rubber body suits. Alice was in for a way more extreme experience than I was.

I ran through his list and put a Y next to almost everything. I added a little smiley face to certain things like spanking and ass play. The only question mark I posed was for sharing. I wasn't sure if I wanted to be shared, or on display in front of others.

When I completed my task, I sent the attachment back without a note. It was my attempt at appearing aloof and all business, just like him. After all the years of feeling detached from my emotions, I hated to admit, when I hit the send button, a glimmer of something simmered within. Or maybe I ate too many chips?

Before I shut my laptop down, I saw an email from Fetish Confidential. *Huh? Weird.* I was sure I closed my account after my run-in with the Dom I met. More like the poor excuse for a human being. He was no Dom. He was an abusive fake. I opened the email. It said:

"Dear Sub-Curious28, your profile has been flagged due to inactivity. Do you wish to

keep it? Please click here and confirm you've received all your messages of interest or complete all three steps to delete your account."

Three steps? *Shit!* Maybe I didn't get rid of it. I clicked on the link, and there was a pop-up flashing "Full" above the message box. I checked them out of curiosity, and my fingers froze over the keys with my heart in my throat. *What the hell?* I had dozens of messages from the fake. He called himself DomAidenLV.

The buzz from my cell snapped me out of the shock of seeing Aiden's name. Before I checked my phone, I completed the three-step exit process with quick precision, and put that horrible experience in my rearview mirror. *Done!*

The text was from Roger. He was awake and ready to pick up Harley. I sent him a message and hopped out of bed. "Come on, mister. Your person is coming."

Minutes later Roger was at the door, sporting a wide-eyed grin. "Hey, Jess. Thanks a million for these last two nights. In a couple of weeks, I should be done with these double shifts. I put my notice in at The Golden Nugget."

"You did? Does that mean you have good news?"

He knelt down to pet Harley. "Yes. I sure do. Guess what, buddy, I got a new job. I've hit the big time at The Palisades working for Adam Maxwell."

"Wow. That was fast," I mumbled.

"What?" Roger asked and stood.

"I mean, congratulations. I'm so happy for you."

I couldn't comprehend what came over me. I threw my arms around Roger's neck and hugged him. He returned my out-of-the-blue embrace with a big, burly squeeze. He even lifted me off the ground a little and patted my back.

"Thanks, Jess."

Harley nudged his way between us, and we laughed.

I took a step back. "Sorry. I hope that was okay. I'm just, excited for you."

"Hey. It's cool. I'm excited too. I got the shift I wanted, a raise, and now Stacy says, she's going to put in for a transfer to a different department. Something a little safer. She has seniority and thinks she can get a similar schedule to mine, so things are really looking up."

I cocked my head. So they were a couple? "This is the best news I've heard in a long time. I just might have to hug you again."

Roger laughed. "You can hug me anytime. And that goes for Stacy too. We were talking about you the other night. After all these years, you've become like family to us. Hell, you're better than our real families. We actually like you. Our relatives get on our nerves."

"The feeling is mutual."

"Oh, and I actually have today off. Stacy and I were thinking of taking Harley up to Mount Charleston and escaping the heat. You're welcome to come with us if you like?"

"That's so sweet. But, I made plans..." Plans to be a sex slave for your new boss! "I'm going out with Tilly," I fibbed.

"Hey, you haven't been out in ages. I thought there was something different about you."

"Different? What do you mean?"

"I don't know. You just look different, in a good way. There's a light in your eyes, a glow, or something. You're not pregnant, are you?"

"Oh God. No! I don't have that warm and fuzzy mothering gene. I think it skips a generation, or in my case two."

"That's not true. You have it. I've seen it with Harley. It's there."

"If you say so. I worry I'll end up as hardened as my mother, Lauren the Ice Queen."

"Never. Not if me and my buddy have anything to say about it. Right, Harley."

I crouched down and smooched Harley's spotted nose. "I do love this snoot. You're a good boy. So, when do I get to have him overnight again?"

"I'm not sure. My schedule is up in the air tomorrow, like always. Boy, I'll be glad when I'm done working there. Come on, Harley, let's get out of Jess's hair. She has big plans for the night."

I patted Harley's head and rose. For a moment, Roger and I stood in silence. The expression on his face was sheer joy. Adam hiring him at his casino gave him a whole new lease on life. I nearly reached out to hug him again but stopped myself. After all, warm and fuzzy wasn't built in a day. I spent too many years being guarded by my walls. But, changes were coming. I felt them from somewhere deep inside. A new chapter was right around the corner ... for all of us.

* * * *

"Good evening, Jessica. You're right on time. Please, come in." Adam granted me a full, gigantic smile, showing off his perfect pearly white teeth.

I sauntered into his penthouse with a bit of false confidence and uber anticipation. "Thank you. You look extra happy, Mr. Maxwell."

He rid me of my small overnight bag and purse, placing them on the couch. "I'm always extremely happy when I get an attachment back from a sub that puts smiley faces next to all the ass play items." He circled around me, like he was taking inventory. "Although, I noticed no smiley face next to the act of taking your ass and making it mine. Do we need to discuss that?"

"No. I put a Y next to it. So, that's a yes. I guess the smiley faces were for the items on my wish list tonight."

Adam stopped and grasped my shoulders. "Sweetheart, I need to know. Have you ever done that before?"

"No. Are you disappointed?"

The corners of his mouth, upturned with a sly grin. "Quite the opposite." His fingertips trailed along my jawline. "It will be my pleasure to train your ass properly."

I swallowed and exhaled. "Um ... that sounds nice ... I think." I glanced down at the red splotches forming on my chest.

Adam touched the back of his hand against my chest. "Relax. We're going to go slow. The most important thing about tonight has nothing to do with kink or sex." He took my hands in his and fixed his eyes on mine. "It's about you. And your submission to me, trusting me to guide you through the scene I've planned."

His voice was so calm, and reassuring, his touch so gentle, and his very presence so captivating, any shred of trepidation vanished. "I do trust you. I want this."

"Good girl. Turn around."

I did as he asked and he unzipped my little black dress, sliding it down my shoulders, and letting it fall on the floor, leaving gooseflesh in its wake. For the first time, I was completely naked in front of him, and I tingled with a new-found fearlessness. I stood tall and proud, patiently waiting.

"Step out of your dress and face me," he ordered.

I turned to him, and the look on his face was pure delight mixed with sin. His deep blue eyes fucked every inch of me before his cock made contact with my skin. Without uttering a single syllable, Adam offered his hand, and I took it.

He didn't lead me into temptation. This was my choice, my curiosity, and my own hidden dark desires. He did deliver me to his penthouse master suite. I was just like Alice in my book, sliding down the rabbit hole, awaiting Wonderland.

The room was dimly lit in amber hues, and the light scent of sandalwood filled the air. I glimpsed at the four-poster bed, and the luxurious chocolate and chestnut colored comforter.

A few deviant treasures adorned the bed. However, my eyes went right to the small stainless steel butt plug.

The blood in my veins surged with warmth, and my pussy bloomed in wetness. The fullness in my breasts caused my chest to heave. But there were no blotches.

Adam positioned himself between the bed and me. "Slow your breathing down just a little bit for me."

I let go of a lungful of air. "Is that better? Oh, was I not supposed to talk?"

"Sweetheart, with me, I want you to talk. Remember, communication is key, even now. Your body is already speaking for you." He brushed his fingertips over each one of my hard, elongated nipples. "I'm very pleased with you. You look beautiful, Jessica." His hand roamed over my breasts, cascaded down my waist, landing on my sex. The pad of his thumb skimmed my outer lips. "So smooth. I approve."

His sultry voice soothed me. I felt so free and tranquil completely naked with Adam Maxwell, the most gorgeous, successful man I'd ever laid eyes on. How was that possible?

An intensity emerged in his expression as he gestured to the bed. "Come. I want you on your knees, face down, ass in the air."

I climbed up on the bed and obeyed. What was it about this position? It made my pussy drip like a leaky faucet. I closed my eyes and focused on my breathing while I heard Adam rustling around. *Please be stripping out of your casual business attire!*

He clasped my hips, maneuvering me closer to the edge of the bed. "There. Hold just like that. I'm going to shackle your ankles to the spreader bar. It will keep you nice and open for me." The silver metal pole with black restraints slid out of my view, and he locked my ankles in place. I smelled the leather cuffs before Adam showed them to me. "I ordered these just for you. They aren't red, they're burgundy. Just like your dress."

I nearly blushed at the thoughtfulness. "Thank you, Sir."

"Absolutely. Hands behind your back." He placed them on me and grazed his fingertips along my sides, stopping at my hips. "Are you still okay?"

I gasped. "I'm better than okay. I'm … amazing."

"You look exquisite, bound and spread for me. Ready to be played with and used for my pleasure." His hands kneaded my ass flesh. "You're permitted to make as much noise as you like. I want to hear you, to know what makes you want to come and scream. But, you aren't allowed to come until I say. Are we clear?"

"Yes, Sir."

He stretched my bum cheeks open. "In case I forgot to tell you Friday, I think you taste like heaven." His tongue made contact with my clit and slithered its way into my hole, fucking me slowly.

The sensation was so decadent and mind-blowing. My body already craved its release. How did he do this me? I moaned into the comforter, offering him my wanton juices in exchange for an orgasm.

Would it please him if I talked like the horny slut that's been buried beneath my guarded walls for years? "Oh, Sir. Use me. Take my pussy. Please, fuck me!"

His mouth came off me. "Easy, sweetheart." His fingers petted my sex. "I know you want to come for me.

But don't rush and chase the orgasm. Relax and enjoy the ride."

The gravelly, deep tone of his voice melted me into the mattress. I exhaled.

"That's it, beautiful," he praised. "You're being so good for me." Two fingers pressed inside me. "It won't be much longer, and I'll let you come."

He stroked me at a leisurely pace, making me quiver and squirm. When he accelerating his rhythm, I heard a little click, and felt a dollop of something warm on my anus.

I reacted with a jerk. And he pressed his palm into the small of my back. "It's just a little lube, so the plug slides in nice and easy. It might hurt at first. Everyone reacts differently. There's no right or wrong. There's only you, surrendering to it. Is it still what you want, Jessica?"

His finger spread the lube over my anus, and a foreign pleasure gripped me. "Yes. Oh, God. Yes, Sir."

Adam pushed the plug into my tightest entrance, slowly, stretching me as he went. "Good girl. It's almost all the way in, sweetheart."

His free hand rubbed my clit, and he gave the plug one final nudge. I detonated like a grenade with zero control. I screamed and flailed, knowing full well I had not been given permission to come.

Once my pants subsided, a silence fell over the room. Without a word, Adam removed the plug, unlatched the ankle shackles and the handcuffs. I wasn't sure what to do or say. Was our session over because I disobeyed him? I hung my head in shame and squeezed my eyes shut. I heard him open and close a dresser drawer. Then, nothing, it was quiet again.

After what felt like an eternity, Adam spoke, "Jessica. Look at me."

I raised my head with my eyes wide open. *Shit!* Adam was shirtless. God Bless America! Nothing but loose-fitting charcoal grey sweats adorned his inviting, tempting body. His muscles were jacked to the max, and his chiseled chest exhibited the perfect smattering of black chest hair. An insane eight-pack of abs, rippled before me, as my gaze traveled down his body to the V. Oh, the V! It always made me stupid!

"Jessica. We need to talk."

"Okay." *Ugh!* "I mean, yes, Sir."

He sat on the edge of the bed. "I'd like you on your knees, by my side."

I crawled across the bed to him, resting my bum on my heels. "I'm sorry."

"What are you sorry for? Tell me."

"I came without permission. Do you want me to leave?"

"Absolutely not." He brushed my hair away from my face. "Remember I said everyone reacts differently." He cracked a smile. "Coming the way you did is a first for me."

"You and me both. I promise I'll try harder."

"I know you will. Especially after a little punishment."

Was he going to send me to the corner? "Oh."

"I'm going to spank you."

"I'm confused. Is it a punishment or a fun-ishment?"

He smirked. "It's both. I'm going to make an exception, just this once. I was planning on spanking you anyway. I've been wanting to take you over my knee since the second I found your tape recorder. I promise you I'm not angry, but the last five slaps will be something to remember me by. Have you been spanked before?"

"No. I never thought I was even interested until recently."

"See, our tastes evolve and change over time. I've always said BDSM is like an endless buffet. You sample what you like. I only spank my subs with my bare hand. I love the skin-on-skin contact, especially with a virgin ass like yours. There's nothing like it. But I suppose maybe someday that could change. I've also sent subs home in the middle of a session for coming without permission if I felt like they were playing some kind of game."

"Honestly, I wasn't."

He caressed my cheek. "I know, sweetheart. That's why you're still here. I'm discovering you might be the least experienced sub I've ever been with. You'll take more training before you're ready to serve." His intense expression returned. "Okay then. Over my knee for your spanking. I planned on making your ass a lovely shade of pink, but now I'm thinking more like red, or burgundy."

He guided me over his lap, and little sparks and twitters zinged through my bloodstream. My torso rested on the bed, and he opened my legs. "Flex your feet and hold still." His tone was filled with authority, which made his voice that much sexier. His fingertips aligned along my slit. "I'm going to keep my hand here so I can feel how your pussy responds. Are you ready?"

"Yes, Sir," I panted.

"Tell me why you're getting a spanking, Jessica."

"Because I came without permission."

His other hand massaged my cheeks to prepare me. "And was that being a good girl?"

My pussy was already heavy with need. "No, Sir."

"I'm going to spank you twenty times. And you're going to count."

"Yes, Sir." Before the first swat hit my bum, I raised my head to look at him. "Sir?"

"Don't tell me. You have a question."

"Just one. Is it going to hurt?"

He grinned and cocked an eyebrow. "Only in the best possible way, sweetheart."

I sighed and lowered my head relishing a moment I had fantasized about a million times. And then his bare hand *cracked* my naked cheek. *Yes!*

"Start counting," he commanded.

"One."

Smack!

"Two."

Smack!

"Ah! Three!"

Smack!

"Oh! Four!"

Smack!

"Oh God... F–Five!"

He stopped for a moment and fondled my newly spanked flesh. "Jessica, you're sopping wet." His index finger made contact with my clit, and I quivered. "I'm barely touching you, and you're already close. Your body has been craving this. You have fifteen more. Focus on your breathing and counting. It will help you. And then I'll let you come."

I did as he asked, counting, breathing, and holding back an orgasm that was on the brink of splitting me in two. Each slap was like a roller-coaster cart inching its way up the incline, building with fierce desperation before it toppled over. This erotic, raging pressure felt different and more extraordinary than my wildest dreams. The sharper the spanks, the closer I teetered to falling over the cliff.

"Ah! F–Fifteen!"

Smack!

"Oh, Shit!" It just happened! I came, again. I smashed my face into the comforter to conceal my primal cries. What and the actual fuck was wrong with me?

My limp, disobedient body went slack across his lap. "I'm so sorry," I muttered.

"Don't be," Adam said in a husky tone. His hands brushed over my cheeks. "It's okay."

I pushed myself up, and returned to his side. "But I'm screwing everything up."

"No, sweetheart." He cupped my face and smiled. "You're learning. And I'm learning too. I've just learned my new submissive comes when she's spanked and during ass play." He rose from the bed, ridding himself of his sweat pants. Standing there completely and magnificently naked. "And she makes me hard as a fucking rock. The rest we'll work on. And I'm going to enjoy it. Come."

He offered me his hand, and we stood face-to-face with our chests heaving in tandem. Our bodies radiated a heat that ricocheted off us, filling the room with electric currents of lust. Adam's head-to-toe Greek god-like perfection was almost too much to feast on. His piercing blue eyes, hooded with hunger, penetrated me, leaving me breathless.

One hand coiled around my waist and pressed me into his brick-like frame. The other grabbed my hair and tilted my chin to him. His lips hovered over mine.

I gasped. "I want you to know, that ... I ... really do want to please you."

"That's everything."

His mouth captured mine with needy possession, ripping the air from my lungs. Adam's tongue met with mine and explored it with urgency. The taste of him filled me like a drug. I was addicted with one hit.

He sucked on my bottom lip and bit it like he was marking me, and I felt the sting all the way to my pussy. His lips found my neck, making a meal of my flesh, while my hands roamed over every contour of his chest.

"Fuck," he growled. "I need to fuck you. Get your ass back in the air. I'm taking what's mine."

I scampered back on the bed, drunk with a longing for his cock. I assumed the position, grabbed my cheeks, and spread them wide.

His tip teased my wet crease. "Just when I think I couldn't want you more, you surprise me. Look at you, stretching yourself open for me. You're a good girl. A fucking good girl."

He speared me to his base in one seamless thrust, and I wailed in ecstasy. His hands gripped my wrists while he pounded away at me. "That's right, you scream. You're mine now, sweetheart. I own every inch of you and your tight little pussy. You're all mine."

My walls squeezed his dick. *Oh, God.* I was about to implode. He slowed, wrapped an arm around my waist, and pulled me to him. "Your greedy cunt wants to come again, doesn't it?"

"Yeah... Ah!" I panted. "Permission to come, Sir?"

"Yes. Touch yourself. I want you to feel your clit while my cock is buried inside you."

I fingered myself while he watched. The room resonated with our heavy moans and his essence invaded my veins.

His hands groped fistfuls of my tits, and it sent me hurling over the edge.

"That's it, sweetheart. Come all over my cock. Jesus. You feel even better than I imagined."

He clutched my neck, angled my face to his, sealing his lips to mine in a demanding kiss. When his mouth released me, his cobalt eyes filled with greater intensity. "How does it feel to be mine, Miss Blake? Tell me. How do you feel?"

"I feel... I feel alive."

"Good girl."

His mouth swooped down on mine, but his lips grew softer, more benevolent, as they made their way to the curve of my neck and shoulder. He slowly guided me back down, with the side of my face resting on the comforter. Adam dug his hands into my hips and revved up the long, luscious strokes of his cock.

This was everything I had fantasized about. I was reeling in this wickedness, as I patiently waited for him to fill me full of his cum.

"Every time you move tomorrow, sweetheart, you're going to feel me. You're going to feel how deep and hard I fucked you. I want you to be reminded who stretched this tight pussy. Who made you sore."

"Ah ... ah!" I whimpered. "My Sir. My Sir made me sore."

He was ruining my pussy, but I didn't care. My body was pumped full of endorphins, with his punishing piston-like thrusts pushing me toward another orgasm.

He tightened the grip on my hips and growled, "Ah, fuck."

A massive tremor rocked me deep inside. "Oh... Oh... God!" I cried out.

And we came. His hot cum filled me, while we rode out our climax together, savoring it like we were one body.

Tiny breaths and sighs of satisfaction filled the air as our satiated bodies eased down on the mattress. Adam was still inside me, and I didn't move away. I actually wanted him to stay there, to hold me, and to fall asleep in his arms. *Who am I?*

He positioned us on our sides, so we were spooning, and pulled out. I'd never felt so peaceful in my life.

His fingers wiggled against my belly. "So, Miss Blake. How did this experience compare to what you read?"

I giggled. "Well, usually the heroine is perfect. She's not a runaway coming train wreck like me."

His lips grazed my shoulder. "Sweetheart, this is reality. Everyone's first time in a scene is fraught with a few bumps."

"I wanted to be perfect for you." I rolled over to face him.

"You were. I'm pleased."

I yawned. "Oh, sorry. I guess I'm a little tired. All those book-worthy orgasms."

He grinned. "So, the orgasms were book worthy? They lived up to the fantasy?"

"They more than lived up to it. They surpassed it. You may have spoiled reading for me altogether." I concealed another tiny yawn.

"You're tired. Let's get you ready for bed."

I nuzzled his chest. "I could probably fall asleep like this."

In the blink of an eye, everything shifted. He sat up and nudged me away. "Jessica, I don't sleep with my submissives." He rose from the bed and put on his sweats. "Come with me. I'll show you to your room."

"My room? I don't understand. You want me to spend the night, but you don't want me to share your bed?"

His eyes turned icy and distant. "It's one of my rules. For me, sleeping in the same bed can blur the lines between Dom and sub. I don't want any of my subs to get the wrong idea, that this can lead anywhere."

"Right. I get it. It's cool. I'd rather just go home." I hopped off the bed. "If I could just use your bathroom, I'll be gone in like two minutes."

He clasped my arm. "I'm afraid I can't let you do that."

"Can't let me?"

"Get on your knees."

I hesitated. "What?"

His jaw flexed in tension. "Now. On your knees."

"Fine." I knelt and was eye level with his erect cock, bulging through his sweatpants.

"Do you see how hard I still am? The only reason I'm not fucking you into a heap is because it's your first time, but make no mistake, I'm going to have you in the middle of the night after you get some sleep. So, you're going to your room and on the way, we'll stop by the kitchen, so I can show you how I like my coffee. Bringing me my coffee is your morning task."

"But I don't drink coffee. I drink Red Bull."

"Sweetheart, the coffee is not for you. What did the email say that I sent you this morning?"

"That you've been easy on me. That I was going to be treated like your other submissives."

"That's right. These are the rules for all of my submissives. I'm afraid I may have spoiled you Friday night. And for that, I apologize. I didn't mean to give you the wrong impression. I've tried to be upfront and honest about what I expect. Are we clear now?"

"Yes, Sir. So very clear."

"Good girl. Come."

I followed behind him through the penthouse, naked with his cum dripping down my legs. After gathering my things in the living room, we made our way to the kitchen so he could show me his Keurig. My room was off the kitchen. It was small and looked like some sort of servant's quarters.

He flipped on the light in the adjoining bathroom, and threw back the covers on the twin bed. "Be sure to clean yourself. I want a fresh pussy to fuck after you've had some rest."

I stared at the ground, wishing I'd never set foot in this penthouse.

"Jessica. Look at me. Are you all right?"

I peered into his eyes, searching for the man that made feel alive for the first time in years. He was nowhere to be found. "Sure. I'm good."

"You don't have any questions?" he said in a matter-of-fact tone.

"No, Sir."

"Excellent. Good night," he said in a clipped tone, and left.

I flopped on the bed. *What the hell?* My head swirled in a sea of turmoil. What was I doing? I trudged to the bathroom and showered, scrubbing away any trace of Adam from my skin.

As I crawled into the tiny bed I realized, my curiosity about BDSM had shifted into confusion. Maybe it wasn't anything like my books. Maybe this wasn't for me. Maybe I would never be a good submissive.

I was clear about two things. Adam Maxwell was an ass. And, I was going home.

CHAPTER SEVEN
JESSICA

"Hey, Jess. I bought you some chips." Tilly held up a bag of Ruffles in the doorway of my office. "It's a new flavor, Honey Dijon."

"Are you trying to bribe me, so I'll spill my guts about last night with Adam."

She bopped in and tossed the bag on my desk. "Oh, you're good, *mija*. That's exactly what I'm doing."

I swiveled in my chair to face her. "Can I tell you tomorrow? I feel kind of—awful."

"You don't look so good either. Are you sick?"

"No. I'm just stupid. Incredibly stupid and exhausted from last night." Not to mention, sore! Even though I snuck out and went home, I didn't sleep a wink.

"What do you mean? You were so excited?"

"I was, but I don't know. Adam is so confusing, and I guess, my curiosity has been satisfied."

"Do you have enough information to write the article?"

I tapped on my keyboard, and looked at my outline on the computer. "Not really. But, I might be able to make it work. It just isn't everything I hoped it would be." I held my head in my hands and sighed.

Tilly came to my side, throwing an arm around my shoulder. "It will be great. I know it. Because you're awesome."

My phone beeped. "Ignore that. It's probably another call or text from Adam. He won't leave me alone."

"Maybe you should talk to him."

"I'm never speaking to him again."

"Jess. You have to tell me what happened."

Hal interrupted with a head full of steam. "Blake, I don't know what you did, or how you did it, but I'm about to adopt you."

"What are you talking about?" I asked.

"I just got off the phone with Adam Maxwell. He's tripling his advertising budget. Whatever you're working on with him keep it going."

"What? I don't understand?"

He dabbed his neck with his plaid handkerchief. "What's to understand? He's on his way here in person to sign a new contract."

I shot out of my seat. "He's coming here?"

"Yeah," Hal answered. "Jess, are you okay? You don't look so good."

"Um … no. I think I'm coming down with something." I coughed and collected my things.

Tilly played along, touching her hand to my forehead. "Oh, she's burning up. Don't you think she should go home and rest, Hal?"

"Sure," he agreed. "Take the day off with pay. Heck, take two. Just feel better, kid."

"Thanks." I rushed out of my office and fled the building like it was on fire.

On the way to my car, Skip flagged me down. "Jess! Wait! I need to talk to you."

"Sorry, Skip. I've got to go. I'm not feeling well."

I jumped into my Nissan and sped off, leaving Skip in the dust. Whatever he wanted to speak to me about could wait.

The closer I got to my townhouse, the louder the whir of sirens became. I barely veered over in time for an ambulance whizzing past me.

I made my usual right at the light and couldn't pull into my cul-de-sac. *Oh, my God!* Emergency vehicles were everywhere. What the hell was going on?

I parked my car on the street. With my heart beating out of my chest, I raced toward the chaos.

"Roger! Stacy!" I screamed.

An officer stopped me at the barricade with police tape. "Miss, you can't go any further. This is a crime scene."

"I live here! Please! You have to let me through!"

With tears streaming down her face, Stacy ran to me. "Let her in. She's with me."

He stepped aside, and she grabbed me, clutching me to her chest, sobbing.

"Stacy, *shh* ... don't cry. Talk to me. What's going on?"

"Roger! It's Roger!" she wailed. "Oh, my God."

"What happened to Roger?" I asked in a steady, calm voice.

"He was home ... sleeping ... and ... and ... they... Oh, God! They shot him!"

"It's going be okay. This is Roger we're talking about. There's no one tougher. If anyone can pull through, he can."

The paramedics wheeled him out as we looked on in anguish.

Stacy hurried to the gurney, calling out to one of her fellow officers following behind them. "Kevin! He's okay, right? Please tell me he's okay."

Kevin shook his head.

She collapsed into my arms. "No!"

I turned her away from Roger's lifeless body being taken away under a sheet, while Stacy wept.

Kevin consoled her too. "He fought like hell. The paramedics did everything they could. They tried to bring him back, but ... I'm so sorry, Stacy. Roger's gone."

She broke our embrace. "I need to see him."

Kevin held her back. "Stacy, don't."

"Please," she cried, beating on Kevin's chest. "I need to be with him."

He wrapped her up in his arms. "There's nothing we can do now."

Stacy busted out of Kevin's hold and threw her body on top of Roger's. "There's got to be something somebody can do. He can't leave me. Roger ... please..."

Everyone stood motionless while Stacy clung to the last bit of warmth Roger's body had left. Then, Kevin looked to me for help, and I went to her, placing my hand on her back. "Stacy, I think we have to let him go."

She wiped her eyes. "I know. I know you're right. I–I just... Damn it. How could this be happening? It's not fair, Jess. It's not fucking fair."

"No. It's not fair. Roger was a good man. He had a heart of gold. I saw it every day, especially with Harley."

Harley!

"Oh, my God. Where's Harley? Where is he?"

Stacy grabbed my hand. "I don't know. Oh, God, Jess. I don't know. You have to find him. Please."

"I will. I'll find him." I tore off to Roger's place. "Harley! Harley!"

Once inside, I ignored the orders of the officers telling me to get out and charged up the stairs. I searched every corner of every room and came up empty-handed.

"Hey, you can't come in here," a heavyset cop snapped when I got to the doorway of Roger's bedroom.

"I know, but Roger had a dog, Harley. Have you seen him?"

"Dog? Lady, there's no dog."

My voice trembled. "There has to be. I've checked the other rooms. He's got to be in there. Please. Let me look for him."

The cop threw his hands up. "Two minutes. Don't touch anything."

"Thank you." I darted inside. "Harley, buddy, it's me, Jess." Where could he be? I stepped inside Roger's walk-in closet. "Harley."

There was no sign of him anywhere. I steeled myself before moving toward the mattress covered in blood.

"Harley." I filled with hopelessness. "Buddy, where are you?"

The faintest whimper sounded from under the bed. I dropped to the floor and inched my way to him. "Oh, Harley." He was shaking, and when I tried to reach for him, I realized his fur was coated in blood. "Oh, God. No." Did those bastards shoot him too? I couldn't squeeze under the bed, so sat crossed-legged and got as close to him as I could, and patted my lap. "Harley, come? Come on. You can do it."

Slowly he dragged himself to me, and crawled into my arms. "There. I got you. Good boy. Oh, thank God. You're okay." I held him tight, choking back tears. "Oh, Harley, I'm so sorry. Roger's gone. You lost your person."

"Good. You found him." Kevin said, coming into the room.

"Yeah." I swallowed hard, regaining my composure. "He was under the bed shaking. I think he's okay, but he's covered in blood," I explained, checking him over.

Kevin handed me a towel. "I know. I was the first one on the scene. Harley was laying on top of Roger. I picked him up, and he hid under the bed."

I wrapped him in the towel. "Oh, Harley. You poor thing. You were probably scared to death."

"I should've told you that outside, but you took off so fast, and Stacy she—"

"She what?"

"She tried to go with Roger. I stopped her and kept her from running in here. She shouldn't see this room. And we need to get out of here too. This is still an active crime scene."

"You're right. Come on, mister. Stacy needs us."

Kevin bent down. "Let me carry him for you."

I cradled him to my chest, not wanting to let go of him. Kevin held out his arms. "I swear. I'll give him right back."

We made our way out of Roger's townhouse and over to Stacy's porch. Stacy was hunkered down on the steps with her head in her hands, rocking back and forth.

I flew to her side. "Hey, I found him. I found Harley."

She lifted her weary eyes to mine. "Is he all right? Please, tell me he's all right?"

"He's fine."

She grabbed my hand, squeezing it tight, and nodding her head. "Thank God," she replied in a hoarse, faint tone.

"He's still a little shaken," Kevin said and placed him on my lap. "Once he has a bath, he'll be good as new."

Stacy kissed his snoot, as a few tears rolled down her cheeks. "He looks perfect to me."

Kevin took out his phone. "Do you know if Roger has any immediate family in town I could call to come get Harley? Otherwise, I'll contact animal control."

"Animal control? You can't call them," I insisted. "They'll send him to a shelter."

"If I don't call them, who's going to take him?" Kevin huffed.

Harley tilted his head, and I peered into his scared, soft brown eyes. "Me," I whispered. "I'll take him. Harley belongs with me."

Stacy threw her arms around me. "Thank you. It's what Roger would've wanted."

Her body trembled for a moment. Then she steadied herself and stood. "I need a minute, I'll be right back."

"Do you want me to come with you?" I offered.

"No. I'm going to grab some sheets and towels for Harley. I'll just be a second."

Kevin waited until Stacy was out of earshot. "Look, I need to check in with everyone. But, I won't be far if you need anything." He started to leave, and he stopped himself. "For the record, I've never seen Stacy like this. I've been her partner for five years, and we've been through a lot. That lady is tough as balls. So, we've got to look after her."

"I hear you. Thanks for your help."

Harley squirmed, and let out a deep sigh, while I petted his head. "I don't know what I would've done if I lost you too. I know I have big shoes to fill, and I'll never measure up to Roger, but I promise I'll try, because, I'm your person now. It's you and me, Harley. I'm your person."

"Jessica!" A deep voice called in the distance. "Jessica! I'm Adam Maxwell, and I demand you let me through."

I kept rocking Harley on my lap and pretended I didn't hear Adam yelling my name. What did this man want from me?

He burst through the crowd, spotted me on Stacy's porch and rushed to my side.

"My God! What happened? Are you okay?" He crouched down and clasped my shoulders. "Is Harley all right?"

"We're okay," I said with my eyes on the ground. "But..."

"What, sweetheart? Please talk to me."

I lifted my gaze to meet his. "Roger, my friend. He's dead."

"I'm so sorry." He sat down next to me and draped an arm around my shoulder. "What can I do?"

I shrugged him off. "Nothing. We'll be fine. I think you should go."

"I'm not leaving you. I've been going crazy trying to get in touch with you."

"Why? Because I left that shitty little room you put me in, and you have some new confusing punishment for me? No—thank—you."

"No. Because I realized I fucked-up. Look, we need to talk, but not now. I need to get you out of here."

"I'm not going anywhere with you. And I'm not leaving Harley. Wherever I go, he goes."

"Of course you're not. Bring him with you. I want you to."

"To your penthouse? I'm not taking him there. That's ridiculous."

"I have a house at The Vegas Edge Country Club." He rose with authority. "So, that settles it. You're both coming with me. Let's go."

"I don't think you get it, Mr. Maxwell. I don't have to do anything you say. You can't order me around, and we aren't going with you."

He shoved his hands in his hair and paced. "You're infuriating. You know that? I'm trying to help you."

"No one asked you to," I hollered. "We're staying here. This is our home."

"Hey, what's all the yelling?" Stacy asked emerging from her townhouse. "Mr. Maxwell? What are you doing here?"

"Stacy, Adam and I are ... we ... well, we know each other. He wants Harley and me to go with him. But I told him we're not. We won't leave you in the cul-de-sac all by yourself."

Adam extended his hand. "Nice to meet you, Stacy."

Stacy stared at Adam in a daze while she shook his hand. "You—You hired Roger."

"Yes. That's right."

"Thank you. We went to Mount Charleston yesterday to celebrate. It was the best day of my life." She brushed away a tear, glanced in my direction and set down the sheets and towels. "Mr. Maxwell, can I speak to you for a minute, in private?"

They moved far enough away from me, I couldn't hear them. Naturally, Stacy's face was etched with grief, but also fear. Adam nodded in agreement with everything she said. Were they talking about me?

Like a newly formed united front, they came back to the porch. "Jess," Stacy said with a shaky voice. "I'm going to be working around the clock trying to figure out who took Roger away from us. You'll be here all alone. I really think you should go with Mr. Maxwell. He'll keep you and Harley safe."

"But, I don't want to leave you by yourself," I protested.

"You won't be. I'll figure something out."

Adam bent down and peered in my eyes. "Please. Come with me. I promise I'll protect you. Both of you. Please, Jess."

He called me Jess.

"Okay," I murmured and held Harley to my chest.

* * * *

"We're almost there," Adam said softly as we stopped at a red light. "How's Harley doing?"

"He's asleep," I answered from the back seat. "I hope we don't get blood all over your car. I wrapped him up with the clean sheet and put towels down, but it's everywhere, including on me."

"Sweetheart, it's okay. It's just a car."

"Well, not just a car. It's a Mercedes."

"Still. It's only a car."

He coasted through the guard gate of the country club. It was like one of those magical places I'd always dreamed of going, but now I was so numb, I couldn't appreciate how spectacular it was.

"Didn't this used to be called The Mountain Heights Country Club?" I asked.

"It did. And then I bought it."

I sighed. "Of course you did."

"Welcome to The Vegas Edge Country Club, Miss Blake. I think you'll find these accommodations more suitable."

"You really didn't have to bring us here. We'll just be in your way."

"Nonsense. I've already texted Claire and Sam. They look after my property for me, and they're excited to have guests. It's been a while."

"Like, how long."

The car rolled up to what was probably the largest and most exclusive estate on the grounds. "Like, never."

Adam parked in the driveway of his five-car garage, and insisted on carrying Harley. I lumbered behind him, and felt like a total reject in my bloody dress. *Wait until Claire and Sam got a load of the first guest.*

The garage door levitated, and out they came with their arms open to us. "Hey, you must be Jessica." Sam extended his hand.

"Yes. Please, call me Jess. I apologize for my appearance."

He shook my hand. "Nothing to be sorry for. I'm Sam, and this is my wife, Claire." He plucked Harley from Adam. "And this guy is coming with us."

Claire patted his head. "Poor thing. Don't worry, Jess. We'll take care of him. We'll give him a bath, and I already made him some chicken."

"Harley will love that. I can help," I offered.

"No," Adam interjected. "Claire and Sam were medics in the army, and they had military dogs. Trust me. He's in great hands."

Claire clasped my hands in hers. "You go. Get cleaned up and then we'll have dinner. Sam's grilling steaks and making homemade chips."

"Homemade chips!" I exclaimed.

"The trick is how you slice the potatoes," Sam bragged.

"Let's go, FryDaddy," Claire teased. "Jess doesn't need to hear every detail."

Before they toted him away, I smooched Harley's head, and the three of them moseyed off joking about Sam and his chips.

"They're really sweet," I said. "Thank you."

Adam cocked his head. "For what?"

"For bringing me here, to your home."

"You're welcome." He took my hand. "Let's get you inside."

I was a nervous wreck making my way through Adam's beautiful house to his master suite. Almost everything was white. There were a few splashes of color here and there, but even those were neutral tones.

Even the bathroom sparkled with white, off white, and oatmeal shades.

Adam laid out thick, fluffy taupe towels on the sink. "Is something wrong?"

"I'm kind of a mess. It's so neat, and clean. I'm worried I'll get everything dirty. Even on a good day, I spill stuff."

He turned on the water on his oversized tub, and then sauntered to me with a grin. "You're fine. Although we may need to throw away your green dress."

"It's aquamarine. And it's a Diane Von Furstenberg wrap dress that I got at a half-price sale."

With one yank on the flimsy, tied belt, the dress unraveled. "I'll buy you ten more. But this one has to go." When I opened my mouth to argue, he stopped me, with a gentle grasp on my shoulders. "Sweetheart, every time you look at it, it's going to remind you of today."

I exhaled. "You're right."

He slid the dress off, crumpled it up, and threw it in the wastebasket. "I think your bath is ready."

I kicked off my shoes. "Thanks. You can go now."

Adam rolled up his sleeves, and turned off the water. "Jess, I've seen you naked. I've been inside you. And, now, I'm giving you a bath."

"I can do it myself," I muttered.

"I know you can. But..." He smirked. "You probably would make an awful mess of my bathroom. Turn around." He brushed my hair to one side and unhooked my bra, allowing it to fall to the floor. "See, such a mess."

When he bent down to pick up my bra, I let out a small laugh. "You really can't leave that there, not even for a minute."

"No. I'm afraid I can't." He folded it neatly, placing it on the sink. Hooking his thumbs into my waistband, he glided my thong off, and I stepped out of it. "Good girl. Okay. In the tub you go."

"Adam. Wait."

"What is it?"

"Why are you being so nice to me?"

"Because you're mine."

"I don't even understand what that means, especially since I left last night. I snuck out as fast as I could."

"I know. And we're going to discuss that, but not now. Sweetheart, get in the tub."

His voice was firm but soft, and it made me all gooey inside. As I climbed into the tub, Adam cupped my bottom, easing me into the warm water.

I closed my eyes, and let the scent of sandalwood and soap invade my senses. I felt Adam's presence calming me with each gentle touch. We didn't utter a word. He just took care of me. He washed my hair, massaged my shoulders, and cleansed the day away. Not that it would ever be forgotten. It was more like a momentary respite from the shock and devastation of losing Roger.

After he had toweled me off, he excused himself. Alone, with nothing but my thoughts, my hands trembled, and I dropped the bottle of expensive hair serum. As I bent down to retrieve it, images of the crime scene flashed through my head. My knees buckled, and I found myself on the cool tile. Stacy's cries echoed in my brain, and I curled up in a ball on the floor with my body reeling in despair.

I blew out a few deep breaths, and mumbled to myself. "Pull yourself together, Jess. You can't fall apart. Harley and Stacy need you."

With my head in my hands, I fought back tears and remained immobile for what seemed like an eternity.

Adam returned with a summer lavender dress in tow. "Claire gave me this. She said it was the smallest thing in her closet, and hey..." He tossed it on the counter, bent down and took my hands in his. "I'm sorry I left you so long. I was trying to... Sweetheart, what do you need?"

"Nothing. Do you think it would be okay if I skipped dinner and stayed up here? I just don't feel like being around people."

"Isolating yourself is not the answer. Look, I'll make a deal with you. Get dressed, come downstairs, and try one of Sam's chips. If you still want to be alone, then, I'll have Claire make you a plate. Deal?"

I nodded. "Deal."

"Good girl." He helped lift me off the floor and slipped the dress over my head. "You look lovely."

"Thank you," I replied, combing a brush through my hair.

"Are you hungry?"

"Yes, I'm actually starving."

He offered his hand. "Come."

The second we landed in Adam's ultra-modern, enormous kitchen, Harley barreled toward me. "Hi, mister. Look at you." I knelt down to kiss his spotted nose. "How's my good boy?"

"Hey, Harley's a gem," Sam said. "We gave him a little once over, and there's not a scratch on him. One of my old army buddies is a veterinarian, so I called him. He's going to drop by and take a look at Harley first thing in the morning if that's okay."

"Yes. Thanks. That would be great." I stood. "I just remembered. I need to call Tilly, and Hal. Oh, no. I don't have my phone, or anything. I'm not even sure where my car keys are. Shit. What am I going to do?"

"It's okay, Jess. I took care of it," Adam said.

"You did?" I asked.

"I made a couple of calls. I talked to Tilly and Hal. Hal said to take a couple of days off. And Tilly connected with Stacy so we could get your things." He bent down to pet Harley. "And I didn't forget about you, buddy. I sent out for some food, so could you do me a favor and tell Jess to relax, I have everything under control."

Harley's little nubby tail wiggled, and I couldn't help but smile. "That's Harley's way of saying thank you."

Adam's crystal blue eyes captured mine. "No need to thank me. Just make yourself at home."

"Sam!" Claire called. "A little help, Captain."

Both Sam and Adam hurried to Claire coming from the garage entrance, with her arms fully loaded.

I followed. "Claire you're a super woman. What can I do?"

"Not a thing. The concierge from the club had a delivery. It's some stuff for you and Harley. Here's your purse." She handed it to me. "That dress looks adorable on you. You should keep it. It was a little too tight in the shoulders for me anyway."

"Thanks. I love it."

"Oh, look what I found!" Sam held up Harley's baby blue shark and squeaked it.

He came running, snatched the toy, and shook it. The room erupted with laughter.

Before we ate Sam's specialty, I touched base with Stacy and Tilly. To my surprise, they were together, in a suite, at The Palisades. Adam's treat. That man thought of everything.

At first, when we sat down to dinner, I did nothing but stare at my plate. Then Adam placed his palm on my shoulder blades, and gave me a slight nod, encouraging me to eat.

I tried one of Sam's famous homemade chips. The wide-eyed look of Sam awaiting my chip review was priceless. I didn't want to be a wet blanket.

"Sam, your chips are banging," I declared and ate a few more.

He popped one in his mouth. "Banging? Is that a good thing?"

Claire laughed. "Yes. You old fart. It's a good thing."

As Sam and Claire teased each other, I wondered if they were going out of their way to cheer me up, or was this really them. Either way, it was sweet and helped me rally a bit.

Smiling at Sam and Claire's playful dynamic, Adam asked, "Would anyone like more wine? I opened another bottle of Cabernet."

"Well, if it's already opened," Sam hinted.

"I'll take that as a yes," Adam said, folding his napkin.

"Here, let me get it." Claire rose.

Adam shoved himself out his chair. "Please. I'm happy to do it. Be right back." He journeyed off to the kitchen.

I sliced a piece of steak, and asked, "So, how did you two meet?"

"In the army," Claire answered. "We were both on our last tour of duty in Iraq."

"Oh. How long ago was that?" Even now, I had to ask questions.

"Ten years. Wow! It went by in a flash too," Sam responded, gazing at Claire. "It's been the best ten years of my life. You know, Adam doesn't get enough credit for it, but he hires a lot of veterans."

"Careful, Sam," Adam warned as he placed the wine on the table and sat down. "We can't let Jessica think I'm actually not an ass."

Claire poured the wine. "Oh, she doesn't think that."

I shot Adam a sideways glance. "It's just a little, joke. I'd actually like to hear more about your work with veterans."

He shrugged. "There's not much to tell."

"Sorry, boss." Sam grinned. "I'm calling bullshit on that. He just hired Claire's little brother, Ben, for his security team. He served four back-to-back tours in Afghanistan. He's been having a rough time, so having a job, is... Well, we're grateful."

Claire reached over and squeezed Sam's hand. Both were late forties, early fifties at the most, in great shape with an incredible spirit. I've never felt so comfortable with people I'd just met before. The way they pitched in to help Harley and me would never be forgotten. They were true heroes in every way.

After more wine, conversation, and chips, we all said good night. Sam and Claire headed to their private quarters—a guesthouse at the back of the property. Harley, Adam, and I climbed the stairs, and we were back in the master suite.

Harley jumped up on the bed and made himself at home. "Hey, mister. You better get down. You'll get black hair all over Adam's clean, ivory bedding."

"It's all right," Adam said ridding himself of his shirt and trousers.

"He's probably going to shed. Come on Harley, let's go." He hopped off the bed. "Just show us where our room is, and we'll get out of your hair."

He stripped off his T-shirt, came to me, and placed his hands on my shoulders. "You're sleeping with me."

"But you said you didn't want to blur the lines."

"I also said I fucked up." He slipped the lavender dress off me, laying it on a chair with his clothes. "Go, get ready for bed, and I'll take Harley out. While you were on the phone with Tilly, Claire put some of your things on the dresser, and the rest are on the sink."

When I came out of the bathroom wearing an oversized white night shirt, Harley and Adam were propped up in bed, like two old friends. Bare-chested and breathtaking, Adam's sharp jawline and cleft chin still made my stomach do back flips, even after a day like today. Was he naked under that sheet? *Ugh!* Those thoughts were not helpful, especially when he had me drowning in a river of confusion.

Adam threw his arm around Harley. "What do you think, buddy? Is there room for one more?"

Harley nestled against Adam with a sigh.

"I guess I'm outnumbered."

Adam smirked, flipped back the sheet, revealing his muscled thighs and navy boxers. "Get in here."

He nudged Harley over, and I settled in between them. "Thank you. You know, Roger used to call him buddy sometimes. I don't think it's sunk in yet. I still can't believe he's gone."

"You've had quite a shock. It's going to take time."

"Right now, it feels like forever."

"Sure it does. I'm just sorry I didn't get to meet him. I had my people fast-track his paperwork, especially when they told me Roger was a veteran."

"He was? I didn't know that."

"Really? I'm surprised."

"I know. It's weird. I knew him for six years, we talked almost every day, but I never asked him any personal questions. Maybe because I wanted to keep my life private, and we lived in close quarters, I don't know.

I realize now that I made a mistake. There are so many things I wished I'd ask him. Now, it's too late."

"Try not to think about it that way, sweetheart. Think about what you're doing for Harley. That's a big deal."

"I'll never measure up to Roger. He was amazing with him. You should've seen them together. Sometimes I can a be little..." I let out a sigh. "I'm just not very..."

"You don't need all that lovey-dovey shit?"

"Exactly."

"That's why I had no qualms about not inviting you into my bed last night, even though I wanted to."

"You did?"

"Absolutely. But, I'd already broken so many of my rules with you. And a little voice in the back of my head said, 'Jessica, won't mind sleeping in this shitty little room. She doesn't need any lovey-dovey shit. She told me herself.'"

"I don't. I would've rather just gone home."

"Would you like to know a secret?"

"Always."

His fingertip touched my nose, and he smiled. "Within thirty minutes, I went to that shitty little room, debating whether or not I should fuck you, invite you into my bed, or both. But you were already gone."

I peered into his ocean blue eyes and saw the man who made me feel alive last night. He exuded power mixed with lust and something else, something indescribable. But after today, opening myself up for more distress was too risky. "Well, it was probably for the best. We're only a business arrangement. Right?"

For a moment, Adam studied me in silence. Then, without a word, he clicked off the light on the nightstand, and rolled on his side, facing away from me. "Absolutely. Good night, Miss Blake."

"Night." I cuddled next to Harley, closing my eyes, and reminded myself, *I don't need any of that lovey-dovey shit.*

* * * *

Harley's anguished cries jolted me like I'd been powered awake with jumper cables. His paws shook uncontrollably. "Oh, it's okay, mister."

Adam flipped on the light. "What's wrong?"

"He's having a bad dream."

"Has this happened before?"

"No. I don't know what to do for him."

Adam jumped into action, leaping over me, and gently waking him. "Come on, buddy. Shake it off. It's just a dream."

Harley let out a high-pitched bark, and his eyes popped open. I wrapped my arms around him, and stroked his sweet head. "Hey, I'm right here. Poor little thing. He's been through hell."

"Let's put him in between us. Maybe it'll make him feel more secure."

I scooted over, and he gingerly lifted Harley, placing him in the middle of the bed.

"There." Positioning both hands on him, and snuggling close, calmed him right down. "Is that better, mister?"

Adam climbed back in bed, petting his shiny coat. "He seems to like being in between us."

"He sure does." When I pulled the sheet up, Harley swatted me with his paw, until my hand returned. "Okay. All hands on Harley. I won't dare move them again."

Adam grinned, leaving one hand on him while he turned out the light. The moonlight streaming through the window highlighted every distinct contour of his flawless face.

My breath caught in my throat. "I—um—I'm so glad we're here with you. This was one of the worst days of my life. I don't think I could've gotten through it without you. Thank you."

"No thanks necessary. I'm glad you're here too." His fingertips grazed the back of my hand. "You know, you're Harley's person now."

"I know," I muttered quietly. "I want to be perfect for him."

"You already are." He gazed deep into my eyes. "Sweet dreams, beautiful."

Beautiful. He said the word like it was my name.

CHAPTER EIGHT
JESSICA

"Morning, sweetheart."

Adam's lush voice, distinct scent, and the gentle caress of his hand on my shoulder roused me and my senses. With the addition of his unruly, black hair and stubble, my eyes quickly adjusted to the delicious feast before me. And there was a tray of goodies too!

"Hi. What time is it?"

"It's a little after nine."

I stretched and suddenly realized I was a canine parent. "Shit. Where's Harley?" I flipped back the sheet, hauling myself upright.

"First of all, you need to watch your language. And, secondly, he's fine. Claire and Sam took him on a long walk while I squeezed in a workout."

"Oh. I could've taken him. You should've woken me up."

Adam covered me back up, and sat on the side of the bed. "I wanted you to sleep. Nothing but rest and relaxation for a couple of days."

"Doctor's orders?" I teased.

The corners of his mouth rose in a wicked grin. "Dom's orders. And they're very strict."

"Whatever you say, Sir Dude." I glanced at the breakfast tray, which was fit for a princess, minus my Red Bull. "Is drinking coffee my punishment for not getting up early and making it for you? I know I'm in the minority, but I don't like it."

"Trust me. You'll like this." He poured a cup from a fancy carafe, and the aroma touched my nose in a surprisingly pleasant way. "Sam roasts and presses the beans himself. It's French."

He splashed a bit of cream in the cup and handed it to me. I blew on it and took a sip. "Oh, my God. This is fantastic. I could drink this every day."

"That pleases me."

"You're spoiling me again. That Dom/sub line is so blurry, it might as well be a blizzard."

He jumped up, moved away from the bed, and kicked off his sneakers. "As you pointed out we have a business arrangement. You have your article to write. But, you must still be in a state of shock."

"So, what are you saying?"

He stripped off his T-shirt and sauntered back to me. "I'm saying. You have a couple of days off. Take a breather from everything. Hang out by the pool. Sam and Claire love having you and Harley here."

"What about you?"

His jaw clenched with his eyes penetrating me. "I have to get in the shower. I'm going to work from home today, while you relax."

He cupped my face in hands, touching his soft lips to my forehead. Just that brief contact sent shivers rippling through me. "Yes, Sir," I whispered.

A warm smile spread across his face. "Good girl."

* * * *

Over the next two days, I followed Dom's orders. Harley and I vacationed at the Maxwell resort like two fat cats on the Vegas Strip. If Sam and Claire weren't doting on us, Adam was. Protective to a fault, he barely left my side. The way he bonded with Harley and interacted with Claire and Sam showed me a different side to the aloof, King of Vegas.

The brief break from reality crashed to a halt on Thursday. Stacy and I held a small, tasteful service at Palm Mortuary for Roger. Returning to the same chapel where I said goodbye to my father brought back so many painful memories. But, I sucked it up and stayed strong for Stacy.

A few of Roger's co-workers attended, along with Stacy's fellow officers. Roger's relatives were a no-show. Granted, his extended family lived out of state, and they weren't close, but only one cousin sent flowers. I learned a long time ago, biology doesn't always make you family.

Adam not only attended the service, but he also footed the bill and hosted a luncheon at Ferraro's. His attention only strayed to his phone once during the entire day at the restaurant. After a brief text to someone, he actually apologized, and then said, "Don't fill up on bread."

As if that was a thing.

Later that evening, we found ourselves back in his master suite. While unzipping my black dress, he spoke in a low voice. "Would you like me to draw you a bath?"

"You don't have to do that." I removed my heels and stepped away. "I was going to pack up my stuff. Harley and I don't want to wear out our welcome. And, I've got to get back to work. Hal's been waiting on our article."

"I've been thinking about that." He struck a commanding stance. "I've decided you're going to move into the penthouse until the article is finished."

I folded my arms, and spouted back, "You've decided? What about Harley?"

"Harley can stay here with Claire and Sam. You and I will work during the day, and I will train you at night. With a week's worth of rigorous sessions, you should have enough material for your article, and enough experience to begin contemplating continuing in the lifestyle. I'll even throw in an evening at The Purple Peacock. You can ask Sebastian and my other associate, Eli questions if you like. This is an excellent deal, Miss Blake. I think you should accept."

"Oh, should I? Is that what you think?" I sniped back, searching for my bag so I could gather my things.

These past two days meant nothing more than a sense of obligation to him. "I don't suppose you happen to give a shit what I think. No, not the great and powerful Adam Maxwell who throws his money around, so he can decide everything."

"Jessica, watch your language."

"Watch my language? How about watch me take Harley and leave tonight."

I flew around the room, shoving my belongings into a bag, not sure why I was so angry. What was I expecting? Some whirlwind romance? Raw emotion pumping through my veins was not my norm. I had to shut this shit down, and get out.

Adam maintained his unshakable demeanor, undid his tie, and rolled up his sleeves. "You're not going anywhere. I hate to break it to you, Miss Blake, but you need me. Otherwise, you're going to be stuck writing 'Sin City Nights.' I'd think about that if I were you."

I whizzed by him to grab my stuff from the bathroom, and ranted, "Well, I'm not sleeping in that shitty little room. Maybe you need to think about that."

"You're absolutely, one-hundred-percent, without a doubt sleeping with me."

I poked my head out of the bathroom door. "What did you say?"

His phone buzzed before he could answer. "It's Hal. Hang on." He faced away and accepted the call. "Hal. What can I do for you? Oh, I see. Well, of course. Yes. I understand completely." He turned around, and his eyes flashed in my direction. "Under the circumstances, I think this is for the best. When will you let her know?" He nodded in agreement, as he listened intently. "Good. And I assure this will not affect our advertising contract. Okay. Talk soon." He hung up, and placed the phone on his nightstand. "Hal will be calling. I suggest you answer."

My cell beeped instantly. Barefoot, with my black dress falling off my shoulders, I grabbed my phone from my purse. How did Adam know that? "Hey, Hal. What's up?"

His voice sounded raspy but full of vigor. "So, first off, I'm sorry about your friend. I tried to get to the service, we all did, but something broke. Skip and I have been on no sleep. We haven't had a story this big in years."

"That's okay. What happened?"

"You're never going to believe this one. Lieutenant Governor, Ronald Sharpe is running for Mayor of Las Vegas."

"But, that makes no sense. Governor Miles has one of the best approval ratings in the country, and his two terms are up. Sharpe is sitting pretty to be next in line, why would he run for Mayor instead?"

"That's exactly right. It seems fishy and doesn't smell right. There's something to it." He huffed. "I've got that gut feeling, and so does Skip. He's going to take the lead on this, and that's where you come in."

"Me? I don't understand."

"There's been another incident in your neighborhood. No one was killed. The perps got away, but our victim, she got a look at them, and the dots are starting to connect. She's a real character too. Her name is Miss Jeannie. Her daughter and son-in-law own Pure and Natural Health. Do you know it?"

"Yeah. It's not that far from me."

"So, this is what I'm thinking. Let's get the community involved. These son of a guns are right under our noses, but we all need to pull together. Do you think your friend, Stacy, the cop, would help us?"

"Hell, yes. Not just Stacy, but her fellow officers too."

"That's what I was hoping you'd say. I want you on this, Jess. This is your story. Cover it from every angle.

We'll have our own tip line, and we'll do some pieces on the families left behind. Heck, do a story about that dog, Harley I keep hearing about. We need to put our readers on alert, but make them feel part of the solution. You get me?"

My head was already spinning with ideas. "Yes. You can count on me." I'd been waiting for a chance like this for years. "I'll be in first thing in the morning." I glanced at Adam, almost forgetting about our arrangement. "Oh ... um ... what about, Mr. Maxwell? We had a deal?"

"I've already spoken to him. The deal is off. He said not to worry. Thought it was for the best, and he would still honor our advertising contract even though he didn't get a chance to sign."

"He didn't?"

"No. Skip told him he got word that something happened in your neighborhood, and Maxwell took off before he signed it. I think he might have a thing for you, kid. He's one heck of a guy. He's what you gals call a choice stud."

"No. No one says that, Hal. And you should seriously never say that again. Look, I'll see you in the morning, and we'll hammer out some more details. Is that cool?"

"Yes. It's cool. Is it okay to say that?" He chuckled. "Sure. That's totally cool."

"I'll see you in the morning then. Congrats, Blake. You are officially a full-fledged feature reporter for the *Las Vegas Times*."

"Thank you. I promise I'll give it my all." I hung up, and placed my phone down on the other nightstand. Adam and I stood on opposing sides of the bed, in silence.

He broke the awkward moment. "So, I guess congratulations are in order. You're a reporter."

I shrugged with a half-smile. "Yeah. I'm a real reporter."

"I thought you'd be more excited. You got what you wanted. Didn't you, Miss Blake?"

His poker face was firm, and as hard to read as ever. The only distance between us was his bed, but it felt like he was on the other side of the world.

"Yes. I did, get what I wanted. Hal said our deal is off. He told me you thought it was for the best. Is that what you really think?"

"Well, what was I supposed to say? I didn't want to stand in your way of getting a big story. And finding out who killed Roger and the other victims. That's what's really important here. Right?"

"Right. I guess I should be thanking you?"

"You absolutely should, but why do I have the feeling you still think I'm an ass."

"I don't. You've been wonderful to me."

His brow furrowed. "You're thinking something. I can see your wheels turning."

Our eyes met, and he held my gaze. With my heart racing, I opened my mouth to speak, but I couldn't spit out any words. It was as if we were engaged in some sort of twisted game of emotional chicken.

There was no reason for me to stay with him for one more night, much less a week at his penthouse for training. Just another deal gone south, that was all I was to him. *"My relationships don't evolve, they just end."* His words clanged in my head like a mantra I should never forget. If only he would say something, anything.

I pressed my lips together to stop them from quivering and exhaled. "So, I guess that's it then."

Adam didn't flinch or make a sound.

I repeated his mantra in my head once more, *"My relationships don't evolve, they just end."*

With nothing but uncomfortable silence between us, I hurried to the bathroom to collect my things. A lump formed in my throat while I threw my toiletries in a small bag. Tears threatened, and it pissed me off. *I have to get out of here!*

At full speed, I hustled out of the bathroom and found Adam retrieving my heels from the floor. My instinct was right. He wanted me gone.

When our eyes locked on one another, he tossed my shoes aside. "Don't go," he said in a hushed, gravelly tone.

"What?" I squeaked out.

"I said. Don't go. Stay. Stay with me."

I clutched my bag to my chest like a life preserver. "Adam, what are you doing to me? I'm so confused. What do you want from me?"

He closed the distance between us, ripped the bag from my hands, letting it fall to the floor. "Stop talking. You talk too much."

With one sharp move, he pressed me up against the wall, and seized my mouth, hijacking the breath from my body like a criminal. His lips found their way to my neck, threatening to steal any ounce of sense I had left.

I pushed my palms against his granite-like chest, and gasped. "Adam, please. I don't understand. You said..."

His arms wrapped around me, holding me close. "*Shh...* There's nothing to understand. I want you. I want to protect you and keep you safe." He released me and cradled my head in his hands. "Don't go. Stay here with me."

"But ... why?"

He kissed my forehead and looked deep into my eyes. "Because you're mine."

Without taking his gaze off mine, he lifted me into his arms, laid me out on the bed, and stripped out of his clothes. He knelt beside me, and slowly peeled me out of my dress and thong. We were naked, and quaking in a heightened state of neediness. The way Adam's nostrils flared and eyes blazed with heat, caused every piece of me to pulse anew. It was as if I couldn't breathe, but my heart vibrated with a fresh awakening.

He lowered his body on top of mine, and I relished the weight of him, pressing me into the mattress. Our skin rustling together felt like tiny, flickers of euphoria floating over me.

His soft lips joined with mine in tender kisses, while my hands gripped his broad shoulders, completely intoxicated by this new Adam Maxwell cocktail.

I spread my legs and surrendered to him, lost in a heady trance of temptation. "Oh, Sir." I sighed.

He clasped my chin, and whispered, "Sweetheart. Right now, we are not just Dom and sub. We are more. This is about you and me ... and this, unrelenting craving between us. This is different. This is—us."

With one smooth thrust, he slid inside me, taking me easy and gentle. Adam was right. This was different. This was beyond anything I'd ever experienced. It was also too good to be true, and I froze in panic.

He slowed his sensual strokes, as his eyes searched mine. "Jess, what is it? Tell me."

"I'm afraid," I mumbled.

"Afraid? Sweetheart, I'm right here. There's nothing to be afraid of."

"I mean, I'm afraid, that, I'll fall ... for..." I couldn't finish my sentence.

"Then fall. I'll be here to catch you."

He swept me into his arms, held me close, and I fell. I plummeted deep and let my emotions take over. We weren't just having sex. We weren't fucking. We were making love. Adam Maxwell was making love to me. I fell hard. I fell for him. My Sir.

CHAPTER NINE

JESSICA

"Hey, beautiful." Adam's scruff tickled my neck. "You awake?"

Not ready to get out of this glorious sex bed, I buried my head in his chest and grumbled incoherently. *What a night!* I didn't think it was possible to come that many times. Adam was insatiable, taking me every which way, and then some. We were two fiends with a thirst that couldn't be quenched. We made love, and then fucked like animals, ate a snack, and fucked some more. I *floved* it!

At one point, Claire sent him a text saying:

> *"Sam and I are going to have a slumber party with Harley."*

Obviously, they knew the deal. We were more. Last night changed everything. Now, we were us.

"Sweetheart, as much as I would love to shut out the world, and keep you here all day, someone has to start her new position."

I rubbed my eyes, and quipped, "I don't think there are any new positions left. You fucked me in every one of them, and made up some new ones along the way."

"Jessica," he reprimanded. "Language."

"Sorry, Sir."

His lips touched my forehead, and he handed me his phone. "That's better. I've got to get in the shower. Claire will be texting. Tell her I'll have my usual Friday breakfast, and let her know what you'd like."

"Okay. I should probably head back to my place and regroup before I go to work. Do you think Harley could stay here for the day? I hate the thought of leaving him alone right now."

"Absolutely. And I don't want you going anywhere near your townhouse. Make a list for Claire. Let her know what you need. She and Sam can pick up your things."

He rose from the bed, naked, with his feet scuffing across the carpet. *Shit!* That ass! And I was the one tapping it!

My question nearly left me. "Adam. Can I ask you something?"

"What is it?"

"Where will Sam and Claire be taking my things?" As my head filled with more questions, I covered myself in his sheets. "I mean, I don't know what we are, or if you want me to stay here to keep me safe, and that's it. What are we?"

"Still hung up on labels, Miss Blake?"

"No. I'm just curious."

His voice turned stern, as he took deliberate steps toward the bed. "Get rid of the sheet. Let me see you. Show me those beautiful tits."

My skin flushed, and I let the sheet drop. Adam's cock stiffened at the sight of my erect nipples. He took one in his mouth, and I panted in the pleasure of his tongue teasing me. Before releasing my breast, his teeth clamped down, making me wince.

"This is what we are, Jess. You make my cock harder than any sub I've ever had. And I could make you come just by sucking on your tits. We are us. Are we clear?"

"Yes." I exhaled.

His mouth hovered over my heaving chest when his phone buzzed. "I'm going to leave you wanting." He smirked. "It will make your orgasm more intense tonight."

"There's a tonight? What's happening tonight?"

"No more questions." He moseyed back to the bathroom. "I'm getting in the shower. You answer Claire's text."

I collapsed back on the bed. *Ugh!* If I were home alone, I'd be firing up my vibrator, Boomer. But, I put my lady wood on hold when I looked at the clock. I promised Hal I'd be in early.

Adam's phone buzzed again. I opened the message, expecting it to be from Claire, but it wasn't. It was from Sebastian. *What the hell!*

> *"Sorry I didn't respond last night. I was doing background checks, and I think I found you the perfect sub when you've finished with Jess. Her name is Teresa. She's brunette, curvy, and never been spanked. We all know how you enjoy that. You kinky fuck. Let me know when you can meet with her. What were you thinking? A week? Oh, and don't forget, Helen is unveiling her new painting at The Purple Peacock Saturday night. It should be a real ripper. She's stoked."*

As I scrolled through their conversation, it was clear. Adam was the one who initiated finding a new sub. *Oh, my God.* Yesterday at lunch when he was texting at Ferraro's, he was confirming with Sebastian. I felt sick.

I sprung into action, dropped his phone, threw on some clothes, grabbed my stuff and fled. Claire intercepted me on my way out the door.

"Jess. Hey, Jess. Wait. I was just going to text you and see what you lovebirds wanted for breakfast." She grinned with a wink. "You must be starving."

"Oh no. I'm not hungry. I've got a big day at work. I've got to go."

"So, Harley. He's staying here? Please say yes."

Shit! Harley. "I should probably take him home. To my townhouse."

"Oh, that's such a shame. He'll be all alone. You said it yourself, you have a big day."

Harley and his speckled paws galloped toward me. "Hey, mister." I crouched down, kissed his spotted nose, and tears welled up. What was wrong with me? "I guess, maybe I could leave him here for the day. Would you like that, buddy? Okay. I'll come and get you right after work."

I rose and plastered a fake smile on my face. Claire was not fooled. She held her arms out to hug me, and I recoiled. "Thank you for taking care of him. I'll come pick him up this afternoon?"

"Jess. Are you all right, hon? You look like you're going to cry."

"No. I'm not." I swallowed hard and stifled my impending tears. I hadn't cried in ten years, I wasn't about to start over Adam Maxwell. "I woke up with allergies. No tears. Just allergies. I've got to go."

"Can I get you anything? Something to eat? A tissue?"

"No. Thank you. I don't need anything."

I scrambled out the door and ran to my car. Before, speeding away, I wrapped my arms around myself and peeked up at the window to the master suite. I didn't mean anything to him. "Adam's relationships don't evolve. They just end." Blowing out a heavy breath, I fired up my car, and said under my breath, "I was right the first ten times. He's an ass."

* * * *

"Congratulations!" Tilly squealed! She danced her way into my office, and plopped a Red Bull with a fuchsia bow on my desk. "Hal told me the good news. You're a feature reporter, and I'm taking over 'Sin City Nights.'

We're crushing it, *mija*. Except, you don't look so happy. What's wrong?"

"Nothing," I lied.

Immersing myself in my first real story didn't block Adam from my mind. Throwing my phone in my desk drawer was also not as helpful as I hoped it would be. But, I could do this, one step at a time. Seeing my beautiful bestie's face lit up, excited for both of us was a step in the right direction.

Tilly put her hands on her hips. "If nothing is wrong then why do you look like you need a hug?"

"No. No hugging." I slouched back in my chair. "But, thank you for the Red Bull. And, congratulations to you too. We'll have to go out and celebrate. My treat."

"Yes! It will be just like old times. I can't wait."

"Me neither. And, I know I thanked you on the phone, but, again, thanks for staying with Stacy at the Palisades. I could tell yesterday at the service you two really bonded."

"Oh, that was nothing. She's a great lady. And the suite was popping! *Dios mio*, that Adam Maxwell knows what he's doing."

I scrunched up my face. "Yeah. I guess, he does."

"So, that's what's wrong."

"Tilly, I swear to you nothing's wrong."

"You can't fool me, *amiga*. Adam gives you the feels, and you're scared out of your tits."

"Do you mean, wits?"

"Whatever. Don't change the subject. You've got the feels for him."

"No. I don't feel anything. Remember me, your friend Jess, the girl who's dead inside?"

"I've never believed that and deep down you don't either. Just admit it. You feel something for him. It's not a crime. No one will take you away in handcuffs, unless, that's how you roll now."

When I opened my mouth to argue, a lump formed in my throat, and I rested my head in my hands. "Shit. I do have feelings for him. And, I hate it because he doesn't feel anything for me. He's already moved on. His next curvy, brunette submissive, Teresa, has already been handpicked by Sebastian. I'm such an idiot."

"No, you're not." Tilly came to my side of the desk, with open arms, and embraced me. "See, hugs aren't so bad, *mija*. Maybe a good cry would do you some good? You've been through a lot."

I pulled away, and popped the tab on my Red Bull. "Nah, he's not worth it." I chugged half of the can. "If I was going to cry about anything, it'd be about Roger. And I'm afraid to even think about him too long, because if I start crying, I might never stop. Life was so much easier without feelings."

"Easier, yes, but not nearly as colorful. You should always use all the crayons in your box."

"But, I can't color inside the lines," I joked.

"Neither can I. That's why we're friends."

"I tell you what I'm going to do. I'm going to find out who killed Roger. I won't rest until the murderer is behind bars."

"Oh, that reminds me. The tip line is set up. The calls will be forwarded to your landline when you're here. Otherwise, they'll leave a message. And a Miss Jeannie is coming into see you in an hour."

"Okay. Cool. Hal told me about her. At this point any information is helpful. I should touch base with Stacy too, so we can work together on this. Is Skip in? Maybe I can go over what he's found out so far."

"Check your email. He said he sent it to you already."

"Thanks." I fired up my laptop. "Man, I thought I got here early this morning. What time did you get in?"

"I got here at six."

"Six? Wow. I feel like a slacker."

She showed me her wristband from the Ghostbar's private section. "Please don't. I haven't been to bed yet. I'll be sleeping all afternoon. I just wanted to come in and help you get the tip line set up and say congrats."

"What about Hal and Skip?"

"We crossed paths in the parking lot. Those two were up all night again."

"Really? Ronald Sharpe running for mayor has them burning the midnight oil."

"I know. Hal is exhausted, but I've never seen him happier. They should be back in a couple of hours."

"You'd better get to bed. It's way past midnight. You should've turned into three pumpkins by now, Cinderella."

"That's so funny because I thought I lost one of my shoes last night. I kept waiting for Prince Charming to find it."

"Life is not a fairy tale. In Vegas, if you lose your shoe at midnight, you're shit faced."

Tilly cracked up. "That's so true. And there's no horse-drawn carriage either. Just an Uber driver with judgy eyes."

"Go get some sleep. And thanks for everything."

As Tilly left, I picked up the phone on my desk to call Stacy. "Shit. Her number is in my cell." Almost afraid to look at my phone, I retrieved it from my desk. Did Adam call? There was only a three-word text message:

"I can explain."

So could I. You're an ass!

I ignored him and called Stacy instead. "Hey, it's me, Jess. Do you have a minute?"

"Hi! Yes. Of course I do. I wanted to talk to you. Yesterday's service was so beautiful, and I still can't believe Mr. Maxwell. He didn't even meet Roger, and he paid for everything. He's so generous. Please tell him again how grateful I am."

"I will. You know. If I see him."

"What do you mean 'if'? You and Harley are staying with him, right?"

"That's kind of up in the air. I might go back to my townhouse tonight."

"I don't think that's a good idea. I've only been back to my place a few times, and it's been during the day with Kevin."

"Where are you staying?"

"I'm still at The Palisades. Kevin's sister, Nola, took in all my cats. She's fostering them until I feel safe again."

"So, our neighborhood is that bad?"

"There's definitely some shit going down. I'm getting more information than I normally would because of Roger. And all I can tell you is this isn't like any other crime spree Metro has seen."

"Crime spree? Don't they mean, killing spree?"

"Not exactly. Keep this off the record, for now, Miss Feature Reporter. Tilly told me the good news. Congrats."

"Thanks."

"So, have you met Miss Jeannie yet?"

"No. She's coming by my office soon."

"We have a couple of suspects in a holding cell. They matched her description and were picked up outside of Pure and Natural Health."

"Do you think they had anything to do with Roger?"

"No. Not these two. They confessed so quickly to what went down with Miss Jeannie. Their stories matched hers to the letter. But, this is what's strange. These are decent kids. Like, nice college kids, political science majors, with no priors. They had a gun, but bought it after Roger was shot. Miss Jeannie will fill you in a little more. But here's the thing. They aren't trying to strike a deal or even seek legal counsel. They are willing to do time, which makes me think, someone else is pulling the strings. And, that maybe what happened with Roger was a robbery gone wrong."

"Oh, wow! You mean they didn't think anyone was home."

"Right. Roger had guns, and he knew how to use them. Monday morning, we went to breakfast, and he said, he was going to work a double shift at four, so after a quick trip to the shooting range, he told me he wanted to take a nap. We were up late Sunday night celebrating his new job." Her voice cracked. "We came back from breakfast, and the last thing he said to me was he was going to drop Harley off at your place before work, and he told me—he told me to... He said, be safe. He was always so worried about me being a cop, and he gets shot in cold blood. I just wish..." Stacy sobbed softly. "I'm sorry. It comes in waves. One minute, I'm fine, and the next..."

"Don't apologize. My God. You've been through hell. I wish there was something I could do."

"You're already doing it. We're going to crack this case together."

"Damn right we are. If it's the last thing I do."

"I've got to go, Jess. Let me know how things go with Miss Jeannie."

"Okay. Take care. I'll be in touch."

I rummaged through my desk and found my emergency chip stash. *Nice.* Original Tostitos. A classic. I tore them open while checking my email and downing the rest of my Red Bull.

Wow! Skip's detailed notes on the case engrossed me. There wasn't much to go on when it came to eyewitnesses, but what the thieves were after was interesting. The only thing stolen from Roger's place was his laptop, cell phone, and cash. *Huh*, not only did Stacy just tell me he had guns, but I knew he was a Yankee fan.

He'd buy and sell memorabilia. So, why cash and electronics, and no other valuables?

A knock on the door jolted me. I glanced up to find a petite, sweet-faced older woman decked out in carrot orange from head to toe. Her outfit beamed brighter than the sun.

"Hi. Are you Miss Jeannie?" I asked.

"That's me." She smiled, adjusting her glasses. "I'm looking for Jessica Blake. I heard she was blonde, with big knockers, so I'm assuming I'm in the right office?"

I jumped up to greet her. Hal was right. What a character. Towering over her small frame, I shook her hand, and offered her a seat.

She flopped down in the chair, and held her brown purse firmly on her lap. "Thanks. It feels good to take a load off. I walked from the store. I do five miles every day whether I feel like it or not."

"Good for you. I appreciate you coming in to see me. I just got off the phone with Officer Sibley. She said they picked up a couple of suspects outside of Pure and Natural Health."

"Oh, I know. I'm going to the station to see if they were the little shits that stole my wallet."

"Is that all they got?"

"I wish. I had the bank deposit too. It's my own damn fault. I was playing Minecraft on my computer at the store. My son-in-law, Sean said to leave the bank deposit in the safe, and one of us would take it in the morning. Well, next thing I know it's dark outside. I decided to bring the money home with me, and hit the bank in the morning. And these two little punk ass bitches tackled me right under the streetlight. They grabbed the money bag, and told me to give them my wallet and my cell phone."

"That's awful. You must've been scared. Did they have a gun or a knife?"

"The dark-haired kid had a gun. They looked like two frightened cats. So, I elbowed one in the eye and said, 'Here's my wallet you little pisshead.' Wouldn't you know the one time I'm not packing my .38 special. I would've shot them right in the nuts."

Miss Jeannie couldn't have weighed more than ninety pounds, but was fierce, and hilarious.

"Did they get your phone too?"

"No. They took off when I said, 'What do you pussies want with my flip phone?' I don't need one of those fancy new things. I'd just surf porn all day."

I cracked up. "Oh, my God. They didn't know who they were messing with. I'm sorry. I should've offered you some water or something. I'm not quite myself today."

She pulled out a plastic bottle and unscrewed the top. "I've got my water with me. But I wouldn't say no to those chips. Are they gluten-free and vegan?"

"No. I'm afraid not. They're about as far away from healthy as you can get."

"Perfect. Lay them on me. Just don't tell Sean and my daughter, Kim if you come to the store."

"It'll be our little secret." While she chowed down on some chips, I fired off a few more questions. "So, do you remember anything specific about the two guys? Did anything stand out, like a tattoo, or clothing, something like that?"

"The only thing I noticed is that they were clean cut, like those Jehovah Witnesses that ride around on bikes. They had on jeans and T-shirts, but couldn't have been more than twenty years old. When I saw them under the streetlight, they looked like a couple of nice kids, so I let my guard down. That was my mistake. Rotten bastards."

"They are. I'm so sorry that happened to you."

"Oh. I've been through worse. You don't work for thirty-five years on the Strip in a cashier cage without running into a few jerk-offs. I'm just glad these two twits didn't break into the store. Sean got a bunch of orders in that day, and for Christ's sake, they could've stolen my computer. What would I do without Minecraft?"

"Speaking of the store, I was kind of wondering, if I could do a piece about you and this incident. I'd like to feature Pure and Natural Health. I'm trying to go with a more personal angle on this thing. I think it would help everyone feel like we were all part of a neighborhood watch."

"Sounds good to me. Together we are safer."

"Hey, I like that. Do you mind if I steal it?"

"You don't have to steal it. I'll give it you for nothing. You're good people, Jessica Blake. I can tell. Anything you need. You got it."

"Right back at you, Miss Jeannie. By the way, my friends call me Jess."

She pushed out of her chair. "Well, Jess. I better get to the station and take a look at the suspects. I hope Metro caught the right assholes. We need to take our community back from these dirty fuckers."

When I rose to walk her to the door, the magnitude of her statement weighed heavy on me. "We will, Miss Jeannie. I'll be in touch soon. Did you need a ride to the station? It's too far to walk."

"I'll just call my daughter. She said she'd pick me up or call one of those goober drivers."

"You mean Ubers?"

"Yeah. That's what she said. I still got my trusty flip phone. So, I'll call Kim."

"Okay. Stay safe. And we'll talk soon."

She rested her hand on her hip. "Okay. Just don't stand there, give this old lady a hug."

I couldn't say no to my star witness, so I embraced her and said goodbye.

The rest of the morning and part of the afternoon flew by as I worked every angle of my story. After checking in with Hal, we decided an introduction to me would help the public feel comfortable calling into the tip line. If I expected family members and victims like, Miss Jeannie, to put themselves out there, the least I could do was offer up a little about me and my background.

By three p.m. my, "Meet Jessica Blake: Las Vegas Times New Feature Reporter," piece was done and submitted for tomorrow's paper. My first real article! I looked around for someone to high-five, but I was alone, and finished for the day.

I should pick up Harley. But, where would we go? I grabbed my phone to call Tilly. Maybe her offer to stay at her place still stood. *Shit.* Her apartment didn't allow pets. *Screw it. I'll go back to my townhouse.* If these crimes are connected, and the criminals are as green and inexperienced as everyone thought. They wouldn't hit the same cul-de-sac twice.

As I forwarded my office phone to voicemail, I heard footsteps in the hallway. Before I could collect my things, Adam was there, leaning against the doorframe.

"Jess, we need to talk," he said in a low, soft tone with his deep blue eyes burrowing into mine.

"I have nothing to say to you."

He waltzed in and shut the door. "Good. Because I'm doing the talking."

"What's the point? You have a new sub waiting in the wings." I jolted out of my seat, snatched my purse, and hurried to the door. "And since my ass has already been spanked, it's yesterday's news."

He caught me by my elbow. "Sweetheart, just hear me out. Please, Jess."

Ugh! My strong will was no match for his drug inducing scent, so I conceded, plopping down in the chair, while he perched himself on the edge of my desk.

"I'm listening," I murmured quietly.

"Good girl," he replied with a hint of a smile. "I know you saw the text from Sebastian. I did ask him to find me someone new, but that was before last night."

"So, the entire time I was staying at your house and you were being, you know, nice, that was all an act?"

"No. I wanted you and Harley with me. If I didn't, I would have stayed at my penthouse. It was more than just a matter of keeping you safe."

"Then what was it?"

He exhaled, and rolled up the sleeves on his crisp, white shirt. "Would you like to know the real reason Monica ended things with me?"

"Are you trying to not answer my question and change the subject?" I snipped.

"No. I'm trying to explain, and you're not making it easy."

My eyes fell to his tempting bulge, and I was momentarily dick-stracted. "I prefer to make things, hard."

He shook his head. "Such a smart-ass, Miss Blake. Would you like me to fuck that smart mouth right here in your office, or would you like to know why Monica broke our engagement?"

Wet with arousal, I squirmed in my seat. How did he do that? He angered me and made me horny at the same time—again.

I cleared my throat. "Actually, I would like to know."

"Okay. So, the real reason Monica dumped me is because I was too controlling. I drove her away with my domineering need to micromanage every tiny detail of her life. She finally had enough and ended it."

"But, being Dom and sub, didn't she relinquish a certain amount of control to you?"

"We weren't Dom and sub. After we broke up, I met Sebastian and Eli. They were well-established Doms that just moved to the states. They approached me about being a silent partner in The Purple Peacock. I immersed myself in the lifestyle, and found my way as a Dom and teacher. Having control in a scene with a willing sub, and having control of my business helped me move on from Monica and avoid future unpleasant entanglements. I learned to compartmentalize everything. Life is less messy that way."

"So, you wrap up everything in neat little boxes?"

"Absolutely."

"But, I can't be tucked away in a box. I don't fit." I glanced down, and my embarrassing red splotches mushroomed across my chest. "I don't fit in anywhere."

He took my hands in his. "That's not true. After last night, I realized saying that you're mine means more. But, I've never had one of my subs be more than a temporary situation."

"I know. Your relationships don't evolve. They just end. I have your mantra memorized like a mission statement."

"With you, I've been tempted to discard those well-worn lines I've drawn in the sand."

"What's stopping you?"

"I'm standing in my own way because I don't want a TPE arrangement with you."

"What's TPE?"

"It means total power exchange. It's more of a twenty-four/seven type of Dom/sub. People sometimes refer to it as a Master/slave."

I withdrew my hands from his. "Oh. That sounds intense. I don't think..."

"Sweetheart, I don't want that. It's not right for either one of us. For the most part, I want to be your Dom in the bedroom only, but even now, I'm wondering what you ate today. Did you only have chips? I'm wondering if I should hire a bodyguard to keep you safe because I know you're putting yourself out there as the reporter for your story."

"How do you know that?"

"Hal told me, because I asked. I was concerned about the angle of the story. It's putting you in danger."

I sprung out my seat. "But, this is *my* story. I know you're our top advertiser, but you can't tell me what to write."

He grasped my shoulders and guided me back in my seat. "Of course, I can't. I don't want to. What I'm trying to tell you is... I want you. But, I'm also worried I'm going to drive you away. What if I can't help myself? What if I lose you because I can't stop trying to control your every move? That's why I contacted Sebastian. I felt those old micromanaging urges returning when you were staying with me, and I panicked. I figured, I'd have a week with you for the article, and then I'd let you go. But, then Hal canceled the article and, I couldn't let you go."

Astounded by his words, I froze up, unable to speak. My eyes peered into his, and I saw everything I had never allowed myself to dream of.

In a sudden, smooth motion, he took me into his arms, embracing me tightly. "This is all new to me. I know I'll fuck up from time to time, but I want you, Jess. I need you to be mine in every way. Please, say something."

"You're hugging me."

"I am. And I'm going to keep hugging you until you tell me what you want."

Oh, God help me! If I said it out loud, it was real. I peeked up at him and took the biggest gamble of my life. "I want you, Adam. And I need..."

"Need what? Tell me, beautiful. Tell me what you need."

I confessed, "I need all that lovey-dovey shit."

His sweet laughter rang in my ears. "Absolutely, Miss Blake."

He pressed his lips to mine in a kiss full of tender, possessive passion. Adam wanted me.

As he pulled away, a smoldering grin spread across his face that accelerated my heart rate. "In the spirit of lovey-dovey shit, Miss Blake. I do have a question for you."

"I have like a million questions for you, Sir Dude."

He retrieved a square box out of his pocket with a bow tied on top, and teased, "You'll note the color of the ribbon. It's not red. It's burgundy."

"Nice touch. That's either a thick deck of cards or jewelry?" *Please don't be jewelry!*

"Don't look so frightened." With the finesse of a close-up magician, he revealed a deck of cards. "I thought we'd draw to see who could ask one question."

Whew! "I'm game." I selected a card. "Did you stack this deck? I got the Four of Diamonds."

Adam chose his card with confidence. "Well, what do you know? The King of Hearts. I win."

"Of course you do. What's your question?"

"I'd like to ask you to go on a date with me."

"A date? Like Netflix and chill?"

"Whatever you'd like. I want to start over. So, if that's what you want to do, then we'll make a night of it, at the penthouse tonight, eight o'clock sharp. Don't be late."

The look in his eyes told me he was speaking to me as my Dom. It stirred everything in me. "Yes, Sir."

He kissed my forehead, and his lips lingered over mine. "Good girl. We're going to find our way together. We're going to write our own rules. Are we clear?"

"Yes. I want this."

"I want it too." He granted me a quick peck. "I'll see you at eight."

He strolled out of my office, leaving me in a daze.

Tonight, at his penthouse.

Netflix and chill.

That means fucking, right?

CHAPTER TEN
JESSICA

"Tonight is all about trust," Adam said in his sensual Dom voice that made me swoon.

After spending the rest of the afternoon with Harley, I arrived at Adam's penthouse, as ordered, at eight o'clock sharp. To my surprise, we watched Netflix and chilled in his media room while enjoying a little wine and takeout from Sushi Max, one of Adam's restaurants.

Once our episode of *The Alec Stone Chronicles* wrapped, my Sir told me to strip and led me to one of the guest bedrooms. This room wasn't as large as his master suite, but was just as luxurious, and beautifully lit with candles.

The king-sized bed was equipped like a massage table. My naked flesh flushed in anticipation.

"Lay down, face up, sweetheart. I want you completely relaxed."

"Yes, Sir." I happily obeyed.

"Good girl." Adam smiled. "As I said, tonight is about trust." He showed me a silky black blindfold he fished out of his charcoal grey sweat pants, and asked, "Do you trust me, Jess?"

"Yes. I trust you."

He slipped the blindfold around my head, and ran his finger between my breasts to my belly button. "This is the perfect place to start."

The palm of his hand circled the center of my stomach, as if he was preparing my skin for something. My other senses intensified. The ginger, citrus scent of the candles was so powerful, I could practically taste it on my tongue. The gentle brush of Adam's hand gave me goose bumps. And his voice! Those rich, gravelly, velvety tones crooned in my ears like a melody of sex. With my mind at peace and my body feeling weightless, I let out a contented sigh.

"Excellent, sweetheart. I think you're ready."

Drops of warm liquid showered my abdomen. Adam's hand smeared it into my skin. "I'm impressed. You didn't even flinch. Your submission to me is so pure. How does the wax feel?"

"It feels so good. It's not that hot."

"That's because it's a soy based candle that turns into oil."

"I love it. It smells amazing."

Another trickle of simmering fluid melted over each thigh. Adam massaged my quads and blazed a happy trail between my legs and stopped. Once my calves and feet were rubbed to satisfaction, his fingertips teased my nipples, making me mewl in delight at the sensuous sensation.

His hands roamed over each breast, making my nipples pebble. "God, you have gorgeous breasts. They're so sensitive too. I can tell how wet you are. You're dying to touch yourself, aren't you?"

"Yes, Sir."

"Do it. Take yourself to the edge."

I slipped my hand between my thighs before he had a chance to change his mind. *Shit!* My clit was so puffy. I could have made myself come so easily if I was alone. But, I demonstrated my obedience to him, by resisting the temptation of my lurking orgasm. Instead, I stroked myself lightly, and my body quaked in response.

"Talk to me, beautiful. Tell me how it feels."

My words came out in breathy wisps. "It's—so—wet! Ah—I'm close to the edge."

Even in the darkness, I could feel Adam's eyes digging into me. His cock must be frothing in pre-cum that I was dying to taste. When I pushed two fingers inside me, I opened my mouth wishing it was filled with his hardness.

Drips of the heated elixir flowed over my nipples, and Adam pinched them, causing me to cry out in sweet anguish. My veins were fueled with endorphins, as my body floated on a cloud.

Adam commanded, "Take your hand away. Only I can make that pussy come. It's mine."

I retracted my hand from my aching need, and he squeezed my nipples once more. Biting my lip to keep from screaming, I hovered in a sphere between pain and pleasure, savoring each ebb and flow.

Adam's hands tucked under my armpits and he rotated my position with my head hanging off the side of the bed. "I remember you said sixty-nine was a good number. It happens to be my favorite. Spread your legs. I'm starving."

I opened them for him. "I'm hungry too. May I have your cock, Sir?"

"Absolutely," he answered, as I felt the weight of him press into the bed. "Hit your right hand on the bed three times if it's too much because I'm going to fuck your throat, and I won't take it easy on you."

With his tip perched on my chin, I exhaled. "Yes, Sir." And he lowered his hard shaft into my mouth, and I guzzled him down.

"That's a good girl. Take it," he growled. "That's it. Fuck."

Adam's fingers pried my outer lips apart, and his mouth landed on my pussy. He rendered me completely immobile with his muscular upper body holding me down, and his massive cock filling my throat. He was using me for his pleasure, smothering me with his balls, eating me like a savage, and transporting me to a hedonistic wonderland.

"I fucking own that mouth now, sweetheart." He grunted. "Get ready for my cum. You've been a good girl. I'm giving you every drop."

He slapped my pussy, and reinforced his hold on me. "Once all your holes are filled. You can come."

One finger slid easily into my ass, and then two digits shoved in deep inside my last empty hole. With quick flickers of his tongue on my clit, I exploded like a Molotov cocktail, while he emptied himself down my throat.

As the orgasmic tremors subsided, he extracted himself from my mouth and cradled my limp body in his arms. I could barely hear his accolades of praise for trusting him and being a good girl. My climax was so intense. I thought I blacked out for a second.

"Tell me what you need, beautiful," Adam whispered. "I'm right here."

"C–can we j–just stay here?"

"Absolutely."

For almost an hour, he held me while I came out of my trance-like state. When I was ready, he cleaned me up, gave me a bath and put me to bed. This was an entirely new side to Adam, I'd never seen before. I'd never been cared for like this. Feeling safe and cherished was a foreign concept to me.

Before turning out the light, Adam gazed at me while we lay on our sides, facing each other in bed.

"What? Do I have some leftover jizz on my chin?" I joked.

He shook his head with a grin. "Such a smart mouth. Now, I'm not going to tell you where we're going tomorrow night."

I poked him in the stomach with my index finger. "Oh, come on. Please, Sir Dude."

He grasped my hand and pulled me close. "You might have an inkling since you saw Sebastian's text.

Our friend Helen is unveiling a new painting at The Purple Peacock. I want you by my side."

"I would love to go." The way his eyes penetrated into mine told me he had more to say. "Is that everything? Why do you keep looking at me like that? All lovey-dovey and shit."

He cupped my face in his hands. "Because, I was also thinking you have the most beautiful blue eyes I've ever seen, and how you've probably been told how gorgeous you are your entire life."

"Um, actually, the total opposite. My mom called me her ugly duckling."

"That's horrible."

"Well, that's my mother, Lauren. She is horrible. But it wasn't just her. Kids at school made fun of me. I had thick glasses, stringy blonde hair, and looked like a cross between a giraffe and a skinny owl. Even you said I wasn't your type."

"I should've never said that. I'm sorry. You were right. I'm an ass."

"No. You're not. I think maybe I reminded you of Monica. She's blonde and thin like me. Is that why you prefer brunettes?"

"You always have a question."

"That's because I'm always curious."

"Yes. You're very curious." He smiled, as he rolled on top of me, with his dick pressing into my groin. "You're also intelligent, a smart-ass, and the most beautiful submissive I've ever had."

Adam guided his cock inside me. Maybe it was to keep me from asking more questions, or it was our unrelenting craving for one another. In that moment, I didn't care, because the demons in my head always screamed loudest at night. With every thrust, Adam was telling them to shut the hell up.

* * * *

"Morning, kid. What are you doing here on a Saturday?" Hal asked from the hall.

"My first piece ran this morning." I held up the *Las Vegas Times* as if it was a diploma. My rite of passage. "I figured the tip line would be busy. Did you see it?"

"See it? Heck, I'm going to frame it for you. Congratulations. You done good."

"Thanks, boss. Coming from you, that means a lot."

He strutted into my office like a proud, literary papa, and helped himself to a seat. "You're welcome. I'm proud of you. I always knew you could do it."

"Sometimes it just takes the right opportunity at the right time."

"You earned that opportunity. I know it's not the secret, salacious Sin City story we envisioned but, with Ronald Sharpe and the crime spree in your neighborhood. Well, it's been a long time since we've had two stories with legs like this. Subscriptions are bound to pick up. But, it's going to take digging, and patience, and keeping our eyes and ears open. I haven't slept in days, but it's been worth it. I can sleep when I'm dead."

"I just hope we find out who killed Roger, and the other person." I rifled through my notes. "Here it is. Josephine Blackburn. She was only forty-three. I'll have to touch base with Stacy and see what I can find out. Do you have any juicy details about Ronald Sharpe that you can share?"

Hal had a twinkle in his eye, I hadn't seen in ages. "Oh, yeah. You need to keep this under your hat."

"Lay it on me. I can keep a secret."

"Old Sharpe has himself a mistress in Vegas." He folded his arms and paused for my reaction.

"What? How did you find out?"

"Skip tailed them. You know those high-rise apartments across from Tivoli Square. That real estate developer, Cole Roberts owns it as well as half of Downtown Summerlin."

"Yeah. They're really fancy. But only one tower is finished. There's always an AJ Construction sign popping up with his unfinished properties."

"Exactly. There are a couple of empty stores in Tivoli Square, and Ronald Sharpe's name is on the deed. We've been combing through his tax returns. He has little pockets of real estate all over the city, most of it is empty or unfinished. So, Skip follows him to Tivoli a couple of days ago. He's thinking he's having some sort of campaign meeting, but this blonde hops in his car in the parking garage and over to the apartments they go. After some nosing around, Skip found out Sharpe's renting two apartments side by side. The mistress cussed out the security guard, so he was only too happy to share their dirty little secret with Skip. Now we just need a name and some proof. Like a photo or something."

"I wonder if his wife in Carson City has any idea?"

"Skip's got contacts there too."

"Good for him. Although, it still doesn't explain why Sharpe is running for mayor and not Governor. There's got to be something he isn't telling the press. You don't think it's because of his mistress?"

"I think there's more to it than that. If we work together, we'll figure it out. Then, we'll all be sitting pretty. People will pay attention to this little paper, just like the good old days before social media took over."

"I'll do everything I can on my end. My loyalties are with you."

He shoved himself out of his chair. "I know that. Keep plugging away."

"You have my word, boss."

Before he left, he stopped at the doorway with a serious expression emerging on his face. "Be careful, Jess."

The ringing phone commanding my attention didn't allow Hal's comment to sink it. I was slammed all day taking down information and possible leads. So far, Miss Jeannie was the only witness with any concrete information. This could be like looking for a needle in a haystack.

I put the tip line to voicemail and worked on my next feature story for "Together We Are Safer." Miss Jeannie and their store was an easy first choice. Although, I was anxious to tell the world what a wonderful man Roger was, I couldn't go there yet.

Before my grief consumed me, my phone beeped with a text from Adam:

> *"Looking forward to showing you off at The Purple Peacock tonight. I'd like you to wear that dress."*

I knew exactly which one he was talking about, but opted to be a smart-ass. I wrote back:

> *"You mean the red one?"*

He texted back one word:

> *"Burgundy."*

This should be a night to remember.

CHAPTER ELEVEN

ADAM

"Evening, Brandy," I said, greeting her with a slight nod. "This is my girlfriend and submissive, Jessica Blake."

As the word girlfriend left my mouth, Brandy's dark eyes widened in surprise. I suppose there would be more shocked faces throughout the night. I was still getting used to the idea myself.

Brandy offered her hand. "Nice to meet you, Jessica."

"You too," Jess responded with a quiet confidence, looking spectacular in her burgundy dress.

"Your table is set up just the way you like it," Brandy added. "Oh, and I almost forgot. Sebastian added someone to the list for this evening. Ronald Sharpe and a guest will be joining us for the unveiling of Helen's painting. I can't remember the woman's name, but they've both been screened by Sebastian and signed confidentiality agreements."

I glanced at Jess, and her wheels were turning. "Thank you, Brandy," I replied in a clipped tone and quickly led Jess to my table before she burst.

"Oh, my God!" she whispered while taking a seat. "Hal just told me Ronald Sharpe has a mistress. He must be bringing her here. If I could sneak a picture, Skip's story would blow up. Damn it! I wish this was my story."

"Language," I reprimanded. "And there will be no pictures. Are we clear?"

Her huge blue eyes pleaded with me. "But, this is major. It could have a massive impact on his campaign."

"Sweetheart, everything that happens in this place is strictly off the record. Be a good girl and take your reporter hat off for the night."

"Yes, Sir."

Every time she called me "Sir," my cock twitched. In some ways, Jess was an unlikely submissive, because of her unyielding feisty temperament. She was two sides of the same coin. There was a vulnerability and strength in her submission to me. Experiencing her high-strung nature meld into a calm peace transformed me as a Dom. It made me want to be a better Dom and a better man for her.

"Well, if it isn't my mate." Sebastian waved and made his way to our table. "You're looking well, Jess. I see you gave this ass another chance."

She laughed with that intoxicating sultry lilt. "What can I say, he wore me down."

I slung an arm around the back of her chair. "Yes. I did indeed. And she's all mine."

"Ah, come now. You've always shared with me before," Sebastian said with a look of desire for Jess.

Her shoulders rose in tension as she peeked up at me. I took her hand, and responded, "We haven't discussed it yet. So, where's Helen? Is she ready to show us her new work of art?"

"Just about. I got a little preview, and I must say it's a real beaut. I like it even better that the peacock. I'm so proud of her."

"That's because you're in love with her," I retorted.

"Fuck off, Maxwell," Sebastian retaliated. "I apologize for my language, Jess, but Adam has a way of being—"

"An ass?" Jess interrupted with her smart mouth.

I gave her thigh a firm squeeze, and she flinched. "Would you like a spanking now, in front of everyone? I'd be only too happy to bare your bottom right here."

She blew out a breath. "Whatever you say, Sir."

"I'll leave you to your discipline," Sebastian quipped. "I need to take care of something."

Sebastian ran off to take care of his cock. There wasn't a doubt in my mind Helen would be on her knees in a matter of minutes. I had my hands full with my own naughty submissive.

"Look at me, sweetheart. Did you think that was being a good girl, calling me an ass in front of Sebastian?"

"No, Sir."

I dipped my hand between her legs. "The thought of me spanking you in front of everybody turned you on, didn't it?" She nodded as I pushed her cotton thong to the side, and fingered her. "You're very wet. I might have a bit of an exhibitionist on my hands." I circled her clit, and she squirmed in her seat. She looked sexy as fuck writhing in pleasure. It gave me a full-blown erection. "If you had been a good girl, you'd be coming right now. Since you weren't, you'll have to wait."

"Yes, Sir," she gasped.

I removed my hand and showed her my glistening fingers. "Look what a mess you made. Clean it up."

When she reached for a purple cloth napkin, I chuckled to myself. This was all so new to her, but her willingness to please me was palpable. "Not with the napkin, sweetheart. With your mouth."

With zero hesitation, she sucked my wet fingers inside. Little moans escaped while she delighted in her task, and her nipples poked through the fabric on her dress. It was all I could do not to fuck over the table.

I pulled my fingers out of her mouth. "Do you like the way you taste?"

"Yes, Sir. I apologize for my remark."

"When we're here, we are Dom and sub. Respect to me and the other Doms is demanded. There's a fine line between light banter and disrespect. Are we clear?"

"Yes, Sir," she said softly, lowering her head.

"Look at me, Jess? Remember I said we're finding our way. You're forgiven." In an effort to see that beautiful smile, I added, "Do you have any questions?"

"Like a million." She beamed. "Even though I'm not writing the article anymore, I still want to learn everything about BDSM. I think I'd like to keep a journal, and maybe one day, write something about the lifestyle. Even if I'm the only one who ever sees it."

"I love that idea. So, ask away, Miss Blake. What would you like to know?"

Her eyes flashed with curiosity. "Are you going to share me?"

"Normally, that would be a definite yes, as long as the submissive is willing. But, with you, I honestly don't know. Did you wish to be shared or watched?"

"I've had fantasies about it, but now, I'm not sure. Maybe I wouldn't mind being watched?"

"You don't have to decide anything tonight. What else would you like to know?"

"Just something I noticed. Brandy is brunette, and so is the waitress over there. Have you ever, you know, Dom-med them?" She giggled. "I guess that's not really a word."

"Not really, but I like it. And, no, I haven't 'Dom-med' Brandy or Lisa. Brandy actually works for me at my headquarters. I trust her implicitly. She's the only person who is a part of this world and Maxwell Industries."

"I saw her sit on your lap when I was here for the munch. She's interested."

"We had a long talk the next day. I was very clear that she and I would never happen. She's too valuable an asset at both places to ever go there."

"But you wanted to?"

I kissed her forehead. "No. I only want you."

She smiled slightly, and her eyes flashed toward the bar. "Oh, look there's another brunette with Sebastian. Who's the tall guy?"

"Tall? Eli? He's not that much taller than me? I'm over six feet, and he's only a few inches more. Tall guy? Is that what you noticed?"

"Well, yeah. I'm almost five eight, so I notice tall men. I didn't say he was sexy, or hot. I only say that about you, Sir Dude."

"Sir Dude. Only you can get away with that, Miss Blake. That's the kind of banter I enjoy." I drew her to me for a kiss and felt the eyes of everyone on us. A gradual applause grew. I tugged on Jess's long blonde hair. "Let's give them something to talk about."

Our public display of domination continued, as whistles and catcalls sounded in the air, taunting us to get a room. At a place like The Purple Peacock, getting a room would be no problem. The only question was, which one?

Sebastian's voice rung out over the ruckus, and we put an end to our little show.

"Attention, everyone! As much as we'd all like to witness the copulation of Adam and his lovely submissive, Jess, we have another pressing matter to attend to. Although, I wouldn't mind another performance from those two, since I'm a kinky fuck."

Eli chimed in, raising his beer bottle, "I'll drink to that, mate."

Sebastian draped an arm around Helen, and proceeded with the presentation. "As you know our friend Helen is an incredible artist. This painting is brill. I think it embodies the reasons why Eli, Adam, and I wanted to have a place like this. We might be a small community, but we're fam. So, without further delay, I give you Helen's latest masterpiece."

With a flourish, Sebastian flung the covering away to reveal Helen's exquisite creation. It was part Andy

Warhol, part Monet, mixed with our BDSM motto, and Helen's creativity. The canvas was divided into four squares, featuring a pair of handcuffs, a collar, a crop, and a blindfold with the words, safe, sane, consensual, and private. The purple hues running throughout were the perfect touch to her painting.

While the room erupted in a well-earned ovation, Jess and I made our way through the small crowd to congratulate her.

Flanked by Eli and Sebastian, Helen clasped her hands together and beamed. "Well, Sir, what do you think?"

I grasped her by the shoulders. "I'm pleased. It's incredible."

As I introduced Jess to Eli and Helen, I coiled a possessive arm around her waist and kept her close to me.

Our small talk came to an abrupt end when Brandy let me know Ronald Sharpe and guest had arrived.

I whisked Jess back to my table, and reminded her in a stern voice. "No matter who Ronald Sharpe walks in with, you're not to have a reaction. He is our guest. Is that clear?"

"Yes, Sir," Jess said with a slight pout, and took her seat.

"If he becomes the next mayor, it could be nice to have friends in high places. The longer we're in business, the dicier it becomes. Our waiting lists to get in for munches are already longer than we can manage. With each passing month, the private part of the club is becoming harder to maintain."

Her head bobbed back and forth, she couldn't help trying to get a good look at them. "Well, I can see him. Man, I thought the camera added ten pounds. He looks so much heavier in person, and that's got to be some sort of dead animal on top of his head. It looks like he bought it at the raccoon house of crap."

"Sweetheart, that's enough. Eyes front. I can't afford to make any waves. I need you on your best behavior."

She settled into the chair and placed her hands on her lap. "Yes, Sir."

"I know reporter Jessica Blake is exploding with curiosity and questions. If you're a good girl, I'll take you into one of my private rooms, and you can explode all over my cock. Do we have a deal?"

A devilish grin flashed across her face. "Deal."

"Good, because they're coming this way. He's definitely not with his wife. His wife isn't a blonde. I have no idea who she is."

With his wrinkled, navy suit and mistress in tow, Ronald Sharpe moved with the grace of manatee, but the confidence of a lion. The well-worn blonde was small framed and seemed to possess a kind of phoniness. As a successful businessman, I had learned to read people quickly and trust my gut. I took an instant disliking to both of them.

My instincts told me to place a protective arm around Jess. When I glanced her way, she'd gone pale except for the beet-red spots on her chest. "Jess, what's wrong?"

She heaved. "Ronald Sharpe's mistress. I know her. That's Lauren, my mother."

Before I could get her out of there, this titanic duo landed in front of us. Ronald jutted his hand forth like a used car salesman. "Ronald Sharpe."

I stayed seated. There was no way I was leaving Jess's side. "Adam Maxwell. It's a pleasure to meet you, Governor."

He shook my hand a little too hard, and corrected me, "That's Lieutenant Governor, and soon to be mayor if you get my drift. You look familiar, little lady," he said, referring to Jess. "You are?"

Jess straightened her spine, shooting daggers at her mother. "You didn't tell him who I am, Lauren?"

No doubt putting on an act, Jess's mom smiled through her veneers. "Of course I did, darling. Ronnie, this is my daughter, the one I told you all about. This is Jessica—"

"Blake," Jess interrupted quickly and offered her hand. "Jessica Blake."

Lauren wrinkled up her pinched face. "Still going by the last name Blake? Interesting."

"Still between husbands?" Jess piped back. "How many are you up to these days, seven? Or is it eight? I lost track."

Lauren let out a fake laugh as her beady blue eyes filled with disdain for her own daughter. "Oh, my, Jessica. Always the comedian. I'm so glad I ran into you. I stopped by your place a little while ago. Did that horrid man with the motorcycle tell you?"

"That was Roger, my friend."

"Well, your friend was ill-mannered and very—"

"He's dead, Mother. Roger was killed. So, you can save your ratchet rant. God, don't you ever read a paper."

"Not that little rag you write for," Lauren retorted.

"Ladies, please," Ronald intervened. "I don't get it, Maxwell. I thought this was a swinging place. And gals just did what they're told."

I rose slowly out of my seat, staring him down. "You thought wrong. You have no clue what this lifestyle is really about. I think it would be best if you both left."

"Oh, come on," he bellowed. "Is that any way to talk to the next Mayor of Vegas? Have you seen my poll numbers? It's practically a done deal. And I know you like deals, Maxwell. I'm about to make your brother, AJ, a hell of a deal. What do you say, you throw him a bone, and we'll all be rich? I hear you're in negotiations to seize control of Bally's and give it a facelift. You know, give it the Maxwell touch."

"How did you know that?"

"So, I'm right, huh? I've got my ear to the ground and my fingers in every pie."

"Get to the point," I huffed.

"The point is, I scratch your back, you scratch mine, and in the process, give AJ Construction the contract for Bally's."

"My half-brother and I don't do business together. He doesn't even admit we're related unless he wants something."

Ronald shook his head, like he was playing me. "That's a damn shame, son. Just trying to make you the richest man in Vegas by the age of thirty."

"I'm thirty-five, and not your son. You're on thin ice, Sharpe. I see right through you, and AJ too for that matter. This is not the kind of business I do."

"Well, that's a major bummer, because we would be all be rolling in it, big league," Ronald said while glaring at Jess. "I wanted to make you a deal too, little lady."

"Me?" Jess's eyes darted between the three of us. "I'm almost afraid to ask, but what kind of a deal?"

Ron helped himself to a seat, and pulled out a chair for Lauren. "We might as well take a load off and have a drink." He craned his neck, looking for a waitress, and came up empty-handed. "Where is everyone?"

I shrugged, and sat down. "Probably off celebrating Helen's painting in the private rooms."

He rapped his knuckles on the table. "Now that's what I was talking about. They do swing here."

"Not in the way... Never mind," I said. "Now, if we could get back to the deal that concerns Jess?"

He leaned back in his chair and leered at Jess. "Yes. The deal. Well, it's like this. I saw your first article this morning, with the nice picture of you. It was about your series of stories. What are you calling it, 'Together We Are Safer'? Meanwhile, I got this little twerp from your paper tailing me everywhere I go. Then Lauren says to me, my daughter Jessica works for the *Las Vegas Times*.

I pulled your article up on my phone and show her, and sure enough, it's the same Jessica. So, here's what I propose. I'll give you exclusive coverage of my campaign. You'll have access that other media outlets won't get. And in exchange, no more twerp following me. I know they've been poking around in some delicate places. I need someone I can trust. Someone like you, Jessica. Now is that a deal, or what? What do you say?"

Jess placed her hands on her lap, took a breath, allowing her shoulders to relax. "I say, no thank you. You're not looking for someone you can trust. You're looking for someone you can manipulate. I'm a reporter. I report the truth. All of it."

"Oh, for Christ's sake," Lauren chided. "You write one lousy article, and now you're a reporter?"

Poised with confidence, Jess spoke calmly. "I have integrity, Mother. Maybe that's something you don't understand."

Lauren wagged her finger. "How dare you speak to me like that, after all I've done for you. You ungrateful freak."

"That's it." I jumped up. "Ronald, I need to speak to you, in private." I placed my palm between Jess's shoulder blades. "Are you going to be okay, sweetheart?"

She grinned like a naughty minx. "Yes, S–i–r."

Oh, my Jess was wicked. She was pushing her mother's buttons, so I helped her along. "Good girl," I said, and petted her hair before motioning for Ronald to follow me to the door.

Besides Patrick behind the bar, the only other person in earshot was Brandy. I could always speak freely in front of her.

It appeared Ronald was thrown off his game. He wasn't accustomed to hearing the word "no."

"Listen, Maxwell, I think you're making a big mistake here. And so is your ... your, whatever you call, Jessica."

"I call her mine. Jessica is my girlfriend and my submissive. I protect what's mine. Like my club. Exactly how did you find out about The Purple Peacock?"

"I just held a fundraiser at The Vegas Edge. Some of us hung around and had a few too many. A couple that lives there, The Petersons. They said they come here all the time."

I nodded, he was telling the truth. "Mrs. Peterson is a lovely woman, but a bit of a blabbermouth."

Ronald laughed. "You ain't kidding. When I said, 'I couldn't risk being seen at some kind of kink club,' she said, 'It's fine, Adam Maxwell's there all the time.' You might want to have a talk with her."

"Indeed. Did you tell anyone you were coming here tonight?"

"Are you nuts? Of course I didn't. That'd be like handing the election to that clown, Crenshaw."

"Good point. I just have one more question. Did you know Jessica was going to be here tonight?"

"Hell, no. Did you see the look on Lauren's face? Look, I'll come clean. I'm not a perfect man. I got some things in my past and present I can't let anyone find out about. It would ruin me. So yeah, one of the reasons I came here was to talk to you about getting that damn paper off my back. It's easy to see you're their main advertiser, so I thought you could tell them to back off, and maybe I'd score some points with Lauren by offering her daughter an opportunity."

"Jessica would be your worst nightmare if she was a part of your inner press core. She's relentless when it comes to pursuing a story, and she'd tell the whole truth. But, I could talk to Hal for you at the *Las Vegas Times*. I could help you if you help me."

"Oh, boy. What's this going to cost me?"

"What do you mean?"

"I've heard about the great negotiator, Adam Maxwell. You just turned the tables on me, so I know this is going to cost me."

Perfect. I had Sharpe where I wanted him. I was going to get what I wanted from this deal. I always did. "I only need your word about Jess and The Purple Peacock. No one can know anything about tonight."

"That's it? Come on, I know there's more."

"There is. It's about my brother, AJ. I don't trust him and you shouldn't either. I won't be in business with him. I don't even have a relationship with him. If you know what's good for you and your campaign, you won't either. But this is what I insist on. He can't know about The Purple Peacock, or that we've had any contact. Tonight never happened. Do that for me, and I will talk to Hal for you. Deal?"

"I can do that, but the negotiations at Bally's will be so much easier for you if you use AJ Construction. I did promise to make your life hell if things didn't go his way."

"That's okay. I like a challenge. And if AJ made you any promises, he isn't going to keep them anyway."

"I guess we got each other by the balls in a matter of speaking."

I extended my hand and gave him an even firmer handshake than he gave me. He winced slightly, and I pulled him closer. "Make no mistake. You're the one with everything to lose. My mother knows, Crystal, your wife."

Lauren's voice reverberated through the club. "You've put that man on a pedestal like he's some kind of a saint!"

I rushed to Jess's side with Ronald trailing behind me. Lauren continued her tirade while Jess remained in her perfect posture.

"You act like I was never there for you," Lauren yelled. "I gave birth to you. And I know things! I know the truth!"

"Enough," I commanded. "Ronald, I think it's time for you to leave."

"Sure," Ronald agreed. "Come on, Lauren, let's go. We'll see ourselves out." He hurried Lauren out, with his tail between his legs.

"Jess, I'm so proud of you." Her body crumbled in on itself, like she was falling to pieces. "Hey, sweetheart." When I hoisted her into my arms, I felt her trembling. "What did she say to you? Tell me."

Her big blue eyes were glassy, filling with tears. She was reeling. I should've never left her alone with that horrible woman.

"I'm taking you to one of the private rooms, so we can talk."

"I—I don't want to talk."

"You have to communicate with me, Jess."

"I will. I promise. But, right now I need. I need you to..."

"Tell me. What do you need?"

"I need you to be my Dom. I need you. I need, us."

* * * *

"You're not going to blindfold me?" Jess asked in a soft voice, strapped to the St. Andrew's cross in one of the private rooms.

"No, sweetheart. I need your eyes on mine."

Even though she didn't shed a single tear, there was still a storm brewing in her beautiful eyes. They gave her away at every turn, and right now I needed to read every moment of this scene with her.

She surprised me by choosing the X-shaped St. Andrew's cross to be tied to, naked except for her burgundy thong, which was soaked in her arousal. I demanded she left it on, just in case that fucker Sebastian wanted to see if I changed my mind about sharing her, and surprised us.

I selected the black leather flogger, and whipped it through the air, untangling every strand. Then, I rolled up my sleeves, and showed her my instrument of choice. A hint of a smile touched her lips.

"I was so impressed with you tonight, Jess. You stood up for yourself, but maintained your cool while your mother came unglued."

"I was doing what you taught me. I relaxed and breathed, and trusted you. I knew you were going to keep me safe. There was no point in giving in to her hysterics."

"That's a good girl. A very good girl." I clasped my hand around her throat and kissed her sweet mouth. She tasted like everything I'd been hungry for my entire life. "You're my girl, Jess. All mine."

I swept the leather strips over her naked flesh, and it caused her to mewl. Those huge gorgeous tits heaved heavy with desire. I couldn't resist feeling how wet she was for me.

I dove two fingers inside, and whispered into her ear, "Do you feel that? Your body yearns for this."

"Ah—ah, yes. Yes, Sir."

From the moment the first lash of the flogger striped her skin, her eyes calmed like the ocean at night. This is what she needed. Her surrender to the pain across her body freed her from the wounds in her heart.

When she lowered her head with a sorrowful groan, I decided she'd had enough even if she didn't say her safe word. She was on the verge of breaking, but I knew she wasn't ready yet.

I released her from her the cross, and she collapsed into my arms. "Good girl." I carried her to the bed, placing her down on the satin sheets. "Lie still for me. There's some aloe vera gel in the drawer."

Once I found the gel, I turned, and the sight of her long, lean figure, branded with my mark made me hard as a rock.

"What?" she asked in a hushed tone, still breathless from the flogger.

"Nothing. It's just, you. You look beautiful. How do you feel?"

She brushed her fingertips over a pink streak on her stomach. "Well, at the risk of getting in trouble for my language. I feel like you helped me tell my mother to fuck off."

"I'll let this one slide."

I squirted the gel on my hands, gently rubbing her hardest hit areas and she purred like a kitten. This woman was unbelievable. She was tough, yet soft, strong, yet delicate, and was almost too witty for her own good.

Any self-respecting Dom would at least ask his submissive if she wanted to be shared or watched when at The Purple Peacock, but I was a selfish bastard. I wanted her all to myself.

I tore off her thong. She gasped, and said with a grin, "You realize, Mr. Maxwell, I'll be leaving this joint commando."

"You think so, Miss Blake." I reached into my pocket and produced a periwinkle panty surprise, dangling from my finger. "I told you, you'd get these back when you least expect it."

"Well played, Sir." Her eyes filled with playfulness. "Shall I put them on now, or will they just get ruined too?"

I tossed them to the side, and stripped. "So many questions, sweetheart. I'll give you the answer." I lowered my voice. "You're going to stay naked for me until I fucking devour you. Are we clear?"

As soon as I said "Are we clear?" the mood shifted. Jess moved to her knees with her hands resting on her thighs.

"Good girl."

I offered her my hand, and she took it, as I guided her to straddle me, with my cock aching for relief.

"Put me inside you," I commanded.

Jess grasped my dick, and I eased into her. With a solid grip on her hips, I slammed her to my base, and fucked the shit out her. Those tits bouncing and her tight pussy squeezing my cock almost made me blow my load immediately.

I slowed down and spread her butt cheeks. Then holding a finger to her lips, I growled. "Suck it."

Her tongue toyed with my finger before taking it in her mouth, and I slapped her ass. *Fuck!* I love the sound she made when I disciplined her. It was part release, part arousal, and a little bit of a pain-slut cry—meaning she craved more. I gave it to her, and her cunt gushed all over my cock.

I pulled my finger out of her mouth and pressed it into her asshole. She shrieked, and I brought my other hand to her chin and held it firm. "Look at me. I need to take your ass. I have to have it."

She whimpered, "Yes, Sir. Now?"

I eased up on my thrusts and caressed her cheek. "No, sweetheart. You're not ready yet. You'll need training. I would rip you in two if I took you there now. We'll go slow, but I'm going to take what's mine."

The sweetest smile lit up her face. "I'm yours."

Our lips came together in a frenzy of fuck lust. I flipped her onto her back, climbed on top of her and buried myself balls deep inside that tight pussy. I was taking what was mine, and Jess was freely giving herself to me with every stroke. She relinquished her body, mind, and soul to me when we came together. It was a heavy responsibility. She'd put her trust, heart, and her very life in my hands. And when she peeked up at me after our climax, all I could think was... *Don't fuck up!*

CHAPTER TWELVE
JESSICA

"Sweetheart. Jess? Are you awake?"

As usual, Adam overloaded my senses while rousing me after our night at The Purple Peacock. The aroma of the coffee I came to love, the rustling of his stubble against my cheek, and his gravelly baritone voice humming softly in my ear. Was I dreaming? This was like waking up to a kinky Prince Charming every morning.

"It's still dark. And it's Sunday," I croaked out. "Can't I sleep a little longer?"

"It's after ten. It only seems dark because it's raining."

I rolled on my back, yawning. "Oh. I don't know why I'm so tired."

He poured the coffee, splashed a smattering of cream in it, and handed it to me. "I suppose I'm to blame for that. I gave you quite a workout last night. Are you sore?"

"Only in a good way. It's like I can feel you in me when you're not there. I like it."

"That pleases me. How would you feel if we started your training today?"

I swallowed hard. "W—w—hat does that mean?"

Adam sauntered to his large off-white large dresser. With safe cracking precision, he retrieved what he was looking for, and presented me with a rectangular kind of jewelry box. *Ugh, jewelry?*

"Open it," he said with a smirk.

I lifted the lid, and was left nearly speechless by rows of stainless steel butt plugs. "Wow! They're all so shiny."

He held it up the smallest one. "We'll start with this one, since you're so tight. It's the same size as the one I used for our first scene. At first, five or ten minutes a day is satisfactory. Then I'll move you up gradually. Are you ready?"

"Can I have another sip of coffee first?"

"Take a sip and then lay on your stomach," he ordered abruptly.

"Did I do something wrong? I'm sorry if I slept in too late."

He sat on the bed, and brushed the back of his hand across my cheek. "There's nothing to apologize for. I'm just a little stressed."

"Then, please talk to me. You're always telling me to communicate."

"I will. But it will have to wait, I have a full day."

"But, it's Sunday."

His jaw clenched. "I'm aware. That's why I wanted to start your training today. It's a way of feeling connected as Dom and sub when we're not together. We're both very independent people with a lot on our plate. You have your story. I have my business. Think of this as your daily task. Every minute you keep your plug in you're pleasing me."

"Oh." I blew out a breath. "I like that."

A slight smile touched his lips. "You're wet, aren't you?"

"Yes, Sir. Wet for you."

"On your stomach, Jessica."

I quickly got rid of the coffee, and flattened on my belly. He threw the sheet back, and my bare butt readied for him. He palmed my cheeks before spreading them open, and wiggled a wet finger inside. My anal walls clamped around his penetrating digit while my pussy pulsed in need. I pressed my sex into the mattress, aching for more.

"Hold still, sweetheart. You do not get to come. That's part of your training too. I want you to be conscious all day long that your ass, your pussy, all of you, belongs to me."

I whimpered into my pillow, "Yes, Sir."

"Good girl." I'm going to wash my hands, and grab the lube from the bathroom. If you don't move, I'll give you the present I put in the nightstand earlier when you were sleeping."

"A present?"

"Don't move. I'll be right back."

When he returned, I heard the click of the lube cap, follow by a cold dollop on my butthole, and a colder butt plug sliding in my anus. I wanted to come so bad. There was no point in begging, groaning, or even promising throaty sexual favors. Adam was not himself. So, I breathed through my arousal and focused on things that weren't sexy, like socks with sandals, or pictures of people's food on Facebook, and hairy backs. *Wow!* That last one did the trick. Lady wood, gone.

"Nicely done," Adam said, kissing the small of my back. "You're learning."

"Did you say something about a present?"

He opened the nightstand on my side, and softened as he revealed my gift. "You mentioned you wanted to start a journal, so I had Claire send out for this before they left on their trip. It's as you would say kind of old school, but I thought you might like it."

I popped up, and practically ripped it out of his hands. "I love it. Thank you. It's beautiful," I said, running my hands over the cloth paisley cover. I opened it, flipped through the empty pages, and even sniffed it. It had that new book smell.

"Did you just sniff your journal?" Adam chuckled.

"I did." I clutched it to my chest. "My dad had one just like it."

"Speaking of your dad. We need to talk about what happened with you and your mother."

"Right now?"

"No. Like I said, I have a full day. But, tonight, we'll open up a bottle of wine, and I'll order dinner in from the clubhouse at the country club. They have a great surf and turf. I can actually have the chef come and prepare it for us."

"They do that for everyone that lives at The Vegas Edge Country Club?"

"Probably not everyone, but since I own it—"

"Everyone has to do what you say."

"You're catching on, Miss Blake." He kissed my forehead. "I'll see you about six. Remove your plug in four minutes."

"Yes, Sir."

"Good girl."

* * * *

After a jog in the rain with Harley, and a shower, I felt refreshed. It was nice being on my own. Adam was right. We both were independent people with big jobs. If he hovered or was too clingy, I'd head for the hills.

Harley was a different story. He burrowed into my side while I wrote in my journal about my BDSM experience last night and what I had learned so far.

Basically, it was what Adam explained when I interviewed him at the penthouse. We all enjoyed different kinks, and had different expectations, and experiences. For me, there was a deeper connection with Adam than any other person I'd slept with. Finding someone to have sex with was easy. Submitting to Adam was like showing him my soul. It was intense, exhilarating, and risky in a way that made me feel alive.

As I wrote, the words, safe, protected, respected, and trust were repeated multiple times. And yet, I had so much more to discover.

Before long, it was approaching six, and Harley was snoring in my lap. "Hey, mister," I said while petting his black shiny coat. "Are you happy here? I know you miss Roger. I miss him too. But, I love you." He stretched, and pawed at my legs like he was pushing me out of the bed. I laughed. "Are you trying to shove me out of the bed?" His eyes flipped open, and he peeked up at me as if he was apologizing. "I know you're not. You're a good boy. You can shove me out of the bed all you want, and I'll still love you unconditionally, because I'm your person."

"Jess! I'm back!" Adam called from downstairs.

Harley leaped off the bed to greet him, and I hung back for a moment. I was going to have to tell him something tonight about my dad and me that I had never told anyone.

I glanced down at the pages of my journal and wrote two words:

My truth.

* * * *

Sipping wine on the balcony off his master suite was the perfect setting for some serious kink instead of a serious discussion. There were so many things to be tied to or bent over. Plus, we were completely alone since Claire and Sam were in California, and for now, Harley was in the kitchen.

Dinner smelled amazing and tasted even better. Harley was probably getting drunk off the leftover aroma of the steak and lobster.

While relaxing on the cushioned teak chaise lounge built for two, Adam placed his empty glass on the small table next to him. "I guess I should've brought a deck of cards out here. On my drive home, it dawned on me you might have a few questions too."

"You were pretty tight-lipped during dinner about why you're stressed. But, I have a feeling it has something to do with Bally's. Ronald Sharpe mentioned it last night."

"You're right. It's about Bally's. It's a lot of red tape and bullshit. The more successful I become, the more people want to bring me down and stand in my way. It's understandable to a point. No one should have a monopoly on the Strip. But, damn it. I'm good for this town. Every time I take control of a property, the tourism industry spikes. And I'm damn good to my employees too. *Fuck!* I really don't want to talk about this."

"You don't have to. It sounds like you had a rough day." I circled my fingertips over the rim of my wine glass. "But, I would like to ask you about AJ. I didn't know you had a brother."

He grimaced. "Half-brother. He's my older half-brother. And we have no relationship."

"I'm surprised he hasn't capitalized on your family's name."

"He's not a Maxwell. Something he's used as an excuse to gain sympathy from my mother his whole life."

"You weren't ever close?"

"No. Never. He's been a pain in my ass since I can remember. There's something seriously wrong with him." While Adam spoke, he stared into the darkness of the night, growing more angry and bitter with each word. "When I had my first dose of success my dad told me a family secret. He made me swear never to tell my mother I knew, but he felt I had a right to the truth, so I would never let my guard down."

"What was it?"

"He told me when I was two, AJ tried to smother me in my sleep."

"Oh, my God. Are you serious?"

"Yeah. My dad came into the nursery to check on me and caught him."

"I'm so sorry. I can't even imagine. What did your dad do?"

"Well, for one thing. AJ was sent away to school. Just one more reason for him to hate his younger half-brother, who he refers to as 'The Chosen One.'"

"Adam, I don't know what to say. I didn't mean to bring this all up." I handed him my glass. "Here, do you want the rest of my wine?"

A slight grin touched his lips as he reached for my Cabernet. "Unless you have something stronger?" He tossed it back like a shot. "Thank you."

"I feel terrible for asking about AJ. I'm sorry."

"Don't be. I've actually never told anyone that before. It felt good to get it off my chest." He gathered me close. "You should try it, Miss Blake."

"Try what?"

"Getting something off your chest. This seems to be a night of bearing one's soul. You might as well dive in, the water's warm."

"I guess I should." I took a long pause. "So, my mother dropped a bomb on me after my father died."

"What kind of bomb? Your mom made a comment about your last name, Blake. What did that mean?"

Letting out a sigh so deep, I found the strength buried in my gut to finally say it out loud. "My dad, William Blake, adopted me when I was a baby. I don't know who my biological father is. I was never supposed to know I was adopted, but my mom decided to tell me after he died as a way to hurt me since I wouldn't give her any of my inheritance."

"Jess, that's. Wow. Now I'm the one who's speechless. That's so incredibly cruel."

"Yeah, well, that's my mother, Lauren. She's heartless. She left us when I was six and bounced around from husband to husband always looking for a bigger better deal. It served her well to lure my dad in, adopt me, and then dump us."

"Who does that to their own child?"

"A narcissistic, soulless person like my mother. Every time one of her marriages failed, she'd come back, and my dad would take her in. She'd lead him on for a few weeks, bilk him out of money, and then move on to someone else."

"Do you have siblings?"

"Nope, just me. I mean there were tons of stepsiblings along the way. But, I never bothered to get to know them. She should've been an actress. The way she pretended to love kids was really convincing. Unless a potential husband didn't have kids and had a parrot, then she loved parrots. Lauren doesn't love anyone, except for herself."

"So, then your real dad is out there somewhere. Did she refuse to tell you who he is?"

"No. She threatened to tell me who he is. That's why I want nothing to do with her."

"You're not curious? Not even a little?"

"No! William Blake was my dad. He was the best father in the whole world."

"Absolutely. But, somewhere out there. You have a real father."

I leaped out of my seat. "I had a real father, Adam, and I lost him."

"Jess, I'm not suggesting trusting your mother to tell you the truth. I don't want you to have anything to do with her either. I'm saying. I could help you find your biological dad. I'll have one of my lawyers start the process tomorrow."

"Are you not hearing me? I want nothing to do with this person. He means nothing to me. He was a sperm donor, that's it."

I marched into the bedroom and contemplated leaving. What the hell was Adam thinking? Why would he even suggest it?

Before I got very far, Adam stalled my movement by locking his arms around me. "Jess, stop. I know you're thinking about taking off. But you're not going anywhere."

"You can't tell me what to do," I argued, struggling to break free from his hold.

As he let go, his tone turned gentle. "No. But I can apologize. I'm sorry."

My voice shook with pure emotion. "Please. Don't ever bring this up again. You have no idea what it's like to lose someone you loved only to find out it was a lie. When my mom told me that he wasn't my real father, it was like he died all over again."

"I have to believe your father was trying to protect you."

"Of course he was. I'm sure he would've told me at some point, when the time was right. My mother kept it a secret to protect herself, and she used the truth like a weapon to hurt me. She's so cold and calculating. And, sometimes, I worry I'm going to turn into her."

His arms cloaked around me like a blanket of comfort. "Jess. That will never happen. You're nothing like your mother."

"I hate her. I know that's a horrible thing to say, but I do. I hate her. I never want to see or hear from her again."

"You won't if I have anything to say about it. I'll keep you safe."

When I peeked up at him, our eyes locked on one another, and I saw my protector, my Dom, my lover, and someone I trusted with the darkest parts of me. Giving him my body was easy. Telling him my secrets and fears was like ripping deeply rooted weeds out of my heart.

Without a word, Adam guided me to the bed and gave me a slight nod of his head. I undressed while he did the same. The yearning for each other surged as he climbed on top of me, and our naked bodies melded in sync as one. There was something different in his eyes as he took me with more intimate, sensual strokes. The perfect Adam Maxwell didn't grow up unscathed. We were both damaged, but our fractured pieces fit together like a work of art. We were our own masterpiece.

CHAPTER THIRTEEN
JESSICA

A few weeks later, the long hot summer was officially over, and Adam and I were swamped at work. I was thankful for my training with the butt plugs. It was our morning ritual, and I cherished each moment his hands caressed my naked skin. Occasionally, he granted me a little extra friction and permission to come if he had to wake me at an ungodly hour. And once in a while, I had a cock in my mouth before my first sip of coffee. But, I longed for a night of play at his penthouse, and neither one of us had time to spare on a decadent indulgence like that.

My typical Friday night consisted of me in my office, with Harley on a dog bed, combing through each and every detail of the case. I was swimming in tips from the tip line, but nothing panned out.

The feature articles on Miss Jeannie and Roger ran, and garnered attention. So, while subscriptions at the paper and interest in "Together We Are Safer," reached a fever pitch, so did crank calls.

Right before I was ready to send the tip line to voicemail, I endured a few more drunken calls. "What are you wearing?"

Ugh! Couldn't they at least be original?

"Hello," I said one last time into the receiver. "This is Jessica Blake. Can I help you? Hello, anyone there?"

"I'm here you little slut." A menacing voice spewed through the phone. "And I have a tip for you. Keep your mouth shut. I know where you live."

As shaken as I was, this man sounded familiar. I had to keep him on the line. "Who is this?" Letting out a long breath, I calmed myself. "It only seems fair you tell me who you are, since you know me. Have we met?"

"Nice try, you sneaky little bitch. You think you can disappear and block me, but you can't. Just keep quiet, or you'll get worse."

Oh, my God! Was it the fake Dom from Fetish Confidential? Before I could utter another word, the line went dead.

"Hey, Jess," a voice called from the doorway.

I nearly catapulted out of my seat. "Oh shit. Skip."

Harley flew to my side.

"Man, I'm sorry. Did I scare you?"

"Um, a little. I didn't think anyone else was here."

"Yeah, I had some work to do. Hal told me to ease up on Ronald Sharpe. So, now I do all my snooping after he goes home."

"Hal told you what? I'm sorry, I've been so busy, I haven't really checked in like I should."

He leaned against the doorway. "He told me to back off on Sharpe a couple of weeks ago. I'm still doing a little digging here and there, but nothing like I was before."

"But Hal was so excited about it. It doesn't make any sense."

"You're right it doesn't. My instinct tells me there's more to it than playing it safe in case Sharpe wins the election. But what can I do about it? I was actually going to see if you needed any help with, 'Together We Are Safer'? I read your articles. Nice work."

"Thanks. But now I feel bad. This was your story first. Do you want it back?"

"No. Your writing is solid. You've got the support of the community. I just wanted to offer to help you with the tip line or flesh out some leads, anything. It's got to be tedious sifting through all those messages, hoping for one nugget of gold."

"You have no idea." I huffed, thinking about my last call.

"I'd be happy to lighten your load, and give you more time to focus on your articles."

"Actually, that would be nice. I think we'll make a good team."

Skips face gleamed with schoolboy innocence and excitement. "Right oh. I think we would too. And if you get any inside information about Ronald Sharpe, pass it along. We can work together on both of these stories. I'd love to scoop everybody about his blonde mistress. But without a name or a photo, there's not much to go on."

Maybe it wasn't such a bad idea that Hal shut down Skip's full-court press on Sharpe. If the *Las Vegas Times* reported my mother was his mistress, it would put me in the middle. She'd have another excuse to blame me when her life fell to pieces by her own doing. Plus, if that last call was DomAidenLV, then it was in my best interest to let Skip man the tip line. I kept picturing his slicked-back dark hair, beady eyes, and leathery skin. The memory of his Axe body spray and greasy soul patch was enough to turn my stomach.

I picked up the receiver on my landline, and hit star nine, punching in his extension number. "The tip line is all yours. Thank you. If you're leaving for the night, just send it to the front desk's voicemail."

"I was going to head out. But, I hate to leave you here by yourself."

"I'm not by myself. I've got my trusted protector."

Harley peeked his head around the desk, sniffed the air and sneezed.

Skip laughed. "I hate to tell, Jess, but your dog is about as threatening as a rose petal."

I patted his head, and Harley yawned. "You may be right. I've always said he's a lover, not a fighter. But, I'm fine. You go on home. I'll be leaving soon anyway."

"Okay. But just be careful. You're the face of a big story."

"I hear you. I'll lock myself in as soon as you leave."

"Sounds good. I'm going to grab my stuff and take off."

"Have a great night."

As Skip left, Harley trotted back over to his dog bed and flopped down.

"I know, mister. You want to go home too. Can you give me five minutes?" He let out a sigh. "I'll take that as a yes."

My landline rang. "Huh, that's weird. I thought I forwarded all the calls to Skip." I answered. "*Las Vegas Times*, this is Jessica Blake... Hello ... hello." Whoever it was hung up. And then I realized I needed to press star ninety-nine. I rerouted the calls to the front desk, since Skip had left.

"Okay, Harley. Just one more email check and then we'll go."

While weeding through the few hundred junk emails I received in the last hour, footsteps echoed in the hall. *Oh no!* I never locked the door. My heart beat out of my chest as I ran to turn out the lights and lock my office. When I hit the switch, someone grabbed my wrist before I could shut the door.

"Let me go!" I screamed, trying to free myself from their strong grip.

"Jess, it's me." The lights flipped on. "What the fuck? Why are you here, alone at night, with the door unlocked? This is unacceptable, Jessica."

I was relieved it was Adam until I saw the tension in his jawline, and the familiar furrowed brow.

He scolded me in his full-bodied Dom voice. "Well, what do you have to say for yourself?"

"Harley forgot to lock the door."

"This isn't funny. I have half a mind to..."

"To what? You want to punish me, don't you?"

His lips pressed together, as he took a deep breath and rolled up his sleeves. "I just want you to be safe. Being here alone with the door unlocked is completely irresponsible."

"You're right. I should've locked the door, and I shouldn't have made a joke. I'm sorry I was an irresponsible smart-ass... I mean, smart ... b–u–t–t–o–c–k."

He appeared to be fighting back a slight smile. "Buttock. You're clever, Miss Blake, I'll give you that."

"Does that mean I'm forgiven?"

"Absolutely."

"If it makes you feel any better, Skip left a mere five minutes ago. And, I handed over the reins of the tip line to him."

"It doesn't. I'm seriously thinking about hiring you a bodyguard. I'm so slammed with the Bally's deal. It would be one less thing to stress about."

"I don't need a bodyguard. I have Harley."

"Harley, are you Jess's bodyguard?"

He rolled over for a belly rub, and Adam cracked up. "I think that settles it."

I shrugged. "Well, I'm not happy about it, but at least you're laughing. I thought you were working late tonight. What are you doing here? It's only nine o'clock. Lately, I don't see you until you fall into bed after midnight."

He pulled me to him and wrapped his arms around my waist. "I missed you. I had a small window for a break, and I took it. The next few weeks are going to be brutal. I may have to start sleeping at the penthouse."

"Oh. I see."

"Sweetheart, this is just temporary."

"It's okay. Claire and Sam are coming back from their trip tomorrow. I'm sure they'd love to have a slumber party with Harley, and I could spend a few nights at the penthouse."

He backed away, and grasped my shoulders. "When things get this intense, I need to be alone. No distractions."

"But what about my training? How we will stay connected?"

"We'll have to put it on hold."

"Maybe Harley and I should just go back to my place."

"No. That's not what I want." He clasped my hand. "Come." He sat in the office chair and put me on his lap.

"Adam, you don't have to baby me. I was just being, a girl for a second. I guess I'm missing, us."

"I am too, sweetheart. Trust me. I'd rather be bending you over the desk, fucking you until you screamed than doing anything else. This is why—"

"Why your relationships don't evolve, they just end. Why you're a horrible boyfriend? Why you're an—"

"Oh, don't say it, Miss Blake."

"I wouldn't dream of it, Sir Dude."

"Good girl."

"So, how long is this break you have tonight?"

"Long enough to swing by and ask you a question."

When I wriggled on his lap, it felt like I was sitting on something hard. "Oh, a question. I was going to say, Mr. Maxwell, there's either a deck of cards in your pocket, or you're really happy to see me."

He laughed and scooted me off his lap. "It's a little of both, but I do have something important to ask you since I'm taking Sunday off."

"You definitely have my full attention. And I'm pretty sure my answer will be yes. Are you whisking me away? Or are we going to go The Purple Peacock for a day of debauchery?

He fished the deck of cards out of his pocket with a sheepish grin. "Just pick a card, sweetheart. This is a big deal."

"A deal? As in a negotiation?" I drew a card. "I swear your deck is rigged. I got the Five of Spades."

Adam revealed the Jack of Clubs. "Looks like I win again, Miss Blake."

"So, what's your question? You look like you're about to bust."

He leaned back, and blurted out a sentence that floored me, "Jess, I wanted to ask you if you would like to meet my parents?"

* * * *

Late Sunday afternoon, on a beautiful September day, Adam and I were driving to his parents' place in the Spanish Trails, an exclusive gated community. Of course, I said yes, even though meeting new people gave me anxiety, especially the infamous Maxwell's. They were an enigma. I knew they existed, but didn't know much about them except for their philanthropic work. I was surprised I didn't have to sign a non-disclosure agreement just to have dinner with them.

"Jess, are you nervous?" Adam asked, placing his hand on my knee.

"A little," I responded, touching my fingertips to my warm chest. "How noticeable are my splotches?"

"You're fine, sweetheart. My parents are pretty down to earth. I would've introduced you sooner, but they just got back from summering in the Hamptons."

I sighed. "Of course they did. Isn't that where all the down to earth folk summer?"

"Fair point, smart-ass. You know it's been a while since I've introduced them to anyone."

"Was the last person they met, Monica?"

"Yeah. They knew her father, Blair. He quit speaking to them when they wouldn't invest in his Ponzi scheme. I advised them against it. One more reason her dad detested me. But, my gut feeling was right. I saved my parents and myself a small fortune. Plus, they're intensely private. Being put on display and hounded by reporters during the trial would've been torture for them."

"Did you tell them I'm a reporter?"

"No. I don't believe I mentioned that."

"Great," I uttered sarcastically. "Well, Paul and Diane Maxwell, guess who's coming to dinner."

Adam chuckled. "Speaking of which, that's them calling." He touched a button on his steering wheel. "Hey, it's Adam. We're just about to pull up to the gate. You're on speaker."

"Oh, excellent. We can't wait to meet you, Jess." A soft female voice sounded in the car. "So, darling. Just to let you know, AJ is here."

"Mother, you can't be serious."

"He showed up unexpectedly. I didn't have the heart to turn him away. He said he's been in a bit of a depression. And he looks like he hasn't slept in weeks."

"Did you tell him I'm coming and bringing a date?"

"Yes. And he asked if he could stay. Your father isn't happy about this either. Last time he came by the house they had a huge fight. But, they are out on the terrace having a Scotch together. So, maybe something's changed. Maybe he really wants to have a nice dinner with his family."

"Okay. Fine." Adam huffed. "But one unpleasant word from him about anything, and we're leaving. I don't want Jess to be subjected to one of his tirades. Especially when he's drinking."

"Understood, darling. Are you almost here?"

"Yes. We just drove through the gate. See you in a bit." Adam ended the call with a sigh. "I'm sorry he had to turn up tonight, of all nights."

"It's okay. Maybe I'll be a good buffer. How long has it been since you've seen him?"

"It's been years. He resurfaces occasionally when I'm about to close on a new property on the Strip. Sometimes he comes sniffing around, hoping for the construction contract."

"Maybe if you gave him a chance, things would be better?"

"That's the last thing in hell I'd ever do. He rarely finishes the jobs he's already contracted for. And yet he'll put on a show about the big time deals he makes importing equipment from Mexico."

"I wonder why Ronald Sharpe pushed so hard for you to give him the contract? There's got to be something to it. Aren't you curious?"

He pulled up to his parents' estate, turned off the car, and gripped the steering wheel. "I don't even want to think about it. Please, forget I said anything. Just consider everything that happens tonight off the record. Deal?"

"Deal. Sir Dude.

"Good girl."

I was completely calm walking into the Maxwell mansion. The way Adam held my hand like a lifeline actually relaxed me. He appeared tense, and it was as if I could feel the weight of his past with AJ bearing down on him.

Diane Maxwell greeted us at the door. She was stunning in her upscale casual coral dress with perfectly matched accessories. She looked like an ad from a Nordstrom catalog.

"It's so nice to meet you, Jess," she said with a warm smile. "Adam has told us absolutely nothing about you."

"You know me, Mother, always private. I learned from the king and queen of discretion."

"Well, you have me there, darling. That's true. I'm going to check with Betty in the kitchen. You kids head out to the terrace. Your father and AJ are having a drink.

Darren has a small bar set up. He'll fix you whatever you'd like."

"Better make mine a double." Adam griped as his mother sashayed to the kitchen.

"Your mother is beautiful. And their house is amazing. I swear I've seen something like this in a lifestyle magazine."

"They've been asked several times to let someone come and do a photo spread, but they are intensely private. Betty and Darren have been working for my parents since I was in high school. With a property this big, they really should have more help, but my parents are very choosy about who they let through the door."

"Then I feel honored."

"Let's hope you still feel that way after meeting my brother. Shall we?"

I took Adam's arm, and we strolled through the doors of the terrace. It looked like a deluxe resort with stone pillars and extravagant landscaping. I heard male voices as we rounded the curve of the ritzy tile. And then every tiny hair on my body stood on end. My heart was in my throat as I halted and hid myself behind one of the thick columns.

"Jess, sweetheart. What is it?"

My body trembled in fear, and I stuttered. "I–I i– it's ... him. Your brother, it's him."

Adam peered deep into my eyes. "Him who? AJ? Sweetheart, you're shaking."

"Aiden," I squeaked out.

"Right. AJ is short for Aiden Joseph. Do you know him?"

"Yes," I gasped. "He's the fake Dom. The one who hit me."

He clutched his head in hands, seething in anger. "It was him? He hit you?"

"Yes. He told me never to tell anyone, or I'd get worse. I've never been more terrified in my life. You're right. There is something wrong with him. Can we just go?"

"No." He grabbed my shoulders with his eyes digging into me. "No one lays their hands on you and gets away with it. You're mine."

"But..."

"You don't move. You stay right here. Don't let him see you. I'm ending this, now."

When he stormed off, I held onto the pillar and peeked around it, keeping myself out of view. With his long, determined strides, Adam lifted his brother out the chair by the scruff of his shirt, and sucker punched him. AJ smacked the ground, and chairs started flying. Adam's dad shouted for them to stop, and his mom ran screaming from the kitchen.

In the chaos, Adam's assault continued on his brother. "You disgusting piece of shit. How dare you fucking touch her!"

Oh, my God! He was going to kill him. I raced to him and hollered, "Adam. Stop! Please! Stop it."

Everyone's heads snapped in my direction, including AJ's bloodied face. He shoved Adam off him. "You! You're that little whore reporter! What the hell are you doing here?"

"Jess, I told you to stay put," Adam reprimanded. "Get in the car. Now."

My legs were like two-ton bricks, frozen in fear.

"Jess, I said get in the car."

By this point, Adam's mom was in tears with Mr. Maxwell consoling her. "AJ, I don't know what you did to this young lady, but this is the last time you will ever be welcomed in this house."

AJ hoisted himself off the ground, wiping away blood. "Really? Well fuck you, Paul."

Adam squared his shoulders and got in AJ's face. "Don't you dare speak to my father like that. And if you ever go near Jess again, I will fucking end you."

"Oh, now The Chosen One is making threats," AJ spat out.

"It's not a threat, dear brother. It's a promise." Adam went to his mom. "I'm sorry, Mother. I'm sorry it's come to this."

"Not your fault, Son," his dad said while wrapping his arm around his mom's shoulder.

Adam's steely glared fixed on me. "Let's go, Jess."

He surged past me, and I followed behind, barely able to keep up with his frantic pace.

Once we were in the car, I noticed his swollen, bloody knuckles. "You're bleeding," I murmured.

"I'm aware," he grumbled.

I handed him some tissues from my bag. "Adam, I'm—"

"Don't! Don't say a word."

"But, I just—"

"I told you to keep yourself hidden. And you deliberately disobeyed me."

"I'm sorry. I thought you were going to kill him."

He pounded the steering wheel, and shouted, "Even now, I've asked you to be quiet, and you're still talking. You don't get it. This isn't over. He saw you. I had a million reasons to beat the ever-living fuck out of him, but now he knows I did it because of you. I had the situation under control."

"Well, it didn't seem like you did."

"Jesus Christ, Jess. I'm begging you. Please. Shut up."

He peeled away from his parents' house, and we drove in deafening silence to the penthouse.

I was at a loss once we arrived inside. Adam hurried to the kitchen, leaving me by the grey sofa.

He returned, carrying an ice pack for his hand and motioned for me to follow. As I lumbered behind him, the enormity of what just happened frayed my nerves and emotions like electrical wires struck by lightning.

The tension between us mounted with each passing second, while Adam paced the floor.

Finally, I couldn't take it anymore. "Do you want me to leave?"

"No," he gritted through his teeth.

"Do you want me to go stand in the corner?"

He shook his head, flopped on the bed, and threw the ice pack to the side.

"Do you think you would feel better if you punished me?"

"Goddammit!" he yelled. "Will you stop asking so many questions?"

"I'm sorry. I don't know what you want."

In the bleak quiet between us, Adam rose slowly, stripping his belt from his trousers, and tossing it on the bed. His piercing eyes penetrated right through me. With the speed and precision of a panther, he came to me, flung his arms around me and held me to his chest. His breathing was heavy, and he clung to me as if he was trying to crawl inside my soul.

"Damn it, Jess." He heaved. "I want you. I want you to be safe. Do you get that?"

"Yes." I gasped, completely overwhelmed by him.

His hands traveled to my face. "If anything ever happens to you. I'd... Jess ... I..."

He didn't finish his sentence. Instead, he tore the dress off my body, ripping it to shreds. Sweeping everything off the dresser, it crashed to the floor, as he placed me on the smooth surface. Raw passion crackled between us as he freed his cock, jerked my thong aside and fucked me like a beast being let out of a cage. He rammed me with ferocious thrusts, while our groans and screams filled the air, like one primal cry.

His mouth ravaged every inch of me until he fucked me so hard the back of my head hit the mirror.

I yelped, "Oh shit!"

"Are you all right?" He ceased, cradling my head. "Come here."

He slid me off the dresser, pressed me to him, and kissed the top my head. "There," he whispered. "All better."

Still needy with lust, I took a page out of Adam's book, tearing open his shirt, sending the buttons flying.

I glided my fingers over his chiseled pecs. "Yes. This is much better."

He rid me of my bra and panties. "I agree. Much better. Now, be a good a girl, turn around and face the mirror." I obeyed, and he splayed his hands over my midsection. "Tell me. What do you see?"

My hair was wild, and my makeup was smeared, but somehow, I saw something glowing from within, something more.

"I see, your submissive."

"What else, sweetheart?"

"I see someone who wants to please you."

His hands lowered to my pussy, and he circled my clit with his fingers. "Did you please me tonight? Were you obedient?"

"No, Sir."

"What do you think I should do about that?"

My wetness trickled all over his hand. "Whatever Sir pleases."

"Good answer. Bend over."

"Yes, Sir."

I flattened myself on the dresser. My breasts were crushed against the cool surface. With my arms outstretched wide, I submitted to him. Peace washed over me as Adam fitted himself inside me, and took what was his.

He gripped my hips, and growled, "That's it, sweetheart. Hold still. You're being so good for me. I might let you come, after all."

He revved up his full strokes, and I fought the urge to climb to the edge. Being in this space with him, fueled my desire to be a better submissive. I would come only if permitted and only when he said.

First, he tested me by rubbing my clit, and I breathed through his heady torment. Then a wet finger nudged inside my ass, and I wailed in pleasure.

He kept encouraging me with his velvety voice. "Don't tense up, Jess. Let me in, all the way."

Expelling a heavy breath, I closed my eyes surrendering to him further, and he went knuckle deep inside. I was completely stuffed writhing in need.

His free hand grabbed my hair. With a tug, my head lifted and was I staring into the mirror.

Adam's thrusts grew more forceful. "Look at yourself. Watch me fill you."

In my reflection, I saw my large eyes double in size as my Dom fucked me as he pleased. Sweat dripped from my hair and poured down my face in rivulets. Seeing Adam thrash my pussy with everything he had, made me feel powerful and free. I was giving into my darkest temptations that lurked beneath the surface, trusting him to take me places I always dreamed of going.

When another finger wedged its way into my asshole, I let out a shriek, then breathed through the pain and relaxed into it.

"That's it. That's my good girl." He grunted. "When you scream like that, it makes my cock even harder. Soon, Jess. Very soon, this ass is going to be mine. Is that what you want?"

Our eyes met in the mirror and in between pants, I grinned at him. "Yes, Sir. I want you to take my ass."

With that, his fingers and dick fucked me in tandem while I stared at this carnal display. It was as if I floated out of my body and watched, lost in the moment. It was wickedly beautiful. It was salacious, yet intimate. It was us.

Adam tensed, yanked on my hair and groaned. "Ah, fuck! Come, Jess. Come with me."

Our climax felt like an explosion that splintered off into rushing surges of pleasure.

My ragged body was plastered to the dresser. When Adam pulled out and released me, my limbs quivered, and it felt like the cloud I was on burst, and I was sinking.

Before panic set in, my Sir cradled me in his arms, whispered words of praise in my ear. Somehow, I ended up in the oversized tub, wrapped in his arms, but I didn't even remember him turning on the water.

"Nicely done, sweetheart. You always exceed my expectations," Adam said softly. "How do you feel?"

"Hungry," I replied with my cheek nestled against his wet chest hair. "I might be beyond hungry, I'm ravenous." I peeked up at him. "Can you cook?"

He laughed. "No."

"Do you have any chips?"

"No. But—"

"You own the joint," I touted in my best Adam Maxwell voice, facing him. "I can have whatever I'd like up here in five minutes. I always get what I want. What do you want?"

"Clever, Miss Blake." He touched his lips to mine. "I just want you. I want what's mine."

* * * *

I yawned, curled up next to Adam. "That was delicious."

"What? The dim sum or the sex?" Adam smirked.

"You're feeding all the hunger in me, Mr. Maxwell. I couldn't possibly choose."

He drew me to him. "I like feeding you, Miss Blake. Your appetite is impressive."

"I wish tomorrow wasn't Monday. Sunday should be forty-eight hours long. Do you want me to leave? You said this week was going to be brutal."

"Don't you dare move. I've already texted Claire and Sam. They were only too happy to have Harley at the guesthouse with them. I've also contacted, Ben, Claire's younger brother. He's going to be your bodyguard. You'll meet him tomorrow."

"I take it, this is non-negotiable?"

"Absolutely not. Especially after what happened with AJ tonight."

"Did you know he was into the BDSM lifestyle?"

Adam jolted upright and spoke in a serious, stern tone. "Jess, what he did to you has zero to do with our lifestyle. He's no Dom. He's a sick fuck that abused you. If I had to spend any time with him growing up, he always did something violent and cruel."

"Like what?"

His expression filled with anguish. "Like my pets. Didn't matter what I had, a goldfish, hamster, or my rabbit, Max. He killed them, and made sure they suffered."

"Oh, Adam. I'm sorry. That's so horrible. I can't even wrap my head around it. Did you tell your parents?"

"I did. And when he was home from boarding school they sent him to therapy, but it didn't do any good. His hate for me grew year after year. As soon as he was old enough, he went to military school, and on his breaks, he was at some kind of a boot camp for troubled teens. Somehow, he always convinced my mother to let him come home. He knew how to manipulate her."

"Can I ask, what happened to his dad?"

"My mother told me he committed suicide. He made a couple of bad investments right after AJ was born, and he lost it all."

"Wow. In my mind, you had the perfect life and family. I had no idea."

"Now you can understand why we're so guarded and private. I probably shouldn't be telling all this to a reporter, but AJ has been in and out of jail too. DUIs, petty theft, that kind of stuff. That's when he likes to make his family connection known, when he gets in trouble or wants something. I prefer to keep our half sibling status a secret. It still irks me that Ronald Sharpe knows."

"All your secrets are safe with me. You know that, right?"

"Absolutely, I do. We need to be completely open and honest with each other. That's why..." He took my hands in his and exhaled. "That's why I want to ask you again. Are you sure you don't want to know who your biological father is?"

I ripped my hands out of his and bounded off the bed. "No. God, Adam. How could you even ask me that?"

"Please. Don't be upset. Just hear me out. Come back to bed."

"I can hear you fine from here."

"Look, I know you have a wall up about your biological dad, but I've been thinking about it. And I just want to say one thing, and then I'll never bring it up again."

"You promise?"

"Jess, you have my word. Now be a good girl and get back in bed."

I hesitated, and then crawled back in bed keeping a little space between us. "Okay, I trust you. Say what you have to say, and then never mention it again."

"I won't. It's just that, my mom used to say the reason AJ was so messed up was because he didn't know his real father. So, I just thought—"

"You think I'm like AJ?" I snapped.

"No. That's not what I'm saying at all."

"Because if you think finding some sperm donor that abandoned us or was used by my mother is going to make a bit of difference in my life, you're crazy."

"I'm not saying that either."

"Good. Because maybe your dad and AJ had an awful relationship, but my dad legally adopted me, because he wanted me. I'm William Blake's daughter and no one else's."

"Fair enough. Consider the topic closed and off the table."

"You left out dead and buried."

He reached for me, and I clasped his hand and shook it like we'd forged a pack. Although, his expression remained strained.

"Adam, what is it?"

"You're beginning to read me like one of your books. When it comes to you, I have no poker face."

"Will you tell me what else is bothering you?"

He readjusted the pillows, and sighed. "I asked Hal to ease up on Ronald Sharpe."

"You did that? Skip told me about it on Friday. Why would you do that?"

"I had to. Ronald was a threat to The Purple Peacock. One word to AJ and everything Eli, Sebastian, and I have worked for would be over. So, I made him a deal. He honors his confidentiality agreement with the club and Skip backs off."

"Thank you."

"Can you say that again? I'm pretty sure I didn't hear you right. I thought you'd be pissed."

"No. I'm grateful. If Skip found out my mother was Sharpe's mistress, she would've taken it out on me. Plus, people need a safe place to find out about the lifestyle. When I think of all those fakes out there online preying on the inexperienced, it makes me sick."

"I wish we could do more. But it's a catch-22 situation."

"I know. But, if you're really serious about it, you can ask around, and a friend of a friend, of a friend, will usually point you in the right direction if they have your best interest at heart. You've probably saved a lot of women from getting hurt, and helped them see if being a submissive is really what they want."

He draped his arms around me. "But, the one woman I wanted to protect more than anyone, I led right into the arms of my brother, by being an ass. I'm sorry, Jess. This is all my fault."

"Please don't blame yourself. I'm the one that came to you with a tape recorder, not being upfront and honest. And I'm the one who went on that website and chose to meet him. And, I'm also the one who didn't tell you he called the tip line Friday night. I know it was him."

"What did he say?"

"He said he knew where I lived, and that I should keep my mouth shut. I'm sorry. I should've told you Friday night. You were right. Being the face of a big story is dangerous. So, I guess if you want to send me a bodyguard, then I won't complain."

His lips touched my temple. "That's a good girl."

"I can't imagine anyone will guard my body as well as you." I grazed my fingertips over his biceps and grinned. "Have you seen these guns? No one would dare harm a hair on my head with these bad boys around. They're lethal."

"You say that now. Just wait until you meet Ben. No one will come within ten feet of you if he's by your side. Trust me on that."

Without waiting for him to initiate, I kissed him, long and deep. Tonight, was a roller-coaster ride, but now, I felt closer to him.

"What was that for, sweetheart?"

"For everything. I do trust you. I trust you with my life."

CHAPTER FOURTEEN
JESSICA

"Congrats, kid. You made the paper," Hal said and placed a copy of the *Vegas Journal* on my desk, two days later, on Tuesday morning.

"What are you talking about? I didn't think copies of the *Journal* were allowed in this building."

He pointed to my name, and teased, "Well, I guess you hit the big time. You've got a mention in Nosey Nadine's column. Read it."

> *"Is the mysterious King of Vegas, Adam Maxwell, off the market? According to my spies at the Palisades, Jessica Blake, who works for that smaller paper that I won't mention has been spotted leaving the penthouse of the elusive bachelor on numerous occasions. Is it true love or business? No one can say for sure, but the word is Maxwell has doubled his advertising dollars with that other paper, which shall remain nameless. Could it be business with benefits? Stay tuned."*

I chucked the paper in the trash. "I never liked her. She's full of shit. Business with benefits. Damn it. That's actually a good line."

Hal plopped down in the chair. "Care to enlighten me? What exactly was that big story you were working on with Maxwell before I pulled the plug."

"Oh, that story? Well, it was ... it was definitely scandalous, but now..."

"Say no more, Blake. I'm not an idiot. There was something between you two kids the first time I saw him in your office. You'd have to be blind not to notice it."

"Can I ask you something?"

"Anything. Shoot."

"Did you bump me up to feature reporter because of Adam increasing his advertising budget?"

"No. I can honestly say I was going to months ago. But you lost your fire. I was waiting for you to get it back."

"So, when you told me you couldn't pay two people to write 'Sin City Nights,' that wasn't true?"

"That was true. But, I couldn't give you a promotion the way you were going through the motions. You've changed. You're ambitious again, curious, and full of life. So, whatever you're doing keep it up."

Oh, if Hal only knew! "Thanks. I promise. I will give you my all."

"I know you will," Hal said, shoving himself out of the chair. "Where are we on our next story. The other victim, Josephine?"

"Blackburn. I talked to her ex-husband. At first, he was all in, and now he's kind of dragging his feet. The second time I talked to him, I got a weird feeling. It would be a real shame if he didn't want to do the interview. Josephine had two daughters. She worked in the employee's cafeteria at one of the casinos. She came home to change before picking her girls up at their dad's house. They were supposed to go see, *Trolls*, at the movie theatre, but she never made it. I wish I knew why her ex seems to be changing his mind."

"It could be—I mean a hate to think this way—but it could be because of someone at the *Journal*. Think about it. Our subscriptions are up. Maybe they want an exclusive interview with the ex and the kids."

"Do you think the *Journal* offered to pay Josephine's family? That's unethical tabloid journalism."

"That doesn't mean it doesn't happen. Take it as a compliment. David is getting to Goliath. Keep up the good work, kid."

My phone beeped as Hal was leaving. It was a text from Adam. We spent Monday night apart due to his grueling schedule. Sunday night felt like a month ago, instead of just two days.

His text said:

"I need to see you, sweetheart, even if it's only to hold you while you sleep. Come to penthouse tonight. I'll try to wrap up early."

I wrote back:

"Yes, Sir!"

He surprised me by texting a smiley face emoji. It wasn't the kissy face emoji, or the one with the hearts, but for Adam, it was pretty darn romantic.

While I was staring at his text, a call came in from Stacy. "Hey, I was just thinking about you."

"Jess. Do you have a second?" she replied in a serious tone.

"Yes. Of course. What's wrong?"

"The person or people who killed Roger. They hacked into his phone and computer."

"So, you have some sort of a lead?"

"No. I wish we did. All I know is they drained his bank account, and got cash advances on his credit cards. They probably have all of his passwords and his social security number."

"How does that happen? Weren't all of his accounts closed?"

"When someone dies without a will or next of kin, it takes time. Only Roger's name was on every bill and document. Except one." Stacy's voice quivered. "And they called me today."

"Who called you?"

"Jared's Jewelry Store." She sobbed softly. "Roger put a down payment on an engagement ring."

"Oh, Stacy. I don't know what to say. I'm just so sorry."

"I am too."

"I wish there something I could do for you. I feel like a terrible friend."

"There is something you could do."

"Anything. Name it."

"Don't do what Roger and I did. We danced around our relationship for years without either one of us making a move, or saying how we felt. If you love someone, tell them. When Adam hired Roger, it gave him a whole new lease on life. Things were looking up and changing, even if it didn't last. I keep thinking of all the time we wasted. Promise me you won't waste a second. Make the most of every day."

"I will. And I promise I won't stop trying to find out who killed Roger. But, I have to admit, I also feel like a terrible investigative reporter. I'm completely stumped. The community is behind us, and the tip line rings off the hook, and still we come up with nothing."

"It's not you, Jess. It's this case. There've been very few breaks. The twenty-year-old kids that mugged Miss Jeannie are in jail, but they won't talk. This is a well-funded, planned operation, using inexperienced college kids with tech backgrounds. That's all we know."

"But what's in it for them? What's the end game? And how is Roger, Josephine Blackburn, and Miss Jeannie connected?"

"That's what we need to find out. But, please be careful. You're putting yourself out there, and it's dangerous," Stacy warned in her official Officer Sibley voice.

"I know. But don't worry. Adam hired me a bodyguard."

"Have you met him yet?"

"No. I was supposed to today."

"Who it is? Do you know?"

"It's someone Adam just hired to work security. It's Claire's younger brother, Ben. I told you about Claire. Her and her husband, Sam, look after Adam's estate at The Vegas Edge Country Club."

"Okay. Well, as long as you're taken care of, I won't worry."

"Oh, holy shit!" I jumped out of my chair.

"Jess? Are you okay?"

Appearing in the doorway was a hulking beast of a man. Saying he had muscles was like saying the Vegas Strip had a few lights. This guy's muscles had muscles bursting out of his tight black T-shirt.

"Yeah, I'm okay. But, I do have to go. I think Claire's little brother just showed up."

I hung up with Stacy and asked the beast, "Are you, Ben?"

"Yeah. Claire's little, brother," he said sarcastically with a crooked smile. "Ben Logan."

He offered his hand, and I flew around my desk so fast to shake it, I almost tripped over my own two feet. While Ben was a tad shorter than Adam, his girth was remarkable. How did he even fit through the door? The wrinkles around his chocolate brown eyes suggested he was also older than Adam, and he had either gone bald or made the bold choice to shave his head, which worked for his intimidating stance.

With my hand in his firm grip, I joked, "I guess I should've said younger brother, not little brother. I've never been more wrong. I'm Jess. It's nice to meet you."

"Nice to meet you too."

"You'll have to forgive me. I've never had a bodyguard before. How does this work? Do you want to sit down and ask me some questions?"

"All I need to do is give you my cell number. And when you go somewhere, shoot me a text. I'd prefer to keep a low profile and not get under your feet. You may not always see me, but I'll always be there to protect you."

Ben spoke in a clipped, professional manner, but there was something in eyes that said he would lay down his life for me if he had to.

I punched his number in my phone, and texted him when I was done for the day. I drove out to the country club to spend a little time with my buddy, Harley, grabbed a few things, and headed off to the penthouse.

When I parked, Ben was by my car to escort me. He was right, I didn't really notice him until I climbed out of the car. He was like an illusionist, disappearing and reappearing when I needed him.

I knocked, and was caught off guard by Brandy showing me in at this late hour.

"Hi, Jess. Come on in. Our favorite workaholic is still in his office."

"Oh. Hey, Brandy. I wasn't expecting to see you."

She tucked her long, shiny, perfect hair behind her ear. "I'm only too happy to help Adam burn the midnight oil. The sooner this deal is done, the sooner things can get back to normal. Can I get you anything?"

What was wrong with me? Brandy was so friendly and sweet, and yet I didn't like her being here.

"No. I'll just pop into the office and say a quick hello," I answered, heading to the left.

"Jess. He's not in his den. He's in his office. You know, the one downstairs. It's through the door to your right."

"Of course. Silly me." I played it off as if I knew that. I didn't. I'd never been down there before. *Damn it.*

My phone beeped, and it was an email from Skip with an attachment. The subject line read:

"Tips worth a second look."

I attempted to open it, but the file was too large. "Shoot. If Adam's busy, I'd really like to open this attachment from work. Would you excuse me, Brandy? I'm going to try to log into my Gmail account in Adam's den."

"Sure. Take your time. I know my boss. He doesn't like to be disturbed when he's working anyway. Do you have the password?"

"Oh, no, I don't. Do you have it?"

"Are you kidding? Adam is so private. He's never shared any of his passwords with me. I don't think he's ever let me touch his cell phone. Good luck. I know he keeps his computers locked up tight."

I lied right to her face. "Well, he gave me all his passwords a while ago, I just didn't write them down. I'm sure it will be fine. Night."

I hurried down the hallway, wondering if Brandy always worked late with Adam. Then, I felt like an idiot and chastised myself for being jealous.

I sent him a text:

"Hey, I'm here. Any chance I could get the password to your computer in the den? Something from work just came in."

He replied:

"Hi, sweetheart. The password is, AMSDJBS69. Please delete this text message as soon as you're logged in. I can't take any chances."

"What's AMSDJBS69?" I asked.

He wrote:

"You always have a question. It stands for, Adam Maxwell Sir Dude Jessica Blake Sub, followed by your favorite number."

I texted back:

"LOL!"

"Work as late as you want. I thought I'd be able to knock off early, but I can't. Don't forget to delete the password."

I plugged in the password, and took a page out of Nosey Nadine's book by checking out his desktop. I shouldn't be doing this. *Hmm...* It looked like boring files, neatly arranged in rows of three in the right-hand corner. I thought he'd have more than a dozen folders, but maybe the real stuff was on his other computer in the office I didn't know was downstairs. *Whatever!*

I logged into my Gmail account and combed through the attachment from Skip. A couple of tips had potential. It was nice to have these narrowed down.

Within thirty minutes, the exhaustion kicked in. Adam's bed was calling my name. As I crawled under the covers, I couldn't help wonder if Brandy was still here.

I fought to keep my eyes open but fell asleep. I vaguely remembered Adam coming to bed. By the time I woke the next morning, his side of the bed was empty.

The exact same thing happened Wednesday night, so Thursday I stayed with Harley at Adam's house at the country club. At least I'd have a snuggle buddy.

At eleven p.m. I curled up in bed with my Kindle and Harley. It had been ages since I'd read, and I had left

Alice in *The Reluctant Submissive* hanging in the balance. After ten minutes of reading the same paragraph over and over again. I gave up. No offense Alice, but you and Lucas just don't cut it anymore. It was all about Adam for me.

I tossed my Kindle aside, picked up my journal and wrote, the word I made up, Sub-curious. I wondered how many women were like me, fantasizing about a walk on the wild side. I learned there was so much more to it than kink. My temptations led me down this road, but it was my choice to submit to Adam.

Outside the bedroom, I was an independent, strong person, wound a little too tightly, with a stiff upper lip. As a submissive, giving up control was a relief. In my surrender, I discovered pleasures I didn't know were possible. The nights after a session with Adam I felt so peaceful and slept like a baby.

I also learned that everyone's journey in the lifestyle was different and that people online weren't always what they pretended to be. AJ or should I say, DomAidenLV, said all the right things in our chat on the website. It was easy to be taken in by him, but I made a mistake. I still couldn't believe how foolish I was. I was ripe for the picking, an easy target. My only regret about not writing the article for the paper was not being able to warn both men and woman of the dangers. Safe, sane, consensual, and private—words to live by.

My phone beeped. Adam was calling. "Hi. I didn't expect to hear from you. It's so late."

His ragged voice still oozed with sexy. "I just wanted to say goodnight."

"How was your day?"

"Brutal. And the weekend isn't looking good. Tomorrow I've got back-to-back meetings with potential vendors. I want to try something that's never been done before."

"Can you tell me? I would love to hear about it."

"Sure. But, don't share this with anyone. Strictly, off the record, Miss Blake."

"As long as I get the exclusive, Mr. Maxwell."

"Absolutely. I want to take the idea of Rodeo Drive in Beverly Hills, and bring it to Vegas."

"I love that idea."

"Thanks. There's just one problem. I need to expand. And that involves... Well ... it has me buried in red tape. So, if I can get some high-end vendors committed, it's a step in the right direction." He let out a sigh. "I miss you, Jess. I'm frustrated as hell with this crazy schedule. You should be in my bed. Not miles away at The Vegas Edge Country Club."

"You're not completely alone. Brandy greeted me the other night."

"She's my right hand, sweetheart. Nothing more."

"I know," I mumbled. "I guess I miss you too."

"How are you and Ben getting along?"

"Great. He's like my invisible shadow. Just when I think he's not around, he appears. He's a good guy."

"I agree." He paused for a moment. "Well, I'm exhausted. I'm sure you are too. Maybe when this is all over, we could take a trip, just the two of us. Nothing but, sun, sand, and lovey-dovey shit."

I laughed. "Sounds good to me, Sir."

"In the meantime, I do need you to do something for me, sweetheart."

"Of course. Anything."

"Keep yourself safe. And be good. Keep being a good girl for me."

"Yes, Sir. I'll be good."

CHAPTER FIFTEEN
JESSICA

"Hi. I'm here to see Officer Sibley," I said and showed my ID to the cop manning the desk at the police station. "I'm Jessica Blake, she's expecting me."

"Jess," Stacy called to me from glass double doors, not wearing her uniform. "This way."

Stacy led me through a bit of a maze, and we landed in a small room with no windows or furniture.

"I got here as soon as I could. What's going on?" I asked.

"Something happened early this morning. I wanted you to come here because it needs to stay out of the papers."

"Of course. You can trust me."

"You can't tell anyone, not even Tilly or Adam."

"I won't. What happened?"

"I went to my townhouse this morning to pick up some stuff. And two guys were at your front door. To me, it looked like they were trying to break in."

"Oh, God. What did you do?"

"I confronted them. I was off duty, but I flew up on your porch, and I lost it. I thought about Roger and couldn't control myself. I beat the crap out of them."

My mouth fell open. "You, what?"

"I'm so ashamed of myself. But, what if I hadn't pulled up and you were there alone. It's too much. This has all been too much."

I hugged her, and she sobbed softly. She was right. This was all too much. And none of it was fair or had anything to do with justice.

"I'm so sorry. Is there anything I can do?"

"Actually, there is. The two guys freaked when I told them I was a cop. I called Kevin, he came and read them their rights, and they confessed to attempted breaking and entering. But, at first, one of them tried to say he knew who lived there. By the time they got to the station, he had changed his story."

"What do you need me to do?"

She flipped a switch on the wall, and a panel rose, revealing two young men on the other side of the glass.

"Is that them?" I asked.

"Yeah. You can see them, but they can't see you. Just in case the blond changes his statement again, I need to know if you've ever seen them before?"

I studied them through the glass, and almost felt sorry for them. They were two skinny kids that looked scared shitless. "I can honestly say I have no idea who they are. Your instincts were probably right. Did they ask for a lawyer?"

"Nope. They didn't even make their phone call."

"Do they go to UNLV too?"

"Yeah. They're sophomores. Why?"

"I wonder... It's probably a long shot, but I went to UNLV. For kids that lived in the dorms, and paid out of state tuition, it was expensive if you didn't have a scholarship, or someone footing the bill. There's got to be a way to figure out if they have student loans in their names. When you're twenty years old, living in Las Vegas, with no money, you'd be surprised what desperate people will do. Somebody, somewhere is dangling a carrot, making it sound like they can make a quick buck."

"You might be on to something. These two are from Wyoming, and the ones that mugged Miss Jeannie are from Oregon. Before I leave, I'll tell Kevin and have him look into it."

"Leave? Where are you going?"

"I'm taking a break. After today, I realize I'm no good to anyone on or off duty. I have to get my head together and try to heal. I have some money saved. Nola's going to look after my cats, and I'm going to get in my car, and just drive."

"When are you leaving?"

"Next week. So, this is goodbye, for now."

She embraced me. For a moment, I choked up, but was able to suck it up and not get emotional. "Hey, Tilly and I are supposed to go out sometime this weekend, do you want come with us?"

"Nah. You two go ahead. I'd be a stick-in-the-mud."

"Are you sure? We could have Tilly meet us at the cul-de-sac, and she could help both of us get ready for girl's night."

"You're so sweet, Jess. But, I have a feeling the bouncer would card me and throw me out for being too old. Speaking of the cul-de-sac, I don't want you going there alone."

"Are you kidding me? With my bodyguard, Ben, I'm never alone. I actually do need to pick up some things."

"Send me a text if you're headed over, and I'll try to meet you, so I can pack up some stuff before I leave town. I don't want to be there by myself either. Not after today."

"Of course. So then, this isn't good-bye, it's just so long. I'll text you tomorrow or Sunday."

"Okay. So long. And, Jess..."

"What?"

"Be careful. Please, be careful."

* * * *

A bag of kettle-cooked chips and Red Bull was waiting for me on my desk. Tilly was probably close by.

Before I hunted her down to thank her, I checked my phone. Adam hadn't answered my text messages from this morning. I sunk into my chair and called him. It went right to voicemail. Well, this was odd. Even during these busy weeks, he always took the time to text me. I didn't even get a chance to mention my night out with Tilly. What if he preferred I go out tonight instead of tomorrow night or vice versa?

I had his office number—his direct line. Should I call it? *Why not*, I rationalized. His cell was probably on silent.

On the third ring, a familiar female voice answered the phone. "Good afternoon, Maxwell Industries, this is Brandy, can I help you?"

"Oh, hey, Brandy. This is Jess. Did I call the wrong number? I thought this was Adam's direct line."

"Hi, Jess. It is. He forwarded his calls to my cell. It's a big day. I thought it was for the best."

"Well, is there a chance I could talk to him, just for like five seconds?"

"Not right now. He's behind closed doors with Monica."

"Monica? As in his old girlfriend, Monica?"

"That's the one. You know how he is about her. I have a lobby full of vendors waiting, but Monica Preston shows up to pitch her overpriced boutique, and everything comes to a halt."

I laughed nervously. "Yeah. Sure. He told me she was coming in today," I lied. "I guess I forgot. Anyway, I'll just talk to him later, or whenever. I've got to go."

I hung up and held my head in my hands. *What the hell?* Adam felt like a million miles away. "It's just business" I kept telling myself, but my stomach knotted in tension. I stared at my phone, willing a text to pop up from Adam. Nothing. It was radio silence.

"Knock, knock!" Tilly posed at the door with a huge smile. "Did someone get their treat?"

"Yes. Thank you so much. This is just what I needed."

"So, what's it going to be, *mija*? Are we finally going out?"

I picked up my phone, since my initial instinct was to text Adam my plan. Instead, I shoved it in my bag. "Oh, yeah, we're totally going out. And we're doing it tonight."

* * * *

"If I didn't see it with my own eyes, I never would've believed it. Jess Blake, in the flesh." My old friend Tony from the Ghostbar said with a grin, "And looking hotter than ever in red."

"It's burg— Oh never mind. How are you?"

"Better now that you two are here. When Tilly said you were coming this weekend, I told her if she delivered, your drinks were on me."

Tilly linked her arm in mine. "Yes! I delivered. We should have champagne."

"I'm way ahead of you." Tony gestured toward the roped-off private area. "There's a bottle of Dom Pérignon at the table over there already chilling. I'll send Amy over in a little while to see if you need anything else."

"Amy?" I replied. "I was hoping to see Suzi tonight. She always used to take care of us."

"Didn't Tilly tell you? Our girl Suzi landed a job as a head bartender at Sash at the Palisades. She loves it over there," he whispered. "I actually asked her to put in a good word for me. This place has gone downhill. Everyone wants to work for Maxwell. He's the best."

Just when I'd forgotten about getting blown off by Adam, Tony's comment reminded me, I still hadn't heard from him.

"Well, good luck with that," I responded with a snip. "Did you say something about the champagne? I could use a drink."

"Bottle of Dom awaits, ladies." Tony did a goofy little bow and headed off.

Once we popped our cork, Tilly raised a glass. "To us, and to our promotions. I couldn't have done it without you."

We clinked glasses and sipped. Then I gulped down a huge swig. "What do you mean, me? You did this on your own."

"No way, Jose. You took me under your wing when I was answering phones, and you fix all my mistakes with your red pen."

"You don't like my red pen?"

"Are you kidding? I love it. I'm learning. I want to be as good of a writer as you are."

"Tilly, you're so much better at writing 'Sin City Nights' than I ever was."

"Are you drunk already?"

"I'm serious. Your voice is bright and funny and full of energy. Mine had more of a sarcastic edge to it. It was all wrong for the column." I tossed back another drink and sighed. "Sometimes, I feel like I'm wrong about everything."

"How can you say that?"

"Just something with Adam. I haven't heard from him today, and when I called, Brandy told me Monica, his old girlfriend was there. I don't know, sometimes I question where Adam and I are going? He's so intense, and gets excited about new challenges, like the deal at Bally's, but then I wonder what happens when he gets what he wants. Does he lose interest?"

"You think he's lost interest in you? That's impossible. You two are in love."

"I'm sorry, what did you say? The champagne has gone right to your head."

"Oh, *mi amor*, it's love. I know it. You've changed, and from what you've told me so has Adam. Remember the day we went to The Purple Peacock. You were after two things, to become a real reporter, and you wanted to fulfill your fantasy. You've done both and then some. You're the face of a huge story, and you're in love with Adam Maxwell, the most sought after bachelor in Vegas. I'd say that's mission accomplished."

What Stacy said earlier rang in my head. *"If you love someone tell them. Don't wait. Make the most of every day."* Was I in love with him? My phone beeped. "Sorry. I should've put it on silent. It might be work."

"Or it could be Adam."

"It isn't. It's Skip letting me know he'll be emailing me potential leads from the tip line first thing in the morning instead of tonight. He wants to know if I'm coming in tomorrow. I guess I might as well. Lord knows when I'll hear from Adam again."

"Ah, Jess, you're killing me. No moping. It's our night out."

"God. You're right. I'm sorry. No moping."

Tilly poured the rest of the champagne in our glasses. "Let's finish this and go see Suzi at Sash at the Palisades. She'll put us in the party mood. It'll be like old times."

I chugged the rest of my Dom Pérignon, and it burned going down my throat. "Sounds perfect. I just need to text Ben and let him know."

"Yes. Text Big Ben. And tell him I'm single and not wearing underwear!"

* * * *

"Suzi!" Tilly squealed.

"Oh, my God! I can't believe it!" Suzi proclaimed with a huge grin. Tiny and sassy, Suzi Lee was one of the highlights from my club days. With her short red hair, and unicorn tat, she was hilarious, tough, and always knew the dirt on everyone. "How the hell are you, Jess?"

"I'm good. You look great."

"Well, I can't complain. And according to Nosey Nadine, you can't either. Are you really dating Adam Maxwell, or is she full of shit?"

"She's definitely full of shit," I joked. "And if anyone is going to get the real dish, it'll be Tilly. She's writing the column now. Just keep it a secret."

"Nice. Congrats Tilly. Your secret is safe with me. Why don't you girls take the table by the dance floor and I'll send some drinks over."

"Thanks, Suz, but it says it's reserved." Tilly pointed to the placard on top of the table.

"It is. But, fuck 'em. You're getting the best table tonight." She pulled us close and whispered, "And just be careful of those two douche bags over there. I call them Man Bun and Beard Boy. They've been in here three weekends in a row. I think they're dealers. Our bouncer, Jack has been watching them."

"What do you think they're dealing?" I asked.

"In the past few years, the clubs have seen a lot more cocaine. I mean, it's Vegas, people get carried away, but lately, it's worse," Suzi explained. "It's one of the reasons I wanted out of the Ghostbar. After you busted that reality contestant dealing there, the place was cool for a long time. Then it started up. I saw some fucked-up things. Now we got Man Bun and Beard Boy, before them it was a couple of ladies that looked like straight-laced businesswomen. You can never be too careful. But, look who I'm talking to. Not one but two reporters. Just think of me as your anonymous source. In others words, you didn't hear it from me. Go, sit, I'll send over the usual. In fact, I'll tell Chris to keep the drinks coming. I'm going on my dinner break, but I'll be back."

Four or seven cocktails later, I checked my phone again, still no word from Adam. "Well, I hope that ass is okay. And if he is, I'm going to kill him. This is bullshit." I giggled. "Did I say that too loud?"

"You're fine, *mija*. You're letting loose. So, are you going to tell me? Is being a submissive like it is in your books? I'm dying to know."

"It's better. In my mind, I imagined it was like being a kept woman in a sex dungeon. Not that there's anything wrong with that if that's your kink, but Adam and I... It's just so ... explosive. And the weird thing is, I feel more confident outside the bedroom. I mean, look at me? No splotches all night."

Tilly laughed. "You're like a fireball again! Oh, Fireball! We should do a shot."

"Heck, yeah!" I motioned for Chris. "We need some Fireball shots, stat!"

"Coming up, ladies," Chris responded with a wave.

"So, have you ever thought about it?" I asked.

"Thought about what?"

"You know, going to The Purple Peacock and getting your kink on. Adam's friend, Eli, is a tall, British, drink of water. I've never been attracted to redheads before, but I picked up on this vibe. He's like a Dominant Prince Harry."

"I like Prince Harry. He seems naughty. But, I don't think it's for me. If any guy told me what to do in or out of the bedroom, he'd get a high heel right to his man berries."

I picked up my empty vodka and Red Bull. "To man berries and Tilly's high feels—I mean heels."

"And to tipsy, Jess. She's my favorite."

Chris delivered our shots, and I downed mine. "Wow! That's some good shit!"

"How long has it been since you've had Fireball?"

"You know what? Too long." I sucked down an ice cube to cool the heat from the shot. "I feel like dancing. Do you feel like dancing?"

Without waiting for Tilly, I sprung into action and jammed out by myself. Normally, I just tried to imitate

Tilly's moves, but I was in my own world, feeling like I ruled the floor.

When the song was over, a pair of hands wrapped around my waist from behind, and I turned to find Man Bun dancing with me.

"Oh, hey," I said, and lost my balance.

"Hey." He coiled his arms around me. "There. I better keep you close, so you don't fall."

"I guess I had too much to drink."

"That's okay. I like a girl who knows how to party. I think we could have fun together."

He pressed his hard-on into my stomach. What was I doing? My head dizzied, and my stomach turned queasy. Where was Tilly?

Out of the corner of my eye, I spotted Beard Boy at our table chatting her up. *Shit!* Suzi said to stay away from them.

"I need ... to go," I slurred.

"Go? Babe, we're just getting started. Would you like to know a little secret?"

Secrets! I loved secrets. I was intrigued or drunk enough to play along. "Sure. Hit me with your secret."

"You go first. What's your name?"

"My name? It's ... um ... Jess... B–l–ack. *Oh shit!* That was close!

"What do you do Jess Black?" he asked more pointedly as the smell of his patchouli touched my nose.

This wasn't just small talk. He was fishing. Probably making sure I wasn't a cop. Maybe I had another big story on my hands. It was too tempting to resist. "Well, you're kind of nosey. What do you do?"

His grip on me intensified. "Let's just say I'm on the ground floor of a major deal. It's big league. I'm getting richer by the day."

"What kind of deal? Maybe I want in. I'm in between jobs."

"In that case. How about we get out of here. And I'll tell you all about it."

"Well, I can't leave my friend. Can't you give me a hint? I'd be into it as long as it isn't anything too illegal." I laughed nervously.

"The laws don't apply to me. I've got friends in high places. You could too. It's all about the game and how you play it."

"I like games," I teased. If only I could keep him talking, I could find out who his friends were in high places.

"Then you, me, your friend, and my buddy, Travis, are going to play." His hands slid to my ass.

"I thought you were going to let me in on the ground floor first. I mean I still don't know your name."

Whispering in my ear, he dug his erection into me. "Justin. And I want to hear you scream it when I fuck you, and then fuck your friend. Let's go."

I wriggled away from him. "You know. I don't think I feel so good."

With the room spinning, he yanked me back into his clutches. "That's too bad, babe. 'Cause shit just got real."

One arm hooked me around the waist, and his hand found its way up my dress. As I struggled to break free, his fingers were working their way to my thong. "No sense in fighting or causing a scene. I'm untouchable."

"Mind if I cut in ... friend?"

Adam! He was here! His hands pried us apart with an icy look of rage spreading across his face. Sickened by Justin's touch, I stumbled backward, into the brick wall of Ben and his muscles.

"Hey. Not cool," Justin griped. "She's leaving with me."

"Like hell she is," Adam spit out. "The only person leaving is you and your coked-out pal over there."

Security guards swarmed the dance floor, with Suzi following close behind. The music cut out, and all eyes were on us.

Justin put his hands up. "Jesus. Fine. We'll go. But I know people in Vegas. Big league people. Wait until the owner of this casino finds out you threw us out."

"Hey, asshole, I'm the owner." Adam shook his head in disgust. "Guys, get them out of here, and escort them to their ride. It's waiting for them at valet. Don't worry gentlemen, we'll see to it that Metro's finest drives you safely to your next location."

"Metro? You called the cops? What the fuck man?" Justin yelled. "This is so fucked-up."

Justin and Travis cussed the entire way out of the club, while security slapped handcuffs on them and showed them out.

"Ben, good work. Make sure Tilly gets home safe," Adam ordered.

They rushed off, leaving me alone with Adam. He glared me with the intense focus of a laser beam.

His razor-sharp jawline filled with tension as he walked to me and whispered, "Grab your bag and get your ass up to the penthouse. Do not say a word. Are we clear?"

I nodded in agreement.

We left the club, and as we advanced toward the elevator, Adam picked up his pace, while I trudged behind, wondering how much trouble I was in. Did Ben rat me out? Did he see Justin's hand up my dress?

By the time I stepped inside the penthouse, I circled back to my anger at him for blowing me off. And Monica! Just what the hell did Brandy mean by, "Oh you know how he is about her, everything stops." But I kept my mouth shut—for now.

When I plopped on the grey sofa and took off my shoes, Adam finally broke the silence.

"Don't bother getting comfortable. You're going right to bed, and we'll discuss this in the morning."

I left my shoes behind on purpose to irritate him and marched down the hall with my bag. Who did he think he was ordering me to bed like a child?

I slipped out of my burgundy dress and into one of Adam's white T-shirts. Then, I waited, and waited some more. Was he coming to bed? Or was he sleeping down the hall?

After a while, I curled up in a ball under the covers and shut my eyes. Maybe I would fall asleep, and things would seem brighter by the morning. Fat chance. The journey from the club to the penthouse sobered me up. I was restless and in need of something that I couldn't pinpoint or understand. The longer I laid there, the faster my heart beat.

The door opened a crack and light streamed into the room. Without a word, Adam padded across the carpet and placed a bottle of water on the nightstand for me.

I glanced up at him. "Thank you." After downing half the bottle, I mumbled, "You're still dressed."

"I'm still working," he replied in a low, gravelly tone. "This is the biggest and the most stressful negotiation I've ever dealt with. I'm up against roadblocks I've never encountered before. Ronald Sharpe wasn't kidding when he said if I didn't give AJ the construction contract he would make my life miserable. I underestimated him. That was my first mistake."

"What was your second?"

"I told you, Jess, we'll talk in the morning."

"But I can't sleep." I popped up on my knees. "My mind is spinning a mile a minute. One second I feel bad, and the next I'm pissed as hell. It's like, I don't know, I feel manic or something."

"You're pissed as hell? Ben called me in the middle of a meeting because my girlfriend was in my club getting wasted. So, I run down to Sash and find some lowlife's hands all over you." He sighed, and headed to the door. "I can't do this right now."

"So much for communication," I groused.

He halted and spun around. "You want to communicate? Fine. Let's do it. I didn't even know you were going out with Tilly tonight. Not to mention coming to my club and letting some asshole paw you in front of everyone."

"Well, maybe if you had bothered to answer either of my text messages or return a fucking phone call, you would've."

"Watch your language. I have half mind to—"

"To what? Punish me? Do it. I've been beating myself up all day feeling like an idiot, knowing everything stops when Monica Preston shows up."

"Monica means nothing to me!" he yelled, taking a step back and exhaling. "Damn it. This is exactly why I didn't want to talk tonight. We both need to calm down. Good night."

"Good night? You've got to be freaking shitting me."

"Jess," he seethed. "You're pushing. Go to bed, right now or I'll..."

In an instant, I realized what everything in me craved. I stripped naked, and assumed the position. Face down, ass in the air.

"What are you doing?" he asked.

I lifted my head and begged him. "Please. Punish me."

His voice softened as he came to me. "Sweetheart, I told you, I won't spank you when I'm angry, and I'm too angry right now. Spankings are for our playtime, not punishments. I don't need you to do this."

Our eyes met, and piercing emotions bubbled to the surface. "But, it's what I need. Please."

The air was thick with silence until Adam whipped off his belt. I rested my forehead on the bed and let out a lungful of air. My breathing already began to slow, and

I focused on a newly discovered peace forming deep within. This wasn't about sex. It was about surrendering control of my body to him in a different way, trusting him to meet a profound longing inside me.

Adam palmed my cheeks and spoke with soothing certainty. "I'm going to warm you up with ten hard spanks of my hand, and then you'll get the belt, five strikes unless you use your safe word. Are we clear?"

"Yes, Sir," I answered.

"Jess, look at me, sweetheart. Are you sure this is what you want?"

With our gaze fixed on one another, my eyes welled up. "Yes. I'm sure."

"Okay. Good girl."

I put my head back down on the bed and braced for the first slap. It cracked across my right cheek and the heat spread down the back of my thighs.

"Count," Adam commanded.

"One!" The second spank clapped loudly on my left buttock with a biting sting. "Two!"

Each one that followed was sharper than the last. By the time he reached the tenth, my ass burned like an inferno, and the tight seal that reined in all my emotions was bursting open. The first lash of the belt sliced into my skin, and a tear rolled down my cheek. More tears threatened, and I finally had the courage not to stifle them, but to let them go.

A wrenching, sorrowful cry ripped free from my gut, and I wailed while I accepted each blow. One last whip of the belt scourged my flesh, and I heard it hit the floor while I sobbed uncontrollably.

Adam gathered me to him. "Sweetheart, come here. I've got you. Just cry it out, Jess. You're a good girl."

While I wept, he held me to his chest and rocked me gently. A cathartic wave of relief swept through me as ten years of grief, anger, and sadness released. My tears were washing away the betrayal of my mother, loss, and pain.

I clung to him, and my breathing became more labored. I thought I was going to hyperventilate.

Adam rubbed my back. "Jess, go to that space when we're in a scene together. Slow your breathing down. Big inhale and blow it out. That's it."

My body and breath calmed as he comforted me. "I'm so proud of you. You're so brave. And you're mine."

When I peeked up at him, I saw such admiration, compassion, and absolute devotion in his eyes. If I was brave, it was because he made me feel safe. I trusted him. I belonged to him.

"Adam ... I..."

"*Shh* ... Jess. You don't have to talk. It's okay. I'll hold you all night if that's what you need."

"But ... I..."

"What is it, sweetheart?"

I gazed deep into his eyes, summoning my newfound bravery. "Adam... I–I love you."

"My Jess," he whispered and brought his mouth down on mine. The fervor of his kiss exploded in my veins with more need, more passion than ever before. He worshiped me like a man who deeply treasured every inch of my heart, body, and soul.

In between his frantic consumption of my lips and neck, he let out soft moans of more praise. "You're so beautiful, Jess. I can't get enough of you. You're mine. My good girl."

I loved him. I loved Adam Maxwell and he... *Oh, my God.* I was so lost in the moment. Did he say it back?

I pulled away and heaved. "Sorry."

"What? What are you sorry for?"

"I'm sorry I said, uh, I mean ... um, I–I have to pee. I'll be right back."

I scurried off his lap and dashed to the bathroom. I flicked on the cold water, and splashed my face. *Oh, Jess, why? Why did you say 'I love you'?* I guess what Stacy said got to me. It just came out.

After doing everything in there I could think of, Adam knocked on the door. "Sweetheart, are you all right?"

"Yeah. I knocked over your basket of neatly arranged towels and spilled my cleanser. I'll be right out."

I didn't do either of those things, but it sounded good. Instead, I was hunkered down on the toilet in a cold sweat.

"When you come out can you bring me the aloe vera lotion in the middle drawer?"

"Okay. I'll be right there."

I grabbed his robe on the back of the door, covered myself, and snatched up the lotion I found in the drawer.

When I emerged from the bathroom, he was naked except for his boxers. "There you are. I thought you fell in. Come. Lay on your stomach. Lose the robe."

I peeled off the robe, plucked up the white T-shirt, and put it on. After I handed Adam the aloe vera, I reclined on the bed face down, and the stinging from the belt set in.

"You're awful quiet," Adam commented. "I thought you'd have a million questions for me."

"I think I'm just tired."

"Okay, sweetheart."

A stillness fell over the room, while he rubbed the lotion over my sore ass. But it was the ache building in my heart that hurt the most. My only comfort was trying to convince myself he didn't hear me.

Adam kissed the small of my back. "There. If you're in any pain tomorrow, I'll give you a couple of Tylenol with breakfast."

I crawled under the covers. "Won't you be too busy? Don't you have meetings?"

He placed the lotion on the nightstand and settled in next to me. "While you were in the bathroom, I canceled my eight-thirty."

"You didn't need to do that."

"I know. But I wanted to, for us." He drew me in his arms. "Now, about tonight, and your punishment. I want you to know, I didn't like doing that to you. In fact, I hated it. But, it was what you needed. I should've seen it coming."

"What do you mean?"

"The night at The Purple Peacock. You were close to breaking, but I didn't think you were ready. I saw it in your eyes. There was a desire for more pain, not to heighten your arousal, but because you wanted to feel the pain and have a different kind of release. Is that something you need? More pain?"

"I don't know. I never thought about it. Is it bad if I do?"

"No, sweetheart. There's no bad or good, right or wrong. There's just preferences, likes, dislikes, soft and hard limits."

"I still have so much to learn. I'm sorry I made you do something you hated."

"Don't apologize. I just want you to know I'd rather spank you in a scene, during playtime, and feel you get all wet, wriggling on my lap." He kissed my temple. "But, if you need more pain, then, I'll make sure you get it."

"Thank you," I said softly with a yawn.

Adam flipped off the light. "Absolutely. And what you need right now is some sleep. Sweet dreams, beautiful."

"Night."

I rolled over, facing away from him, exhausted from the outpouring of emotion. My eyes were heavy, but my head reeled in confusion. He acted like I never said those mammoth three words that carried the weight of a freight train. The three words I could never take back. It was as if my heart opened up and hung in the balance. My "I love you" to Adam existed in limbo on a desert island. In some ways, it was like me. Alone.

CHAPTER SIXTEEN
JESSICA

"Jess, you awake?" Adam's morning stubble brushed against my shoulder.

For a split second, everything felt right in my world, then I remembered my "I love you" was still out there blowing in the wind like a forsaken tumbleweed.

I rubbed my eyes and groaned, "What time is it?"

He flung an arm around me, pulling me close. "It's a little after eight. My first meeting is at ten. I'm going to grab a quick shower, and make us breakfast. You can stay in bed a little while longer if you like."

"That's okay. I need to get to work, anyway."

"Not until you eat something." He gave me a quick peck. "I'll be right back."

While he hit the shower, I retrieved my bag and checked my phone. As suspected, it blew up with text messages from, Tilly, Stacy, and Skip touching base. No doubt news of the scene at Sash and the arrest of Travis and Justin caused a stir. The local media would be eating it up like candy.

There was also an email from Skip that read:

> *"Please check these leads from the tip line ASAP. Any chance the guys that got arrested at Sash are connected to, "Together We Are Safer?"*

Justin and Travis didn't fit the profile of the other suspects, so that was doubtful. But, I was anxious to see what Skip sent me.

Once again, the file was too big. I threw on my dress, and shouted through the bathroom door, "Adam, can I use your computer again for work?"

"What? I can't hear you."

I popped my head inside the door. "I said. I need to use your computer."

"Hang on a second. I'll be right out."

"Take your time. I remember the password. It's cool."

After tossing my phone back on the bed, I hurried to his den, plugged in the password, and his desktop illuminated. *Huh?* There was a new file separated from the twelve folders I spotted the other night. JB-F. JB? Was it about me? Curiosity got the best of me, and I clicked on it. It was a letter from a law office:

"Dear Mr. Maxwell,

While William Blake adopting Jessica, and Jessica's birth certificate are a matter of public record, the information you're seeking is not. There is no biological father listed on her birth certificate as you can see in the attachment. If you wish to continue your search for Jessica Blake's biological father, the next step is to get Jessica involved. If that's not possible, I have someone who can help us."

"Oh, my God!" My body shook uncontrollably. "Adam, what've you done?"

He rushed into the room, still wet from the shower, with a towel around his waist. "Jess, don't..."

"You're too late. I already saw it. How could you do this to me?"

"It's not what it looks like. I can explain."

I jolted out of my seat, and yelled, "You can explain? There's no explanation for this. I begged you to let this go, not once but twice. I don't get it. Why? Why would you do this?" I broke down sobbing. "It's so cruel."

He flew to my side. "You have to believe me. I was trying to protect you. You're out there in the public eye. Isn't it better to know who he is and what we're up against?" He grasped my shoulders. "I never meant for you to find out this way."

I shrugged him off. "You never meant for me to find out at all. Admit it. You didn't do this for me. You did it for yourself. It wasn't some stranger coming after me that you were worried about. It was the Maxwell fortune you were trying to protect. I get it. My mother's an opportunistic whore, and my biological dad could be God knows what. I'm a liability."

He clutched my hands in his. "That's not true. You're not a liability. You're mine."

"Don't touch me." I recoiled from him, and fled to the door.

"Jess, stop. You're not going anywhere."

"No. You stop. You told me you didn't want to micromanage me, and that you didn't want to drive me away. But, my God, Adam, you can't help yourself. You knew searching for my biological father would crush me. And you did it anyway." My lip quivered, and I covered my face with my hands. "This is not okay. It's not okay!"

"Sweetheart, you have to know I did this for both of us. For you and me."

With tears spilling down my cheeks, I shouted, "You and me are, nothing!"

"Please don't say that. Jess... I love, I love ... what we have."

"You don't love anything."

I wiped away my tears, and squared my shoulders with my heart thundering in my chest. For an instant, our eyes met, but he didn't utter a single word. Adam released a heavy sigh, calmly sat in his chair, and stared at the computer screen.

In the dead air between us, I walked out. There were no hysterics, no attempts to stop me. There was just he and I. We weren't boyfriend and girlfriend, we weren't Dom and sub, and we weren't us. We were, nothing.

* * * *

On my way to pick up Harley, I pulled myself together. Oddly enough, breathing deep, like Adam taught me helped calm my frayed edges. It was going to take time, a long time, to get over Adam, but I wasn't going to curl up in a ball and cry over him. If nothing else, being his submissive bolstered my strength, and my resolve.

By the time I parked in the driveway of Adam's house at The Vegas Edge Country Club, my walls were under construction. After all, I was pretty good at bouncing back and shutting myself off from the world. I always said it was better to want people in your life, not need them. I didn't need anybody, except for Harley.

"Hey, Jess. What are you doing ringing the bell?" Claire asked with a sweet smile. "Come on in."

"Thanks. I'll just be a minute. Is Harley around?"

"Sure, hon. He's out back." She placed her hand on my shoulder. "Are you okay? Do you want to come in the kitchen for some coffee? It's Saturday, no sense in rushing off to work."

"Thanks, but I really need to get going."

I dashed upstairs, changed clothes, and shoved all of my things in a couple of oversized Coach bags I'd been carting around. I loaded them into my car and came back for Harley.

I hated the idea of taking him away from this beautiful home with nonstop attention from Sam and Claire, but what choice did I have? I'd never move on from Adam without a clean break.

Harley jumped into the front seat, ready for our new life together. From now on, it would just be the two us.

The normally inconspicuous Ben was parked a few feet away in his grey Prius. I waved before sending him a text that said:

> *"Heading to my townhouse. I need to pick up a few things."*

Fingers crossed he didn't alert Adam I was going there. I wondered if the micromanaging Maxwell would keep Ben on as my bodyguard. Well, I suppose if he did, I'd be safe staying at my place, and so would Stacy when she returned from her trip.

Speaking of Stacy, I should give her a call and let her know we are headed over, so she can meet us and pack her stuff before leaving town.

I climbed in the car, and Harley put his paw on my leg. While petting his head, I said, "Okay, mister. It's time to say goodbye to country club life. It was fun while it lasted, but I guess we don't belong here. You know what I just realized? We both were adopted by amazing men, and we lost them way too soon. Maybe you and me were meant to be. What do you think?" His ears perked straight up, like he understood every word I said. "You totally get me, don't you?" He licked my nose. "You're a good boy, Harley. I love you. I love being your person." I glanced up at Adam's house and a lump formed in my throat. "We don't need anybody. We're going to be okay. Right? Hey, you want to go back to our old neighborhood and see Stacy? Yeah! Okay, let me call her."

When I picked up my phone, she was already calling me. "Hi. I was just getting ready to dial your number. Harley and I are headed over to the cul-de-sac. Ben is following me over. Do you want to meet us?"

She sounded winded. "Hey, I'm so glad you picked up. I'm at the paper with Skip. Can you come here first?"

"Sure. What's going on?"

"Kevin has a friend in narcotics, and he called me this morning. At first, they thought those two guys from Sash were connected to Roger's death, so they thought I could help."

"You mean, Travis and Justin? I guess everyone heard about them getting arrested last night."

"Yeah. It's everywhere. I thought you'd already be at work, so I came over here. Skip told me the tip line has been out of control the last couple of hours."

"Do you think Travis and Justin are connected to Roger? They don't fit the profile, so I ruled them out."

"They definitely don't have anything to do with Roger or any of the other victims, but they're about to break and give up who they're working for. These two guys aren't willing to go down without a fight. They're with their lawyers. Between you, me, Skip, and the tip line, I thought maybe we could put some pieces together. This could be huge for the *Las Vegas Times*. The rest of the media is hanging around the courthouse, thinking they're going to get a statement. They aren't."

"Say no more. Harley and I will be right there. I just need to text Ben my change of plans. I'll see you in fifteen minutes."

"Headed to work instead."

—I wrote to Ben, and fired up my car.

"You ready to go to the office? Maybe if you help us solve the case, I'll change your name to Scooby Doo."

* * * *

With Harley by my side, we ran to Skip's office. "Hey, I got here as soon as I could. Where's Hal?"

Skip adjusted his glasses. "His wife fell down the stairs this morning. He took her to the emergency room at Summerlin Hospital."

"Oh man. That's awful. I hope she'll be okay. What about Tilly?"

"She won't be in until later."

Harley put his paws on Skip's desk and sniffed. "Hey, there. How's it going, boy?"

"Sit, Harley. This is Skip's office. I don't think you'll find any chips in here."

"Harley?" Stacy's voice sounded from the doorway. She knelt down with tears in her eyes, and they had a reunion. "You haven't forgotten me, have you? I've missed you so much." She plopped on the floor, and Harley crawled in her lap. "He looks great, Jess. Just as beautiful and sweet as ever."

"Thanks. I'm afraid I can't take too much credit. I've had some help." I pulled up a chair. "So, what do we know so far? What's Kevin been able to tell you? Anything new?"

"Yeah," Stacy answered. "I just got off the phone with him. Until we know something definite Kevin says for now it's strictly off the record."

"You have our word," Skip said.

Stacy continued, "His friends in narcotics have been close to cracking a drug ring for a while. They've caught a few low-level dealers, like Travis and Justin, but they're just the bottom feeders of the operation. Whoever recruits must have some kind of connection to money or power."

"This is going to sound like a stupid question. But, where do the drugs come from? Where's the source?" I asked.

"It's not a stupid question at all. I'll tell you what was stupid. That Travis guy snorted a line right in front of Tilly in plain sight. Those two dummies had enough coke on them to cover Vegas in a blanket of snow. Now that their sobering up, Kevin said the whole tough guy act is starting to wane."

"Justin did try to sound tough. He bragged about getting richer by the day, and his friends in high places. Big league deals. Big league, who says that?" Something clicked in my memory, and I flashed back to Ronald Sharpe at The Purple Peacock.

"Jess, what it is? I've seen that look before," Skip urged. "You know something. Tell us."

"It's nothing, probably just a coincidence. So, did Kevin say, anything else?"

Stacy rose from the floor. "Like what?"

"Like, where they think the cocaine is coming from?"

"Well, yeah," Stacy answered. "There's no proof, but everyone in the department suspects it's being smuggled in from Mexico."

"Oh, my God!" The pieces started to fall into place.

Skip popped out of his chair. "Oh, my God, what?"

I jumped up and shut the door. "Okay. I guess, maybe I do know something. But, what we do with this information is crucial. If I'm wrong, it could put us all in danger, and if I'm right, it could get us all killed. So, if you don't want to know, I'll go it alone."

Stacy put her hand on my shoulder. "You're not alone. You can trust us."

"Right," Skip agreed. "We've come this far. And as a wise reporter said, 'Together We Are Safer.'"

"Okay. I can't tell you where, but a while back, I had a run in with Ronald Sharpe. And I'm sorry, Skip, at the time, I just couldn't tell you. I was with Adam. Sharpe was trying to make him a deal. And he used the words. 'Big league deal.' It's the same phrase that Justin used. Which I know, sounds like a random coincidence, except that Justin said he was untouchable, and he had friends in high places. Which still is not enough to go on. But Sharpe was trying to talk Adam into using his brother's construction company, AJ Construction."

"Mr. Maxwell's been our lead advertiser since I started working at the paper. I never knew he had a brother," Skip replied.

"It's his half-brother, and until that night, I didn't either. Most people don't, but somehow our possible future mayor Ronald Sharpe did, and he wanted to make a deal with Adam. But Adam said no."

"What do Sharpe and AJ Construction have to do with the drug ring?" Stacy asked.

"Adam told me something." I paused, debating how much I should divulge. "He said one of the many reasons he doesn't want to do business with AJ is because he almost never finishes the projects even though he brags about the deals he gets on construction equipment imported from, Mexico."

"So, you think AJ Construction is a front for smuggling cocaine from Mexico," Stacy concluded. "Wow! Adam's brother could be the kingpin the narcs have been looking for."

Skip nodded. "Makes perfect sense now. No wonder Sharpe is running for Mayor of Vegas, instead of Governor. He needed to be close to his partner in crime, and use our city to hide behind. Damn, Jess. I think you nailed it. What do we do now? We can't just sit on this. It's like a powder keg."

"You guys," I warned. "We need to be beyond careful. AJ is dangerous, and Sharpe is well-connected. One mistake and they get off and possibly come after us."

Stacy nodded. "You're right. I'll text Kevin and have him meet somewhere away from the station, and tell him all of this. I just wish we had something else more concrete. Something that ties AJ and Sharpe together, anything."

Skip tore off his glass. "Well, I've got that. Remember, Sharpe released his tax returns." With a couple of clicks of the computer, documents were spitting out from the printer. "It lists his real estate holdings in Vegas. Most of the properties are empty, unfinished buildings, and the contractor is..."

"AJ Construction," Stacy declared while studying the papers. "Can I take this?"

"Sure." Skip beamed with that schoolboy grin. "What do you think we should do while you're talking to Kevin?"

"I think we're in a holding pattern right now. It really depends if Justin or Travis give up Sharpe in exchange for a lesser sentence. Don't do anything until you hear from me. And don't tell anyone. Not Tilly, not Adam, no one. Are you okay with that, Jess?"

"Yeah. I don't think I'll be talking to Adam anytime soon."

"Okay. So, I'll text you when I'm done talking to Kevin, maybe we should meet some place other than here?"

"How about my townhouse?" I offered. "I need to go there anyway, and get Harley settled."

"Do you think that's safe? Is Ben with you?" Stacy asked.

"Oh, yeah. I'll let him know I'm headed over. Don't worry. I'll have Harley and Ben guarding me. I'll be fine."

She saluted me. "Ten-four. I'll be in touch."

"That sounded awfully official," I responded. "Does this mean you're not going to leave town next week?"

She smiled. "Yes. I'm staying. And as soon as we nail these bastards we're going to find out who killed Roger. I'm never giving up."

I bent down and cuddled Harley. "We won't either. Will we, buddy? We're never giving up."

* * * *

I took the longest shower of my life back in my old bathroom, where I was free to be as messy as I pleased. *Shit!* That felt great. It was liberating, even though I checked my phone twenty times to see if Adam called or texted. There was nothing. *Hmm ...* nothing. Not very long ago, I was the queen of nothing. I felt nothing, I experienced nothing, and I was content with my nothing.

Then Adam came along and put my world on blast. But maybe that was all he was meant to do. *Yes!* That was what I kept telling myself, and then I checked my phone again. Nothing.

I glanced around my bedroom and laughed. "What a mess." I remembered the first time Adam came over here and asked if I'd been robbed.

Since it was a warm September afternoon, I opened the window, and the let the fresh air in. There was no sign of Ben's car. He was probably trying to stay out of sight, and not make me feel uncomfortable.

From the second floor, the cul-de-sac looked sad. Roger's place was boarded up. There was still police tape on the front door. I was tempted to sneak in there and nose around, but for once, I listened to my better angels and stayed put.

Harley appeared in the doorway with a sigh. "Hey, are you hungry?" He twirled in a circle. "Okay. There should be some dry food in the pantry, right next to my chips. Let's go eat."

He led the charge downstairs and into my kitchen. Of course, I carried my phone with me, telling myself that I needed to keep an eye out for word from Skip or Stacy.

My heart sunk a little when there was still nothing from Adam. It seemed like an eternity since I left the penthouse and walked out of his life. God, I hated this. Life was so much easier when I was dead inside.

After we were done chowing down, Harley went and stood by an extra leash I kept by the back door. "Sorry, mister. We better stay put. Stacy should be texting me any minute. Let me look." It was another excuse to glimpse at my silent phone. "Do you think I overreacted?" Harley trotted to me resting his head on my knee. "I know. I still love him, but he doesn't love me. It's a dog-eat-dog world, buddy. We'll just have to suck this up and move on. I think Adam already has."

To kill time, I fired off a text to Hal checking on his wife. I desperately wanted to talk to Tilly, but I held steadfast to what Stacy had said.

The noise of a car door slamming shut echoed in the quiet. I messaged Ben. The poor man had been following me around all morning. Maybe I should invite him in and order some real food and ask him if he had to use the restroom.

Another loud door banged outside. It could be Skip and Stacy. "Come on, Harley. Looks like we have company. Let's go."

I unlocked the bottom bolt, and peeked outside. *Shit!* I didn't know those two guys. Before I could relock it, they were pressing against the door. The only thing holding them back was the top latch.

"We're getting in one way or another," one of them shouted. "Why don't you be a nice lady and open up?"

"Get out!" I screamed. "I have a bodyguard. He'll kill you."

"We already took care of him, baby doll."

Oh, my God! Ben! Our only escape was to flee out the back. "Harley, run. Run, Harley!"

We got halfway down the hall when they kicked the door open. "Let's not make this more difficult than it has to be," the taller one said with the menacing eyes and longish dark hair.

With his hackles on end, Harley bared his teeth and growled. I clasped my hand around his collar. "It's okay, buddy. We're okay."

The short, stocky guy appeared nervous. "Ah! Fuck, Pete! AJ didn't say anything about a dog."

"Will you shut up, dumb ass," Pete bellowed. "Take the mutt out. Shoot him."

"But, man, I don't think I can," the short one said.

"Do it, Cody." Pete pulled the gun out of Cody's waistband.

I knelt down and held Harley close. "No one has to shoot anyone. AJ, the guy who sent you here, is a psychopath. You can't trust him. If he promised you money, you won't get it. I'll give you whatever you want. Just don't hurt him. Please. Don't do it."

Cody pointed a shaky gun at us, while I covered Harley with my body. His growls turned to whimpers, and I whispered in his ear, "Get ready to run. Run with me. Run with me. Run with me." I repeated it over and over like I did on our jogs together.

"For Christ's sake, Cody. Shoot him!" Pete yelled.

"Run! Harley run!" I screamed and sprinted full speed toward Cody, knocking him off balance.

The gun went off and fell to the floor. I spun around and grabbed it, just as Pete kicked Harley making him yelp.

"No! Don't! Don't you touch him!" I cried, turning the gun on him, with adrenaline tearing through me. "Get out! Get out of my house! And tell AJ to go fuck himself."

A crazy smile formed on Pete's face. "Sure. We'll be happy to go, won't we, Cody?"

From behind, Cody pawed at my arm, and I whipped around, pointing the gun at him. Pete snatched me by the hair yanking me into the TV room. "Drop the gun, or I'll slit that mutts throat."

I let go of it, and his grip tightened on my hair. Out of nowhere, Harley barked like I never heard him before. Deep, guttural sounds came out of him as he smacked his paws on the ground ready to pounce.

Pete released me for a split second before saying with a shrug, "You're not worth going to jail for. AJ can kill you himself."

I exhaled in relief, and then he body slammed me into the wall. My headed smashed into the picture of my dad and me. Shards of glass ripped open my skull as I sank to the floor.

"Cody, give me the gun, let's finish this," Pete yelled.

I was drowning in a river of excruciating pain. The only way out of this alive was to play dead.

Somehow in my dizzy state, Adam's voice sounded in my head. *"Slow your breathing down, sweetheart. That's it. Good girl."* It was as if could feel him coaching me, praising me. Oh, Adam.

An enormous weight fell across my midsection. It was Harley. He draped himself over me so they couldn't see my chest rise and fall.

Cody's words were barely audible. "Let's go. Look at her. She's already dead."

"Yeah. You're right. Neighbors might call the cops if we fire the gun again. Let's get out of here."

I fought to stay alert long enough to hear the door close. I opened my eyes, and Harley was staring into them. With the last bit of strength I had left, I touched my hand to my head. When I saw the blood dripping from my fingers, my body tensed up and then quivered in chills.

Tears rolled down my cheeks. "I'm sorry, buddy. I– I don't think I'm going to make it. I'm so tired and cold. I–I love y–you. You're, you're the b–best dog. Be, be g–good to A–Adam. Adam..."

I blew out one breath after another until my eyes shut, and it felt like I slowly disappeared, into nothing.

CHAPTER SEVENTEEN
ADAM

"I'm such a fucking ass," I muttered to myself, staring blindly at the computer screen. What was wrong with me? The most incredible woman I'd ever met just shut the door and walked out my life. And, I sat here and let her go.

She gave me her trust, and I threw it back in her face. There was no going back after this. I felt like shit, and I had no one to blame but myself.

Who knew how long I stared into space, acting like a gutted zombie. Finally, I clicked on the file about her biological father, dragged it into the trash, and mumbled, "I'm sorry, Jess."

I forced myself out of the chair and shuffled back to the bedroom. The room seemed so empty. I bent down, picked up the T-shirt she wore and breathed in her scent. I contemplated canceling my ten o'clock meeting. Hell, I wanted to cancel the entire day, and just be with her, but what could I say that would make a difference? I didn't even tell her that I loved her. Why couldn't I say it?

"I love you, Jess," I whispered. "I do. I'm in love with her. I love Jess."

What the hell was I doing? I had to go fight for her. I had to get her back.

In record time, I was dressed and headed out the door when my phone vibrated. *Damn it.* It was Brandy. "Hey, Brandy. We need to cancel the rest of my day."

"Cancel?" she exclaimed. "Your ten o'clock is already here. Where are you?"

"I'm headed out. Tell them it's a personal emergency."

"It's Jade. You cut your meeting short with her last night because of a personal emergency. You can't cancel."

"Fine. I'm on my way."

When I got downstairs, Brandy was waiting for me. "Where's your suit?" she asked.

"I told you I was headed out. This will have to do."

"Okay, just button your shirt and cover up that T-shirt. And don't come out until Jade's a happy camper."

My mind was all over the place during the meeting with Jade. I couldn't focus on her presentation, and I found myself giving in to all her demands during the negotiation. How much longer was she going to press every tiny issue?

Desperate to end it, I said, "I think we can work out a better deal for you, if I had a little more time to crunch these figures. Maybe we could meet for lunch next week?"

"Lunch?" she snapped. "I don't eat lunch, and I'm traveling next week. I'd like to finish this now, but it seems like you have somewhere else to be?"

"No. Not at all. Let's continue."

Brandy busted through the door. "I'm sorry to interrupt. Ben insisted you take this call. He says it's an emergency."

"Oh great, another personal crisis," Jade chided.

Brandy handed me the phone. "Ben, what's going on?"

His voice was frantic. "Is Jess with you? Have you heard from her?"

"No. I assume she's at work. Where are you?"

"I was in a car accident. A couple of assholes in a white Range Rover cut me off when I was headed up Lake Mead. I hit the brakes and got rear-ended. When the cops showed up the person behind me said I was speeding. It's a fucking mess. They almost arrested me."

"You were headed up Lake Mead?"

"On my way to Jess's place."

I moved away from Brandy and Jade. "Jess is at her townhouse, alone?"

"Yeah. I'm still here. The cops won't let me leave. I had to beg them to make this call. I thought you should know."

"Thank you. I'm on my way to Jess's. Meet me there if you can. Knowing the sick way my brother's mind works, he's probably been stalking her every move. He'll stop at nothing to get his revenge. She isn't safe."

"I'll be there as soon as I can."

"Ladies, I do have to go. My apologies, Jade," I said as I rushed toward the door. "Brandy, cancel the rest of my day."

"Cancel? Adam, you can't be serious? What am I supposed to tell everyone?"

With my hand on the doorknob, I turned to them. "Tell them it's a personal issue, or tell them I'm sick, whatever you want. I don't care. The woman I love needs me. That's what matters. All of this is meaningless without Jess."

* * * *

I drove like a maniac and was finally close to Jess's place. After I pulled onto her street, I passed a white Range Rover, and turned into her cul-de-sac. *Damn it.* The door to Jess's townhouse didn't look right to me.

I raced inside, calling for her. "Jess! Where are you?" Oh God! No! Her lifeless body laid in a pool of blood with Harley trembling on top of her. I flew to her, ripped off my shirt, and wrapped her head with it to stop the bleeding.

Harley whimpered. "It's okay, buddy. I'm here. I promise nothing's going to happen to our girl." I dialed 911 and fought to keep it together.

"911. What's your emergency?" the operator said.

"I need an ambulance, immediately at thirty-seven, forty-two Durango Circle. It's The Willows, right off Lake Mead. Please hurry. She's lost a lot of blood."

"They've been dispatched. Stay on the line, sir. Is she breathing?"

"Hang on. Come on, Jess. Breathe, sweetheart." I pulled Harley off her, and felt for a pulse. "Yes. She's breathing, but she's not conscious."

"Where's she bleeding from?"

"The back of her head. I wrapped my shirt around it. She needs help! Where are they?"

"They'll be there soon. Please stay on the line. Apply a little pressure on the wound. Do you know what happened? Was it blunt force trauma? A fall?"

I pressed my palm against her head, and she bled right through my shirt. "I don't know. I think she was attacked." I jumped up to go find something else to tie around her wound, and I spotted the smashed photo of her and her dad on the floor. She loved her dad more than anyone. He was her person. *God, I fucked up!* This was all my fault.

"Are you still there, sir?"

"Yes. Sorry. I'm looking for something else to stop the bleeding." I grabbed the small throw blankets from her couch. "I found a couple of blankets."

"Good. Try not to move her head. We don't know if she has a neck injury. Can you tell me how old she is?"

"She's twenty-eight. Her name is Jessica Blake." I choked up, brushing my fingertips along her cheek. "She's my whole world. Please, Jess. Please be okay."

"Try to stay calm. After you wrap her head, put the other blanket over her. The ambulance should be there shortly."

"Okay. I'm on it."

After I covered Jess, I checked her pulse again. Thank God. It was strong. Then I heard a noise and looked out the window. *Fuck.* It was the white Range

Rover. "I think the people who attacked her are coming back."

"I'm sending the police. Do not engage. Sir, sir, are you there?"

"I'm still here. But I'm going to set the phone down. Don't hang up." I placed the phone on the end table and hid along the wall in the TV room.

Footsteps sounded on the porch, and my blood went cold when I recognized a familiar voice.

"I can't believe you two dumb fucks don't know if she's one-hundred-percent dead. Do you know how risky it is to come back here? If she's still alive, I'm going to fuck both of you up. Wait here. I'm going in."

There was no mistaking my brother's raspy voice filled with venom. The sorriest excuse for a human being tried to take away the best thing that ever happened to me. After thirty-five years of being his punching bag, I couldn't take one more second.

AJ rounded the corner into the TV room, and I lunged at him, seething. "You fucking bastard! Did you do come back to finish the job? It's not enough for you she's over there fighting for her life?"

"Fuck. She's not dead?"

"Is that what you wanted? Say it?" I yelled, loud enough for the 911 Operator to hear me. "Say it. Say you wanted her dead."

"Hell, yes. I wanted your precious slut dead. My own mother won't speak to me because of that bitch. But, mostly, I wanted to watch The Chosen One suffer. So, yeah, I ordered those two fucktards over here to kill her, while I had a drink at the bar around the corner. I did it. You happy now? It was me. I did it."

"That's all I need to hear."

The ambulance sirens whirred in the distance, and I picked up my phone. "Did you get that? Good. Thank you for your help. They're almost here. Absolutely. I'll stay on the line." I placed my phone back on the end table.

"Who's almost here?"

"The ambulance. I should've asked for two. You're going to need one."

"Like hell I am." He lifted his T-shirt, revealing his gun, before whipping it out, and pointing it at me. "Who's it going to be first? You, her, or that damn dog? Since we're family, I'll let you choose." He laughed and lowered the gun, aiming it right at Jess. "Just kidding. I chose your slut."

In a blind rage, I tackled him to the ground. The gun flew out of his hand before he could fire. I slid it out of reach and pummeled him with my fists. Blood spurted from his nose, and he pushed against my chest, calling for his goons. They ran into the townhouse, took one look at AJ's face and fled.

"There's no one to help you now," I growled with my hand squeezing his windpipe. "Not Mother, my father's money, nothing."

I was draining the life from his body when I wrenched back my fist for one final blow to finish him once and for all.

"Adam, don't!" Stacy screamed from the doorway. "Don't do it! We got this!"

The cops stormed in behind Stacy with their guns drawn. "She's right, sir. Let him go."

Completely out of breath, I shook my head in disgust. "Fine. Get him out of here."

AJ squeaked out, "I knew you didn't have the balls."

I clocked him right in the jaw. "There. Now, you can take him."

Chaos erupted as the paramedics charged through the door with their gear and a gurney.

"She's in here," I hollered, jumping up, and glancing back as my brother was being taken away in handcuffs.

"Her pulse is strong, but she's not conscious. She's lost a lot of blood."

"Okay," the female paramedic said. "We need some room."

I had to pry Harley away from Jess. "Come on, buddy. They're here to help."

"I've got him," Stacy offered, picking him up. "Come with me, sweet boy. It's okay."

"Do you know how long she's been out?" the male paramedic asked.

"I have no idea. I don't think it could've been that long. When I drove into the cul-de-sac, their white Range Rover was pulling out. I passed them."

"That's good." He nodded.

The female paramedic rattled off Jess's vitals, gave her oxygen, and said, "She's stable. Let's get her to the hospital."

Jess's eyes fluttered opened as they moved her to the gurney.

"Did you see that? Her eyes. Did you see it?" I blurted.

"Yes. The sooner she regains consciousness, the better," the female replied. "We're taking her to Summerlin. We'll meet you there."

"I'm coming with you," I demanded. "I love that woman. I'm not leaving her. Not ever."

* * * *

"I hate seeing her like this," I said, standing by Jess's bedside with my friend, Doctor Lou Parker.

"She's lucky you got to her so quickly and stopped the bleeding. If you hadn't shown up when you did, there's no telling what kind of shape she'd be in," he explained.

"She woke up a couple of times in the ambulance. They kept asking her questions."

"That's a good sign. I was with her when she got the stitches. She was semi-conscious, and dizzy. She kept saying her head hurt. They gave her something for the pain. There's no sign of a concussion, but she's lost a lot of blood. I'll be honest with you, the next few hours are critical."

"She looks so helpless."

"She's not. She's young and healthy, and a fighter. Hang on to that, and don't give up hope. I'm going to check on some other patients. Text me if she wakes up. I'll be back as soon as I can."

"Thanks, Lou."

"Oh, and there's a crowd out in the waiting room. They're about to knock the door down to get to Jess."

"Let them in. It's what Jess would want."

"She's only supposed to have immediate family in here, but seeing as how Maxwell Industries built this wing. We're making an exception. Just don't tell anyone Harley isn't a service dog. I may have fibbed."

He shook my hand and left, while I kept my eyes glued to my beautiful Jess.

Moments later our friends filed into her room. Stacy had her arm around Tilly, consoling her. Skip and Hal's eyes were glassy, and Claire and Sam held hands, leaning on each other for support, with Harley in tow. Helen, Sebastian, Eli, and Ben hung in the back of the group.

I picked up Harley and put him in Jess's bed. When he laid down, with his head resting on her stomach, falling right to sleep, you could hear a pin drop. Everyone's energy focused on Jess, as if we were willing her to open her eyes and come back to us.

When I looked at each one of their heartbroken faces, I realized Jess was right all along. Biology didn't mean anything. Her family, our family, was in this room. This was the family we chose, and the one that chose us and had our backs. We were family.

"Adam, what did the doctor say?" Tilly asked through her soft sobs.

"That the next few hours are critical." I touched my lips to Jess's forehead.

Tilly wiped her eyes. "I just want to hug her. She would hate it, but I want to anyway."

"I want her to wake up and start asking me questions," I added.

Hal nodded with a slight smile. "She'll not only be asking questions. She'll probably win a journalism award for solving the biggest cocaine ring in the history of Vegas."

"She'll what?" I asked. "I don't understand."

Stacy replied, "Jess, put all the pieces together. Your brother, AJ, was smuggling cocaine in from Mexico. He used his construction business as a front. Ronald Sharpe was his partner. It looks like her theory is already panning out."

I squeezed Jess's hand. "I'm so proud of you, sweetheart. You're incredible."

"Keep talking to her," Claire suggested. "I bet she can hear you. She's going to pull through. I know it."

"Claire's right," Stacy agreed. "But, I think we should go. Jess needs her rest."

One by one, everyone said a goodbye to Jess, until it was just Eli, Ben, and I. Ben kept his distance, looking like he was going to crack.

"Ben, stop blaming yourself," I said. "Jess is in this hospital bed because of me. This is my fault. I'm the one who fucked-up. And if she doesn't wake up soon and give me hell, I'll never forgive myself."

He punched the wall. "I should've been there to protect her."

"If it weren't for me, she never would've been headed to her townhouse in the first place," I replied.

"Come on, mates. Stop beating yourself about," Eli interjected. "It doesn't sound like anything would've stopped AJ."

"You're right. He's no brother of mine."

"Forget AJ." Eli placed a hand on my shoulder. "You don't need him. You've got us. Right, Ben?"

Ben approached the bed. "A hundred percent. If you and Jess still want me, I will guard her with my life."

"Absolutely." I nodded. "We protect what's ours. If one of our girls needs us, we're there for them."

"Well, in that case, I better find myself a submissive. Maybe it's time to settle down and make a proper commitment. How about you, Ben?" Eli asked.

"What's a submissive?" Ben replied.

Eli patted his back. "Oh, Ben. We need to have a drink at our club, The Purple Peacock, when we leave the hospital. I'll fill you in, if that's okay with your boss."

"Yeah," I said, staring at Jess, hoping her eyes would open. "Would you guys mind giving me some time alone with her?"

"Say no more. Ring us up if there's any change or if you need me to come back and pick up Harley. He can stay at my place tonight," Eli offered.

I petted Harley's head. "Neither one of us are going anywhere. We have to be here when she wakes up. Right, buddy?" Poor little guy was so tuckered out he didn't move a muscle.

"Okay, mate. We'll be in touch."

Eli and Ben headed out, and I pulled up a chair by Jess's bed. I remembered what Claire said, and I held her hand and talked to her. "I'm so sorry, Jess. Please, sweetheart. Please wake up. I need to see those big blue eyes. I need to hear your voice. Tell me you're pissed at me, fight with me, call me an ass, anything. I need you. I want you. No matter what happens, you'll always be mine."

She squeezed my hand, and I shot out of my seat. "Jess, can you hear me? Can you open your eyes?" They fluttered, and she squeezed my hand again. "Good girl. I'm right here. Harley and I are right here." I put her hand on Harley, and he snored. The corners of her mouth upturned in a faint smile. "That's it, beautiful. Your hero is snoring. Harley's your hero."

She pointed at me and whispered, "You." Her eyes flipped open. "You."

"What are you trying to say? Do you want me to get the doctor?"

She scrunched up her face. "No. You, you're a hero too. You, you saved me."

"No, sweetheart. I'm no hero. I'm the one who fucked-up. Don't you remember?"

She closed her eyes, and let out a heavy breath. "Give me a second."

"I'm getting the doctor."

"Adam, please don't leave me. Please. I remember. I remember everything."

I sat on the side of the bed and took her hand in mine. "Tell me. Tell me what you remember."

"I–I remember being slammed into the wall, and they were going to shoot me, so I played dead. That's when I felt you, or I heard you in my head. I know it sounds crazy. But, it was like we were in a scene. You were calming me down, helping me to breath. Then, Harley laid on top of me. They figured I was dead." Tears sprung to her eyes. "And then I got really scared, and I thought I was dying. And... I–I..."

"*Shh*... You're okay now. You're safe. I'm not leaving your side. I just hope..."

"What?"

"I hope you can forgive me. You were right. I told myself I was looking for your biological dad to protect you, but I was also trying to protect myself. I betrayed you, and now I get it. It doesn't matter who he is. Biology is irrelevant. I know I screwed-up trying to control everything, and I'm sorry." I swept her up in my arms. "I'm so sorry. Can you forgive me?"

She broke down. "I already have. Right before I blacked out, it was you. You were in my heart. You've been there the whole time."

I held her to my chest, feeling like the luckiest man on earth. She came back to me. I wasn't wasting another second. "Sweetheart. Look at me." Her weepy blue eyes met with mine. "I love you."

"You, you love me?"

"Yes. I love you. I think I've—no—I know I've loved you from the beginning. I was just too much of an ass to admit it."

She let out a chuckle mixed with a sob. "I love you too."

Our lips came together in a gentle kiss. I placed my palm on her shoulder blades, easing her back down on the pillow. "There. Close your eyes, sweetheart."

"Will you stay with us?" she said softly, with heavy eyes, petting Harley.

"Absolutely. I'm not going anywhere." I slid into the bed, and drew her into my arms, touching my fingertips to her white bandage. "You lost a lot of blood. I should probably text my friend, Lou. He's the doctor that was with you when you got your stitches. He'll want to check on you."

She exhaled. "Just two more minutes. After those stitches, I feel like a pincushion. I'm a little foggy, but I think I remember them cutting off my hair." She rubbed her forehead and winced.

"Are you in pain? Should I get the nurse?"

"No. I'm just worried I'll wake up and you'll be gone. That this was all a dream. This is real, right?"

"Yes. It's real. You're not dreaming. I love you, Jess. You're my person. You're mine."

CHAPTER EIGHTEEN
JESSICA

"Good morning, Sir," I whispered, kneeling by the bed, nude.

A huge smile spread across Adam's sleepy face. "What are you doing? I usually bring the coffee."

"I wanted to please you."

He glimpsed at his tray with coffee and a stack of newspapers. "And, you wanted to see which Sunday papers ran your latest article."

I giggled with a shrug. "Busted. It's still exciting to see it in print."

He pulled me to him. "Come here."

I let out a squeal and straddled him. There was nothing but a thin sheet separating our naked bodies. Ever since I got out of the hospital six weeks ago, we were in a new place with each other. It was more playful, yet more intense, and more satisfying than I ever imagined.

Adam took such good care of me, that when I felt like myself, I took care of him. I found little ways to please him. Some mornings I'd lay out his suit and tie. Other times I greeted him on my knees when he got out of the shower, and ask permission to suck his cock. Pleasing him pleased me. I craved it. And in return, he gave me everything I needed, and then some.

He lured me to his lips for a sweet kiss. "You look so pretty. I have half a mind to skip your training with the butt plug this morning, and take your ass right now."

"Mr. Maxwell, you're bad."

"I am. I'm a bad man in love with his beautiful submissive."

I touched a hand to my short hair. "I'm not beautiful. I look like a teenage boy with giant tits."

He laughed. "No sweetheart, you're my sexy Tinkerbell."

A phone beeped, and I asked, "Is that yours or mine?"

"It's probably the famous journalist's phone. It never stops ringing." He patted my ass. "Go ahead, answer it."

I climbed off him, and glanced at my cell. "It's Tilly. I can call her back. I'm just going to check my office email, really fast."

He grabbed his coffee. "Okay. But, if you're going to be longer than five minutes, put some clothes on." He threw back the sheet revealing his massive erection. "You're driving me crazy."

"Whatever you say, Sir Dude." The first email that loaded turned my stomach. "Oh, my God!"

"What is it?"

"My mother. She wrote me a letter."

"You're kidding."

"It says, Jessica, I just wanted you to know I've left Vegas for good, and I've cut ties with Ronald Sharpe. We were just friends anyway. And I had nothing to do with his shady business dealings. I'm not enclosing my new address, because I know you don't care. I've met someone, and we're going to travel the world together. No need to write back. This email address will be deactivated. If anyone asks, you never heard from me, you don't know how to reach me, and you don't know where I am. The best gift I can give you is your freedom. You will never hear from me again. Lauren." Staring at the phone, I sighed. "Just friends my ass!"

"Language," Adam warned.

"Sorry. But do you believe her?" I deleted her message and tossed the phone aside. "Bye, Felicia!"

Adam laughed. "I think it's for the best. Don't you?"

"Oh. Totally. It's just, I don't know. It's so like her to fuck Ronald Sharpe when he was poised to be the next mayor and then skip town the second he's arrested."

"Jess, that's two. You know how I feel about cursing."

"I'm sorry."

"What's going on?"

"It's her. Lauren. Her email brought back some of my old demons."

"Are you sure that's all?" He held out his hand. "Come."

He positioned me, so I was straddling him once again, with his hands resting on my hips. "I know it's been a while since we've played. I've been reluctant to take you back to the penthouse for a serious session. I wanted to wait until you were ready and fully trusted me again."

"Adam, I do trust you. The past is in the past."

"I still regret looking for your biological father. Now, I realize no good would've come from finding him. I promise to make it up to you if it takes the rest of my life."

"You already have. Being here with you at the Vegas Edge, and making love has been incredible. The past couple of weeks, I've wanted to go to the penthouse, but it's just been so crazy for both of us."

"Thanks to you, my deal at Bally's is all wrapped up. With Ronald Sharpe's roadblocks out of the way, it's been smooth sailing."

"I've been busier than ever. I guess you should be careful what you wish for. I wanted a salacious story, and I got one. Cocaine smuggling, political takedown, and AJ behind bars. I just hope Skip isn't too bummed I got the byline on this story, and I'm still working on 'Together We Are Safer.' I'm not going to stop looking for who killed Roger."

"I know you won't. I'm hoping Ronald and AJ will be sharing a cell with Blair Preston. I don't think any of them will be seeing the light of day for the rest of their lives."

"I wouldn't be too sure. According to my anonymous sources. Old slick Sharpe talked. He might get off easy in exchange for nailing your brother to the wall."

He glided his fingertips over my thighs. "Looks like I have my very own Lois Lane."

I circled my hips and teased, "Then that makes you, Superman."

He yanked me to him, flipped me on my back, and pinned my arms over my head. His voice was low and husky, and his eyes were smoldering with intensity. "Well, it's not the penthouse, but I think we can improvise. Tell me what you want."

"Whatever pleases, Sir."

A look of pure lust emerged on his gorgeous face. "I want your ass."

"Yes, Sir." I gasped.

"Don't move," he ordered.

He bounded off the bed, grabbed the lube, a butt plug, and the belt to his robe. Even though I remained still, I couldn't help the wetness forming between my legs. Just one glimpse of his ripped, naked body caused my nipples to protrude. He hadn't laid a hand on me, and I was already crazed with need.

"Turn over, Jess. Face down, ass in the air."

I quickly obeyed, while my nerve endings pulsed and warmth flowed over my skin.

"Good girl," he praised with his hands caressing my cheeks. "We're going to take our time and go slow. And you have my permission to come as much as you like. It will help relax you. Are you wet, sweetheart?"

"Yes, Sir."

"I'm going to feel for myself." His fingertips glided over my pussy, and he pushed two fingers inside. "That's my good wet girl. I'm putting the plug in to stretch you. I'm going to leave it in while I make you come."

He spread open my cheeks, and I moaned in anticipation. He lubed my opening and slowly pushed the plug inside. After grasping my wrists, he bound them together, and I quivered in response.

His fingers drummed over my clit. Then he applied the exact amount of pressure I longed for, and rubbed it vigorously until I came.

"Nicely done, sweetheart. Can you come for me again?"

"Yes," I panted.

He cracked my right buttock. "Yes, what?"

"Sir. Yes, Sir."

"That's better." He placed one hand on my sex, and smacked my left cheek with the other. Renewed wetness gushed all over him. "So, this is what you need?"

"Please. It's been so long."

"Absolutely. Hold still." His two fingers remained at my entrance, and he spanked me with steady swats, alternating the spot of contact, so my ass burned evenly.

I reveled in this space of pain and pleasure, cherishing every slap. Adam knew how to amp me up and fuel my dark temptations. At the perfect moment, the spanking ceased, and he dove two fingers inside of me and quickly got me off once more.

He soothed my sensitive flesh with his hand, and his voice oozed in a sexy, gravelly tone. "I'm going to fuck your pussy until we're both ready to come. Then I'll remove the butt plug and take your ass. No more coming until I tell you. Are we clear?"

"Yes, Sir."

"Good girl."

His hand clasped my wrists and eased his length inside. "Fuck. Your pussy feels so fucking tight with the plug in. Your ass will feel even better."

I learned to steady myself when he fucked me from behind, and let him use me for his pleasure. The brutal thrusts and the animalistic groans enflamed my submission to him. Another orgasm beckoned, and I held on until he was ready for my ass.

He slowed his thrusts and pulled out the plug. The extraction nearly toppled me over the cliff, but I breathed through it. When his lubed finger pressed inside my anus to prep me, I cried out in anguish, needing to come.

His cock released my pussy, and his tip touched the only hole he hadn't fully claimed. I braced for impact and exhaled.

"Lay on your side, sweetheart," he said while untying my wrists.

I lifted my head, and our eyes met. "What? Why?"

"You have a question? Now? Trust me, Jess."

"Of course. Sorry." I heaved, reclining on my side.

"Draw your knees to your chest," he commanded in a soft tone. "That's it. Good. I want to be able to hold you."

I nodded with a smile. "I want that too."

My back was sealed to his front, as he brought his lips down on my neck. "Remember your safe word. Don't be afraid to use it."

"I'm never afraid when I'm with you. I love you."

"I love you too, sweetheart."

His tip wedged inside me, and we breathed together as he slid in a few more inches. His fingers stroked my clit, keeping me relaxed as his cock continued to pry me open with slow thrusts.

This was an all-consuming addicting kind of sweet pain. Endorphins shot through my bloodstream as

Adam held me, and praised me, bringing us to a new level of intimate intensity.

Our movements grew more primal when I raised my top leg, begging for more. Insane lust gripped me, and I screamed, "Oh God. Yes!"

"Yes, what?" he grunted.

"Yes! Sir! Oh, Sir! Ah ... Ah!"

"Good girl. Ah! Fuck! Come. Come now."

We catapulted over the edge together, filling the room with sounds of pants and groans, until our climax was milked to the tiniest of tremors.

Adam withdrew his cock, and coiled his arms around me. "You're incredible."

"Are you pleased?"

"Absolutely. You've surpassed my expectations as my submissive, my lover, my..." His voice trailed off.

"Your what? Hey, where did you go?"

He jolted upright. "I just realized something. I have somewhere I need to be."

"Dude, slow your roll. Your dick was just in my butt. Isn't it impolite to rush off?"

With a chuckle, he scrambled out of bed. "Normally yes. But, this can't wait. I want you at the penthouse tonight, eight p.m. sharp."

"What about Claire, Sam, and Harley? We were going to go for a hike with them."

"I'll explain it to them after my shower. I'm sure they'll understand." He hurried toward the bathroom.

"But, Adam. I don't understand. Where are you going?"

He turned and looked me right in the eye. "Jess, do you trust me? Do you really trust me?"

"Yes. I do."

The most gorgeous smile lit up his flawless face. "Then, I'll see you tonight at eight."

* * * *

"Well, look at you, hon," Claire said in the kitchen. "You look great. Off to the penthouse?"

I smoothed out my black pencil shirt. "Yeah. I just wanted to say goodnight. Thanks for looking after Harley. Actually, thanks for everything. You and Sam have been amazing to us."

"No need to thank us. It's our pleasure. We love having both of you here. You and Harley, you've become our family."

Without any hesitation, I threw my arms around Claire and embraced her. "That means a lot to me. Thank you."

She patted my back. "Now, you go. Have fun. The two of you work so hard, you deserve a night together."

"Okay. Say goodnight to the guys for me."

"I will, hon. Drive safe."

On my way to the car, I checked my phone. I guess I was on everyone's mind. I had text messages from Stacy, Tilly, and Hal. I sent them all the smiley face emoji with the heart. That ought to thoroughly confuse them. Maybe their formally unfeeling, dead inside, don't hug me, friend was turning into mush. I liked to keep them on their toes.

There was no need to text Ben. With AJ behind bars, my trusty bodyguard was in charge of security at The Purple Peacock. The vetting at the club got much tougher after I was thrust into the public eye. Nosey Nadine devoted her column to outing Adam and I as a couple, which Adam felt could potentially threaten the privacy of the club.

Ben seemed to enjoy his new job. Last time he came to see his sister, Claire at the house, he mentioned Eli was keeping him busy, showing him the ropes, and probably the handcuffs or a nice crop.

I texted Adam and let him know I was on the way. He sure had me in a curious tizzy all day. It wasn't like him to rush off after sex, especially after a spanking.

As I drove to the penthouse, my mind wandered back to the first time he showed up at my townhouse. He told me he wasn't an overly affectionate Dom, and said I didn't need all of that lovey-dovey shit. I suppose we'd both come a long way. I wondered if he'd notice I was wearing the same outfit from our initial train wreck of a meeting. It was the opposite of a meet/cute. It was more of a meet/disaster.

Before I rang the bell on Adam's penthouse door, I touched my fingertips to my chest. It felt a little warm. Why was I so nervous?

I took a breath remembering the temptation that led me to this very spot months earlier. With my index finger, I pushed the button, and the chime rang. I waited, and waited some more.

The door flung open, and Adam appeared in nothing but his charcoal grey sweat pants. *Sweet Mother of Christ!* The only thing better was no pants.

The gleam in his eye told me he recognized my outfit and played along. "Miss Blake, would you like to come in or conduct our business in the hallway? You seem rather fond of that particular spot on the carpet."

"Of course. I was just a little nervous. I'd love to."

I barged right past him, and strutted into the penthouse like I owned the joint. Once inside, I was surprised by the soft glow of candlelight radiating throughout the room, with a hint of sandalwood wafting in the air. A giant burgundy balloon bouquet adorned the coffee table like a grand centerpiece, and shiny silver gift bags filled up the sofa.

"Adam, what is all this?"

From behind, his arms snaked around my waist, and he said with amusement in his voice. "It's lovey-dovey shit."

I laughed and angled my face to his. "I can see that. But, why?"

He kissed the bridge of my nose. "You'll find out. Come." He took my hand, and led me to the couch. "I did recall you saying you weren't that girly and could give a rip about flowers and all that crap. So, I went with balloons."

"I love balloons. And the color. Nice touch, Mr. Maxwell. What's in the bags?"

He grinned. "Chips. I believe you'll find all your favorites, if you want to take a look."

"Okay." I selected the bag closest to me, and chucked the tissue paper to the side.

Adam shook his head. "Not that one."

"How about this one?" I asked, referring to the bag in the middle.

"I'm going to go with, no."

I placed my hand on the bag closest to him. "So, then, this one?"

"Yes. I think that's it."

"Okay. These better be some killer chips, Sir Dude."

I thought Adam would laugh, but he remained silent with his eyes glued on me while I pulled out bag after bag of my favorites.

Then I saw it. The velvet box with the burgundy ribbon, it was Adam's deck of cards. "Oh. Um, you left your cards in this bag."

"I did? How did that get in there?" He fished them out and handed them to me. "That's right. I had a question. Open it."

With shaky hands, I untied the bow and lifted the lid. It wasn't a deck of cards. "Oh, my God." I gasped. "It's so beautiful."

He got down on one knee, and my heart nearly burst right out of my chest. "Adam, what? What are you doing?"

Adam extended his hand to mine. I took it and clasped it tight. With a slight nod of his head toward the box, I placed it on the table, so he could pull out the ring with a diamond so bright it sparkled in the candlelight.

"Jessica, will you be mine? All mine. My submissive, my lover, my best friend, and my wife. Will you marry me?"

I nodded, with tears spilling down my cheeks.

Adam exhaled. "Is that a yes?"

"Yes!"

He slid the ring on my finger, and I fell into his arms. He cradled me close, showering me in kisses, and whispered, "I'm so glad you said yes. You scared me for a second."

"Of course I said yes. Adam, I love you."

"I love you too. I'm going to spend the rest of my life protecting you, spoiling you, and loving you. I'm still going to be your Dom, but your husband too. Are you sure this is what you want?"

"Yes. It's what I want. I want to be your submissive and your wife. You were worried I wouldn't?"

He touched his lips to my forehead, and expelled a sigh of relief. "No. But I thought you'd have a lot of questions."

I glanced down at my beautiful ring, threw my arms around his neck and kissed him. I kissed him with everything I had in me.

My temptation for wanting more pushed me and led me to this moment. I was a journalist. I was a submissive. I was his. Adam was my person. I had no further questions.

In submission, there is discovery and strength.
In dominance, there is respect and compassion.
In both, there is love.

THE END

AUTHOR BIOGRAPHY

Rosemary grew up in Pennsylvania, one of six children. Her parents, Charles, and Dorothy, always supported all her creative endeavors, from acting to singing to Erotic Novelist. Yes, they are super cool.

She's been living in Las Vegas for over eighteen years with her husband Bill Johnson and their rescued pooch Harley.

In addition to writing, she also teaches ten fitness classes a week. Her limited spare time is usually spent at home with her hubby enjoying a home cooked, healthy meal and all things HBO and Netflix. When she ventures out to a restaurant, she normally splurges on her favorite dish, Mac and Cheese. It's just like Nia says in, *Running Away to Home*, "Sometimes it's good to be bad!"

Connect with Rosemary

http://rosemarywillhide.com/

ROSEMARY WILLHIDE

LUMINOSITY
PUBLISHING

Made in the USA
Columbia, SC
21 June 2017